CHILDREN OF A GREATER EVIL

21st Testing Protocol Book 2

IMOGENE NIX

Print ISBN: 978-0-6484841-6-5

Book two of the 21st Testing Protocol raised many questions for me, not just what is the path of humanity into the future.

But I also have to reflect on just how lucky many of us are to live in stable democracies, where the ability to overturn the governments of the day is more than just the removal of the current head of state.

My understanding of these things is largely influenced by—of all people—Mr Nix. Thanks to his degrees in Cultural Policy and Political Economy I have someone to ask about the intricacies of government and governing.

This year too, is extra special as he was recognised for this in the Queens Birthday Honours with a Public Service Medal.

So, it seems fitting that above all, this book is dedicated to him.

Of course, thanks to the usual suspects too of Keri, Suzi, Sassie and Tracey.

Thanks to our daughters Charlotte & Beth and Mr Patrick too.

As always, though, this books wouldn't come to light if not for the efforts of Pamela and Willsin.

Lastly, yet never forgotten, are you—my wonderful readers.

Imogene Nix
2019

21st Testing Protocol

- Cyborg: Redux
- Children Of A Greater Evil
- When Evil Came To Stay
- Finis: The War To End All Wars

Chapter 1

Daniella swirled the deep red wine in her glass. The fire flickered in front of her, jumping and flashing in the fireplace, the occasional spark landing on the hearth before dying away. Not many these days could afford the luxury of a real open fire. Even for her, this was a treat, as was the unallocated time where she could simply sit and relax. It had taken months of effort to clear the evening for this event. She wouldn't have missed it for the world though.

Closing her eyes, she basked in the unusual tranquility of the moment. The ticking of a clock, a replica from the twenty-first century, lulled her until deep bongs echoed. The seat creaked below her, the fine, old leather protesting as she pushed forward, rising to her feet before she slid them into the high, formal shoes. Daniela groaned as the familiar ache settled deep in her bones.

Glancing down, she noted that the material had remained wrinkle-free in the flowing, turquoise *salwar kameez* which Clarissa had chosen for her to wear.

Her brother, Michael, and his partner, Clarissa, would be here soon for the ceremony that would join them for life. However long that might be given the circumstances...

"No time for that kind of thinking, Daniella," she muttered to herself.

A tap on the door captured her attention, and she turned with a jerk. "Who is it?"

Agent Fairburn—a member of the team of special investigators allocated to her—peered through the doorway he'd just opened. During her team's investigations, those who were open to the knowledge learned Clarissa had received extensive bio-cybernetic enhancements at the hand of Dr. Jeremy Colvert. His work with nano-infused embryos shocked all who believed in the sanctity of life.

As the senator with the task of advising on population control and evolution, it also meant Daniella was in charge of the examination of facts and, if necessary, ushering the prosecution of those guilty of circumventing the rules.

To date though, her newly acquired title remained unofficial, and top-level clearance was necessary to ascertain precisely what she was supposed to be doing, apart from the more public information handed out about her previous responsibilities.

"They've arrived at the gate," Kallee, her assistant, called from beyond the door, drawing her from her thoughts and concerns.

Daniella swallowed a sip of wine and took one last moment to enjoy the fire's warmth. A chill seemed to have taken up residence in her body since the instigation of her new designation. Senior Senator for the A'Garve Quadrant wasn't quite as fabulous as it sounded, but it was at least one she could openly claim.

"Senator?" Kallee called to her.

"Coming." Daniella slid the glass onto the wood table and strode toward the door.

JONAH ADJUSTED HIS TIE, grumbling until Franklin flicked his hands away. "Michael invited you to be his *Bachelier Serviteur* today. I honestly don't know why, when you complain endlessly."

Swiping his hand through his slicked-back hair, now worn long,

Jonah grunted. "I didn't realize I'd have to dress like a clown on the day."

The door opened behind him, and Jonah turned to watch as Michael entered the room. The first thing he noted was the wobbly smile on his friend's face.

"Ready to give your life away?" Jonah drawled.

Michael's gaze zeroed in on him. "I'm not giving my life away— I'm joining it to the most fabulous woman who completes me."

Jonah's words had done the trick though, as the strained look melted from Michael's face.

"Good. So, let's get this event started." Jonah moved in and hugged his friend hard before he shoved him away. "We better get out there."

As the three men stalked to the vehicles, it seemed incongruous that they were about to celebrate the occasion of Michael and Clarissa's union. Only months ago, she'd turned up—a waif, damaged and unsure of herself and the world around her, on the run from an evil man whose sole aim was to breed enhanced super-soldiers.

Clarissa had captured his best friend's heart, and shown resourcefulness and internal strength of character that humbled the entire team. Bio-cybernetic implants aside, Jonah had been privy to some of the most fundamental concerns, including the difficulties in reconnecting with her family and classification as *cybe: non-threatening*. It had also made the legalities of the union tenuous until their therapist had petitioned the president himself. At least Michael's family had associated with President Yin and his family for well over twenty years.

"You've got the ring?" Michael's query cut through Jonah's thoughts.

"What? Oh, yes." He patted the small pocket at his breast, able to feel the smooth, round metal beneath the layer of wool. "I've got both of them."

Michael settled against the squabs as the car moved swiftly through the night, and though the journey itself was short, it took just under fifteen minutes by the time they cleared the security zone outside Daniella's house. Their identification disks were carefully checked, to ensure they should access this area.

They waited for the driver to open the door then stumbled out and headed up the steps. The concrete of them appeared artfully aged so it took on a stone-like visage, and as always, Jonah shook his head. "I don't get the whole 'pretend it's something else.'"

Michael simply laughed until he caught sight of another vehicle, lights cutting through the wintry gloom. "Is that..."

The question hung in the air as the driver ushered them up the steps. "Yes, sir, but they request that you be in position before they park."

"Well then, let's not keep my bride waiting!"

Jonah gave a bark of laughter at Michael's joyous words and followed him up the steps and into the building.

JONAH SIPPED SLOWLY at the wine in his hand. The deed completed—Michael and Clarissa married—he now waited for the chance to make his getaway.

If only it were that simple. The senator watched him from the far side of the room, her svelte body wrapped in a bluish-green costume, reminiscent of the pale champagne one the bride wore. A *salwar kameez*, Michael had informed him, in honor of their long-ago ancestry. It didn't exactly hide her lithe figure, yet even though there was nothing suggestive in the cut or fit, he found himself unable to steer his gaze in another direction. Her hair, which was tugged up and back in a soft tumble, glinted below the gems of the light.

"She's something to look at, isn't she?" He hadn't heard Franklin's approach and mentally reprimanded himself for the lapse.

"Michael's sister is a beautiful woman." It took every ounce of willpower to keep his voice neutral, but Franklin's snort informed him that he hadn't managed to keep his interest to himself.

Movement caught his eye; Agent Fairburn weaving toward him. With a murmur, he headed in the direction, Franklin following him.

The three men halted in the hallway, while Jonah checked carefully to ensure that none of the guests would overhear them.

"What?"

The agent's gaze met his. "We have a lead, sir. A teen boy believed to be around fourteen, at the emergency room at Velspar Community Care. He's showing signs of hypothermia, damage to extremities, however, his recovery does not indicate long-term exposure, and there is a general belief that his healing factors are through the roof. He was admitted at seven o'clock with compromised digits on one hand, and the other at about fifty percent. By nine, his observations show them once again at close to optimal. His file was flagged as requiring further investigation. Internal organ damage has been noted in the data tagged by our monitoring systems."

Accelerated healing factors were among the few triggers they'd managed to lock down so far. The children and teens carefully sown in the lab of Dr. Jeremy Colvert had received injections of organic-based cybernetic growth hormones at the point of conception. The children they'd located had a wide range of specialist factors from enhanced linguistic abilities and hearing, through to hyper-speed, strength, and strategic capabilities. For all the advancements though, many displayed tendencies to rages, extreme mood changes, and in some cases psychoses.

Jonah scratched his head, considering the information Fairburn had just imparted.

"Any further information on location, carers..."

"Negative. The boy appears normal but is either mute or has been taught not to respond. No family has been tracked down, and the trace DNA—as we've found with the few other children—is proving inconclusive."

Sucking in a deep breath, Jonah made a lightning-quick decision. "Inform Michael and Clarissa. However, unless this turns sour, we'll continue this investigation without them."

"And the senator?" Fairburn's words shot straight to his gut.

She'd want in, and while he might need the presence of a female depending on the teen, it went against everything he'd been taught to involve a civilian. Even one of her position. "No. We'll inform her after the fact."

Jonah spun on his heel and headed for the door, refusing to look back, because he just knew that if he did, she'd be there. That's the way his luck always turned. The butler at the door took one look at the two men striding purposefully forward and hurried to hold the glass door wide, eyes darting to and fro as if embarrassed by the testosterone they exuded. All the while, Jonah held his breath. Only when the door thudded closed did he exhale.

<hr>

Chapter 2

<hr>

Daniella tapped her fingernail against her lips, scanning the room. The revelers were thinning out, and the happy couple had taken their leave. Jonah and his sidekick, Franklin, had decamped at some point during the dancing, and Agents Sevres and McNally were also frustratingly conspicuous with their absence. Only Fairburn remained, and he'd dodged her, only coming near when there could be no opportunity to interrogate him.

Her ire rose as he slipped back into the room while she stood beside President Yin. At least, if she cornered the man now, he'd be able to talk freely. She spun, making to track her underling, when Yin stopped her, his hand encircling her arm.

"Do you think that wise?"

A hiss escaped between gritted teeth. "Perhaps not, sir, but my men have—"

"Yes, I'd already come to that conclusion. Come, let's talk in your office. I want an update, and given your office is almost fortress-like, we should be able to speak openly."

Frustration wound through her, a ribbon of steel that slid under her ribs. "Of course." *I can't deny the leader of the world.* The aging,

Asian man was in the mood to know how her team was faring, even if her results to date appeared less than stunning

Once the door was closed, her fingers still resting against the wood paneling that hid the soundproofing she'd had installed, he harrumphed. "So, where are they?"

Gathering her temper on a very tight leash, Daniella slowly rotated on the ball of her foot. "I don't know. They headed out about an hour and a half ago. Their destination is unclear at this point."

Noting how the president's mouth tightened, white lines radiating from his lips, Daniella contained her growl of frustration.

"They don't do this often, and I believe that the mission arose during the festivities. Unwilling to call notice, they would have reacted swiftly to determine the threat level. Given I've heard nothing—"

The strident wail of her palm communicator interrupted, and she started hunting through the ornate clothing, searching for the pocket where she'd secreted the small digital device.

The president watched her as she found and activated the unit, lifting it to her ear. The screen glowed, and she saw Jonah's name. "This had better be good news."

"It is, and it isn't. We've located a teen who arrived at the emergency department at Velspar. He's one of the missing. That's the good stuff. The bad part is he refuses to talk. I need to bring him into the unit so we can assess the situation."

"Guardians? Parents?"

"As with most of these cases, none that we can find."

"Fine. Let me know as soon as you have more details, and I want the report on my desk tomorrow morning at eight."

The sound of him sucking in his breath whispered down the line, and her gaze narrowed. So much for them keeping her apprised of what was going on.

"I'll bring it to your home office." The terse voice made it clear he was unhappy. "No. My senate office." She pressed the button, ending the connection, as she turned back to Yin.

"Problems?" He scanned her face as if seeking some hint of

frustration, but she'd blanked out the emotions as she'd turned toward him.

"No. Just organizing a meeting for tomorrow morning."

He blinked. "We have the vote on the Protocol bill."

Daniella's stomach wobbled. "I thought we had put that off for a little longer."

The 21st Testing Protocol required all young adults to report to a testing center on a mandated day, four times a year depending on the day of birth, to be tested genetically and physically to see if they were suitable for warrior training.

"I was overruled." Yin spoke quietly, but the importance of the information wasn't lost.

"*What?* Who? Who was lobbying to push this through?" She tottered to the chair and sat down, waiting as Yin settled into the large, red armchair opposite with a sigh.

"My people are sifting through the layers, but there's a wealthy backer who doesn't want to be found. Contacts are to various senatorial PA's but never the same one or from the same origination point. My people aren't trained for this, that's why yours must find the source and deal with it. I don't need to remind you, senator, that time is running short. If this bill gets through..."

There it was. The unspoken words hung in the air between them. *If my people don't find out who's behind this, then a war on a worldwide scale, never seen before, will be unleashed.*

The citizens had become restive in the months since Clarissa had appeared and Michael's transformation. Now they demanded soldiers of the highest caliber in case more of the biocybernetics attempted to overthrow the world. No matter how careful Delspar's delivery, the threat lay heavy. It was all garbage of course, and Daniella privately had grave concerns that Delspar's reasoning might tip the hand of Colvert's unknown backers.

"I can't argue with them."

Yin nodded. "Your brother."

"And now Clarissa." The fact that two bio-cybernetically enhanced people were part of her family proved too great a barrier.

Any argument she might put forward would be negated because of her 'affiliation' to bio-cybes.

The thought of these genetically engineered super-soldiers they'd detected after Clarissa's abduction and escape, at one person's beck and call, meant the annihilation of anyone who stood in their way. The end of the government as they knew it if the other faction won.

The entire planet ruled by one person, with the power to unleash deadly force and nothing to hold them back. That very idea left her shuddering, and her mouth dried as the knowledge settled in her mind like cold, hard marbles striking a tiled floor.

"I understand, sir. My people are currently following up a lead, but I'll see if we can't step it up."

"I can't make any more people available to you, Daniella. You understand my situation. They have someone on the inside. Right now, I've stretched and prevaricated with the truth, hiding the true mission, but I can't stretch it any further or they'll suspect we know. That would be worse."

Daniella nodded. Yin was right. Once questions started as to why she required extra personal assistance of the military and investigative kind, then nothing would quell them until the truth was outed.

"Yes."

He rose and slid his hand over her shoulder. "I have every faith in you, my dear. It won't be forgotten." Then he moved toward the door, stopping with his hand on the knob. "I'll bump that meeting down to say, ten? That should give you enough time to complete the briefing."

The click of the door as he closed it felt like a spike driven through her brain.

THE BOY EYED JONAH, mutiny glaring just from the other side of the table.

"So, how did you get here?"

The boy shrugged, and Jonah's frustration ratcheted up yet another notch. He'd been here for over an hour, and the boy had yet to answer any question verbally.

The doctor hovered at Jonah's shoulder, but he didn't acknowledge him. Instead, he centered his gaze on the man-child ahead and allowed a fraction of a smile to emerge.

"I think he should be returned to his bed and allowed to rest."

Jonah shook his head, his gaze remaining focused on the boy. "No. I don't think so. I'll be taking him into custody now."

"What?" The doctor's shock echoed in the room, and Jonah detected fear from the professional. From the boy came a smirk.

Thrusting his hand into his pocket, he withdrew the leather identification unit and held it up so only the doctor would see what was on his card. "Check with your supervisor, doctor. This badge allows me to detain and interrogate anyone suspected of representing a danger to the state and the citizens of our planet."

"But... He's just a kid!"

The kid visibly paled, and Jonah yawned, stretched, and kept up his attitude of 'don't care'. It was a front, of course. He was deeply concerned about the boy and the action he was about to take, but he was also aware that striking quickly was the only way they'd have any hope of finding out where he came from.

With slow movements, he rose, his peripheral vision showing that Franklin too moved. The boy scootched back in his seat, and the doctor fumed, "I'm getting the head of my department."

The door slammed shut, and Jonah narrowed his gaze. "You do that. Meanwhile, young man, you and I have a date with my people."

The boy jumped, aiming at him. Franklin shoved himself in front of the door, cutting off his means of escape. They'd been down this path before, and they knew once the teen eluded them, it would be difficult to retrieve him.

Extending his arms in a lightning-quick move, Jonah grabbed and held the wiggling body. Teeth sank into his arm, and he grunted and shook the nameless teen off, just enough to make him unclench his jaw.

Jonah grappled and captured the boy's wrist—thicker in his opinion than the average teen's—and held tight. Franklin moved in behind him, applying the poly-oxide material cuffs to the man-child. Once they clicked onto the boy's arms, Franklin tightened them while the boy twisted and turned, attempting to break free of his bonds.

"Don't bother trying. We've had adults that can't break out of those."

The teen grinned. "They can't do what I can," he snarled, and Jonah laughed.

"True. However, the adults we tested these on can do more." He turned and left Franklin to move the child forward as the door was flung open.

The doctor and his superior scurried in. "You can't take him."

Jonah sneered and extended the ID with his bloodied arm. "Yeah, I can and am. Now get out of my way."

"What happened here?" The older man—the tag fastened to his long, white coat read *Professor Venos*—peered over his glasses at Jonah. "You're hurt. Doctor, go get supplies to clean up his wound."

The younger doctor scowled but hurried to do the professor's bidding.

"No time to stop." As Jonah brushed past the professor, the older man reached out and clamped his hand over Jonah's wound.

"No, you're not leaving right now. I saw your ID, and I know you can take the child, but I will attend to your injuries first."

Jonah grunted, spun, and looked at Franklin. "Get him to our facility. Twenty-four-seven watch. Food is okay, bedding as necessary and ablution. No visitors until we know more."

Franklin nodded and shoved the teen forward. "I'll go with the others and send Fairburn to you."

"No. Leave him with her for now." He daren't name the senator of course, but Franklin narrowed his eyes and nodded his understanding, then pushed the teen out the door and into the hall beyond.

Franklin would get him to their holding cells quickly. What's more, he did grumpy and scary really well, although it was just an act, but Jonah had no qualms with that.

Jonah retreated to the small table where they'd attempted to interrogate the child, hoping he might be able to loosen some information from the professor. "He the first you've seen like that?" he queried and hunkered down on the chair before starting to roll up his shirt sleeve so the man could inspect his injury.

The doctor they'd dismissed earlier hurried into the room, dropping supplies to the tabletop, his gaze roaming. "Where'd the boy go?"

I guess all professions have those who won't take no for an answer. "Gone. In secure custody."

The way the doctor acted set off alarm bells, and Jonah made a mental note to follow up on the younger man. Dr. Alan Figueroa. He forced the name into his mind. Perhaps he knew something, given his reaction to the incident. Jonah had long ago stopped believing that the klaxon that regularly went off in his head was an overreaction. Experience—bitter and painful— reinforced that trusting his instincts was always wise.

"But you can't take a child. They have rights and—"

"That's enough, Figueroa! Return to your post and attend to your patients." The professor's voice was firm.

The man gaped then huffed and left the room, the billow of his white coat following him. The door slammed shut.

"I apologize for my young colleague. He's eager and unruly still. That will change in time."

Jonah grunted and relaxed into the chair. "So, tell me, professor, is the boy your first?"

He waited as the man cleaned his wound.

"No, he's not. We've had a few. Usually my residents deal with them, but tonight things were crazy. There are some specific things we notice with the children and teens who've presented. They tend to be alone. They've come in with a range of accidents and ailments, usually associated with high-impact sports or wilderness challenge type accidents, in my opinion."

Considering the answer, Jonah frowned. "You mean, they have similar types of ailments?"

"Yes and no. We question them carefully. The first few were chatty and told us about their injuries—hiking, rock climbing, wrestling, that kind of thing. By about the fourth they must have worked out where our concerns lay, and from there they started to clam up on us. They only shared the necessary facts. This one though, he didn't tell us anything. We had to work it out by trial and error."

"Who collects them when they're released?"

The professor shook his head as he applied salve and a bandage to Jonah's arm. "That's the thing. They've disappeared on us, usually after a day or two here. We know they've recovered because tracking their healing factors has become something of a marathon. They seem to heal up mostly overnight once they've received appropriate treatment. We go to the bed allocated and it's empty. Drips disengaged. Catheters tugged out. They're just gone." He sighed. "There, now keep that covering on. Here's an antibiotic inhaler. Twice a day. Two puffs. No alcohol." He shoved it at Jonah.

"Could I trouble you to see their charts? I believe they're connected with a case we need to find an answer to quickly. Your records would assist us greatly."

The professor sniffed. "I'm not supposed to share them, as you know. Even under the new act, you're meant to have an order. However, if you promise to update me with details, and when the time is right, let me have a look at what you find—purely for professional reasons— then I'm sure if they were accidentally messaged to you, well..."

The professor rose as Jonah handed the man a card. "I appreciate your care and attention."

Then Jonah stood and rounded the table, heading for the door.

"One last thing. These kids, or whatever they are, can be dangerous. Be on your guard if more come in." He left the professor standing there watching him.

BLEARY-EYED, Jonah stared out the window as dawn crept over the horizon. He'd spent long hours hunched over the keyboard as his arm throbbed. The report was almost complete, but Franklin had indicated the boy was currently sleeping in the practically bare cell, so Jonah had begun the process of organizing what they knew. Not that there was much.

The reports from the professor had come through, and they'd made interesting reading. So far it seemed only one girl had presented, her injuries similar to those of the boys. Broken bones, some hypothermia, two had suffered extreme wounding, one losing a hand. It was partially grown back when the boy disappeared from the hospital.

On a groan, Jonah stood, stretching his back to release the tension before striding to the coffee machine and pouring some of the liquid into his cup.

McNally stuck her head around the corner. "You've probably had enough of that. Water will ease your thirst."

He slumped into his seat, taking a drink. "It's not thirst. I need to stay awake long enough to present the report, then come back and question the kid. After that, I might get a chance at some shut-eye," Jonah rasped.

She shrugged. "Your kidneys, not mine. But when the transplant is scheduled, just remember that I warned you."

"So, what was it you wanted?" He couldn't control the bite in his voice, but she didn't take offense, instead loosed a burbling laugh.

"You might also like to take something to soothe the aggravation in your voice. Here's the documents you wanted on hard copy from the hospital. There's some interesting stuff in there, and I high-lighted it." She tossed the folder onto his desk. "Now, if you intend to reach the senator's office by eight, you should have left maybe ten minutes ago. Traffic's a snarl, and unless you intend using lights, I don't like your chances."

He bolted upright at that, checked the chrono on his wrist, and cursed. "Dammit!" Jonah launched out of his chair, grabbing the wrinkled jacket from the back. He snapped up the folder and shot forward, leaving his office at a run.

McNally thrust a small tin of teeth cleaner pills into his pocket. Jonah hurtled past McNally, who stepped sideways amid the chorus of her laughter.

———

DANIELLA STARED OUT THE WINDOW, the sense of unease spreading throughout her body. Jonah was due there any minute, but the fact that he'd left Michael's wedding without a word to either herself or her brother didn't bode well.

Oh, they'd ensured that she had the information and she could understand the urgency in following through after the fact, but she didn't cope well with being left hanging.

Two sharp raps echoed. "Enter," called Daniella.

The door behind her opened, and she spun on the thick, wool-substitute carpet. Across the room, she read exhaustion in the tense set of Jonah's shoulders and the deep lines at the sides of his eyes.

"Coffee?" Daniella moved before he could answer, heading for the carafe, but he shook his head. "All right then, let's get down to your report." She changed direction to her desk then sank into the seat, grateful for the expanse of wood that separated them like a wall. "What do you have to report?"

His gaze narrowed. "You're not chewing me out?"

"Is there any likelihood that it would stop you from doing that again? Of fixing the fact that you keep haring off without authorization and adequate backup?"

His snort answered her query more effectively than words.

"Fine. So, show me what you've found."

He thwacked the old-fashioned file onto the top of her desk, and Daniella flinched.

"Lots. The teen we picked up last night is not the first of this kind. It seems they've started on their training. The ones that arrive at the ER have similar problems. Some with hypothermic issues, others with broken bones—ribs, etcetera. One lost fingers, another a hand. The few admitted to wards are canny. They escape before anyone can bring them to the notice of the appropriate authorities."

Daniella bit her lip, considering the harsh, bare-bones report he'd just given. "How did we get the notification then?"

Jonah quirked his brow. "The protocols you had us put in place? The ones we all complained about?" His tiny grin had her heart thudding a little faster in her chest. "They paid off. The tags on hospital systems automatically reported to them once the terms 'accelerated healing' and 'no traceable DNA' were entered. The third string was 'no guardian or parental consent on file.'"

"Dammit. These kids can't just appear from nowhere!" Frustration welled, a core of scalding wire that wound tightly inside her mind and body. Her fingers curled into claws against the wood of the desk. "Kids and teens aren't disposable commodities. So where did the parents go? Why can't we trace any that used the service all those years ago?"

"Because their files were changed. The names they used don't exist, and the files that would give us the answers also don't exist."

That stopped her raging, and she stilled, turning her gaze to the man in front of her. "Changed? How?"

"It's a simple matter of changing the encryption log, senator. I've got people working on it. Have had for months, but the system keeps overloading or imploding, depending on how we attack each backup. Our best minds haven't been able to overcome the fail-safes they instituted in the programming."

At every turn, her team remained stymied. Daniella rubbed her now aching brow, trying to consider options. This situation had to be closed down as soon as possible, but unless they could find the head of the beast, it would be like the legend of Medusa with heads growing back at twice the rate. "What about Clarissa? Can she—"

"Already tried it. And before you ask, we've already attempted to clone her data sequencing. No success. Colvert's newest files are also encrypted, using a different set of parameters. We're having even less luck as the kill commands are more robust and better hidden. Someone on Colvert's side knows his stuff."

Daniella groaned. "Okay, so we've had no luck so far with

anything in over, what? Twelve months? How did you get on with the current patient files?"

"As far as we can tell, he hadn't yet entered them into his system, so there's nothing to track. We think it's because Colvert likely had paper-based copies, which he subsequently destroyed. Or e-versions encoded to destruct under certain circumstances. We've only tracked down four hundred of his more recent patients, and while some chose to take immediate action, the rest are now receiving extended care through our safe network of specialists. Our genetic testing is showing that these children received advanced nanos that don't carry the same issues as earlier iterations, though we won't be completely sure for some time."

"Fine then. See if you can get Colvert to assist." A long shot, she knew, but her team could be mighty persuasive.

"Can't do. Colvert attempted suicide three nights ago, and we can't use him in the short term."

That news crashed down on her. "Why wasn't I informed?" Breathing became difficult, the oxygen sticking in her throat and lungs.

"I tried communicating that, but if you remember, you were unavailable as there was a night vote, then you had a meeting with the president, followed by a security briefing, an overnight trip to—"

Jonah's words pealed over her. "Okay, so I've been harder than usual to get in contact with." Daniella exhaled heavily. "We need to devise a more efficient system for sharing intelligence." The instant the words were out, his mouth thinned.

It wasn't his fault she'd been hard to contact. Nor was it hers. The demands of her senatorial position and the high security of this case meant he couldn't just leave her a message on her communicator, nor could he explain it to her personal assistant, Kallee.

His jacket snagged, and he reached to the back of his head and hissed, face pulling tight and paling.

"What's wrong?" Daniella was half out of her chair as he waved her back.

"Nothing. I just had a run-in with some teeth."

"Teeth? The kid bit you?" A rumble of anger started in her belly. "Have you sought medical assistance?"

His lopsided grin further destabilized her emotions. "The professor took care of it. He seemed to think it was important it be dealt with immediately too."

Now that she looked at Jonah more closely, it was clear the exhaustion wasn't a short- term situation. "When was the last time you and the team had a break?"

He laughed. "Why? Going to force us to shut down?"

The bite of sarcasm was hard to accept. Daniella straightened her spine. "No. But you've been run ragged with this, and we need to recharge our batteries. Perhaps a break will give us time to re-assess what we've achieved and how to move forward."

"You're the boss, senator. Whatever you decide is what will happen." He stood, brushed off his jacket, and the action grew in her mind, like an omen. Her stomach clenched.

"Fine then. I'll be in touch after the reading of the bill."

Now he frowned and leaned heavily on the chair. "They're still pushing it through after all the information we've tabled?"

Daniella nodded. "They want the protocol passed by the end of the year. If I could tell the others why it's a bad choice, I know they'd understand and pull it, but right now, without any evidence to show who's pulling strings, I don't dare make full disclosure. President Yin agrees. We need to continue and hope we can uncover who's behind the plot before it can go much further. But there's only one more reading and the final vote after today."

Unconsciously, Daniella lifted her thumb and bit down on the nail. The crunch centered her attention, and she groaned, dropping her hand down to her side.

"Go back to the office, bed down the report, then you're off duty at least until tomorrow morning," she ordered. "If I need you, I'll be in contact."

He straightened to attention, feet clapping together as he saluted, then left her, alone and confused in the office, wondering how the hell they could sort this mess out.

Chapter 3

The senate was full, everyone attending in their official capacity, along with the largest recorded audience to see democracy in action. Except Daniella knew there was nothing democratic about the process unfolding before her eyes.

"The 21st Testing Protocol will allow us to seek the best and strongest among us. Allow us to preserve our way of life. To keep our homeworld safe and secure."

God help her, she wanted to vomit as Senior House Opposition Senator Delspar spouted the lines they'd instituted in their media campaign. The Protocol wasn't about truth. It was to enable the military to detect and seize the children for their benefit.

The only thing was, at least they'd have time to fight, even if the policy moved on to the next reading. After all, it would be years before the first of the genetically engineered children reached the required twenty-first birthday. Except something felt wrong about the scenario and the speed at which they wanted to shunt it through.

"We seek not to remove people's freedoms, but to request sectors of our community, those most capable..." Delspar paused for effect, scanning the crowd who lapped it up and smiling in a mock-benign fashion. "...to protect our sovereign state."

Daniella's fingers curled as she sat, perched on the edge of her seat, stomach congealing in a mass of nerves.

"We don't believe that the selection should begin immediately. We feel that a process of education and preparation should begin soon, but that it will take years to implement the process, to set in train the equipment and testing regime. We are therefore seeking a ten-year lead in process—beginning immediately—where we meet and process the evaluation of those who would be our forerunners. Those who'll be the first of the class, so to speak."

Those words hit her like a fist in the stomach. *Ten years. Evaluating those who'd be the first.* The genetically engineered children who would be turning twenty-one as the front runners were little more than children now. The first intake barely eleven now.

What was being suggested was that they already be tagged, and their education prospects amended to their specific skillset. Her mouth dried at the thought of them taking children into the twisted regime they proposed.

Daniella had expected to hear of the introduction within twelve months, then to start with a planning process of several years before moving onto trials.

A ripple of uncertainty spread through the crowd, echoes of whispers a wave that washed over her. Maybe all wasn't lost? Delspar, the career politician who'd been groomed since his early twenties—some two decades ago—frowned at the sound. She could see the way his eyes moved, considering and weighing options on how best to sway opinion in the chamber.

He shook his head—the mane of silver locks he'd kept artfully long and curled shivered in response—his hand extended, and the crowd responded, settling and hushing to hear more. "No, no, no! Clinical testing and trials will be taking place, and a suitably chosen expert providing leadership. It will all be for the benefit of our people. When taken in tandem with the push to populate the planet of Centaura Minor, we will be advertising ourselves as adventurers and colonizers. We open ourselves to a level of visibility our species has never before faced, and as a result, to increased danger from without. Our testing regime and training must be completely re-examined. The ever-changing needs of our military forces demand consideration. This is why we need the time and funding. This must be a project of planetary significance. It requires immediate and adequate funding, ensuring our success. That is why the 21st Testing Protocol requires enaction now! To provide certainty for our future and those of our children."

Delspar flung his hands out and upward, affecting a supplication, and the cheers rose, a wild cacophony that echoed in the chamber. His dominant performance spelled the death-knell of their hopes.

He turned, faced Daniella across the table, and smiled.

Your turn. The words and sentiment were there in his gaze.

Then he collected his sheaf of papers and returned to his seat. It was theater, and given the hollers and hoots, he'd done his job. It would be a hard act to follow. Daniella would start with her appeal then move in with the facts and figures—the little she could share anyway.

Daniella rose, stepped up to the speaker's box, and inhaled. "I come not to argue that our needs are not foremost in planning for the future. To remain unprepared for the eventualities that could exist once we move beyond our planet and solar system would be madness. However, at what point are the needs of the few so carelessly and cavalierly thrown to the four winds? We claim to love our children, and yet we, as legislators, are removing rights from children who are born. Those who have begun contributing to our society. When did their needs become unimportant?"

The first whispers began, dissent growing, but not against the regime—no, against those who fought the protocol implementation. She'd expected it, though not as vociferously or viciously relayed. A woman screamed at her, the words lost in the echoing chamber.

She glanced up, addressing the gallery. "*Your children.* Your grandchildren. They are the ones who will pay. They are the ones who won't have a say—"

The words had barely left her mouth when an object struck, hitting her in the head. She fell as blood spattered her hands and the seat in front of her, and uproar ensued.

Guards took position around the senators, while the plasglass emergency screens shot up, protecting those in the chamber from the gallery. Someone grabbed her, dragged her from the podium to the seats behind, and she slumped boneless to the floor. Her mind spun in circles and she couldn't tell who assisted her. Gray mist formed around her mind as the pain ricocheted throughout her system, then exploded and stole her senses and she fainted.

COMING BACK TO REALITY, the ache in her head pounded as people milled around her. "What happened?"

A doctor, clad in a white coat, stepped in front of her and batted away the hand she'd raised to feel the damage. "You were hit at the beginning of the vote." Her stomach bottomed out. "They stopped the vote?"

His gaze met hers. "No."

She knew what that meant. *The vote was lost.*

Chapter 4

Settling onto his bed, Jonah tugged off his shoes. "Oh, man!" His body ached, and his eyes were like sandpits—gritty and sore—while sleep was little more than a desperate dream from long ago.

Pondering his choices of stripping down or crawling on the bed fully clothed was replaced by 'who cares?' as he lay back. The soft, pillowy surface beneath him seductive as it lulled him.

Jonah closed his eyes, sighing and allowing his mind to wander. His brain began to settle, and sleep curled itself around him. Then the peal of his communicator split the air. He jerked back to wakefulness. For a second he considered ignoring it, but instead he burrowed his hand into the pocket of his pants and retrieved the tiny device.

"Yeah? Hello?"

"Where are you?" Michael asked.

He shot up in the bed, knowing that Michael would have only contacted him from his honeymoon in an exceptional circumstance. He opened his eyes as his mind whirred back into action. "What's up?"

"There was an attack at the senate. Daniella was hurt."

Michael's terse wording increased the suddenly ragged cadence of his heart rate.

"What? I'm on my way."

Even as he shoved his feet into the shoes he'd just discarded, he dialed the senator's security team office. No answer. He tried again, and still there was no answer.

Fury peaked inside him, and he contacted Kallee. When she picked up, he ignored all pleasantries. "Is she all right?"

"Jonah? Yeah, kind of. Look, are you—"

"I'll be there in ten. I'm coming in hot with sirens and lights."

"Good. Use the side entrance and engage the armor. You may need it."

Nausea rose and he shoved it away, pounding through his apartment to the front door. It slammed behind him, but he ignored that, knowing his locks would kick in automatically.

His car sat in its spot, and he remotely started the engine before tugging the door open and sliding inside. "Senate House. Side entrance at speed. Full armament. Lights and sirens."

The vehicle moved—auto-driver engaged—pushing the car into traffic while the blare had people moving out of his path as it rocketed forward. The town passed by in a blur as he called up the secure feed and rewound long enough to view the attack on the chamber.

"Fucking assholes." Nothing else seemed appropriate as his shoulders set in an attitude of rage. His hands fisted. He'd find who did this, and they'd face retribution.

Daniella. He saw the blood on the screen. His brain felt tight, as if ready to explode.

"I'll kill them," he vented before grappling with the morass of emotions. This ball of seething rage wouldn't help her now. The best thing he could do was get her home, where she would be safe. Then he'd call the team together, because this smelled like a setup.

Rewinding the video, he watched every movement, pinpointed the location of the combatant, and grimaced as he realized they'd been fully aware of the eyes in the ceiling and walls. They'd been careful to hide behind others so no identification could be made.

"Goddammit!" His hand thudded the steering wheel.

"Do you require the vehicle to stop?" the automated voice asked.

"Negative. Proceed to the set location."

The building loomed, the stone structure imposing, and he took control of the vehicle, smoothly navigating to a small side door very few knew of. He jumped out of the car, pressing his hand to the print reader before gazing at the retinal scanner.

The door slid wide, and Kallee, a small woman with dark hair and worried brown eyes, met him. "She's coming now."

The door behind Kallee slid open, and Daniella appeared, the pristine white pantsuit she'd worn rumpled and bloodstained, her hair matted, and a doctor in a white coat was keeping her upright, muttering about foolish women.

"You're her escort?" The doctor pinned him with a sharp gaze.

Jonah reached out, needing to be sure she was still alive, and disbelieving of what he saw. Instinct forced him to cup her jaw, inspect the darkening bruise and jagged injury. "Yes. I'm taking her to a secure location."

"She has a slight concussion. Will there be a medic on hand in case she takes a turn for the worse?"

Jonah's blood curdled. "Is she likely to?" *Maybe we should stay here until the danger has passed.* The thoughts made no sense, but it was all he could do right now to hold onto his sanity in the face of her injury and weakness.

"No. But I want some assurance my patient will receive adequate care. Otherwise, I'm not——"

He released the breath he'd held onto at the doctor's words. It whistled through his teeth, and he gritted them together, thinking swiftly before answering. "Rest assured. I have a physician I can call in at a moment's notice should it be required. Is this the worst of it?" Jonah indicated to the head wound.

"Yes. She needs to be watched, fluids, and rest. Nothing more."

Jonah grunted his response, slid his arm around Daniella——the senator, he reminded himself——and tugged her close. "Thanks."

She was shaky—wobbly and unbalanced—and on an oath, Jonah picked her up in his arms.

"What are you..." Her voice slurred, and he held her just a little tighter until she wiggled.

"Shh, senator. I'm going to put you in the car as quickly as I can, then we're getting out of here."

With care, he slid her onto the seat, fastened her seatbelt under the watchful gaze of both the doctor and her PA, then closed the door with a soft thud before he stalked around to the other side.

Just before he clambered inside, he turned back and pinned Kallee with his glare. "I'll get them, and they'll wish they hadn't done this."

He dropped into the seat, closed the door as rage simmered below the surface. They'd pay. No one hurt the senator; on his watch or not.

THE HAZY FILM that inhabited Daniella's consciousness dissipated slowly, like a frost on a cold winter's morning. She vaguely remembered Jonah lifting her into the vehicle and the sense of movement. Now peeking through the veil of her eyelashes, she noted the tension in his jaw. A muscle ticked in his cheek, and his gaze narrowed as he concentrated on driving.

"You were supposed to be home. Sleeping." Her voice echoed in the silence.

He whipped around to scan her. "You're awake." The breathy quality of his words settled in her stomach, warming her.

"I wasn't exactly asleep. Why did you come?"

"You needed me. Now lie back and let me drive." He returned his attention to the road, and she sighed.

"We lost the vote, Jonah. I wasn't there because of—"

"It was organized. I'd lay my life on that. The whole situation, from his speech and the look he gave you at the end, was carefully planned."

"What?" She pushed up in the seat, only to stop and moan, her hand flying to her head. Her movements jarring her brain and sending shooting pains rocketing. In response, her eyes closed, and she groaned.

"Lie still, and the pain will pass."

Daniella licked her dry lips. "And you'd know that how? Are you a doctor?"

His grunt was followed by, "No. I've just had enough concussions and head injuries to know."

Cracking open one eye, she peered at him. "When?"

Now he glared back. "During the war and before. I used to play contact sports until I joined up."

"Oh." For a moment she wondered what he'd played. The positions he'd fielded and, much to her dismay, what he'd looked like in the uniform.

Come on, Daniella. He might be an above-average looking man, but you're not interested. No time. Career is your focus!

No matter what she tried to tell herself, it didn't work. The warm, tingling sensation made a mockery of her attempts to stifle any form of romantic interest.

Blaming the split in her thinking on the head injury, she pondered his earlier words. "So, you're sure it was a setup?"

"Yeah. On my way, I scanned the feed. The perpetrator knew exactly where they needed to be. Hiding behind others, face obscured, and turned away from the viewer." He scrubbed his hands over his eyes. "I need to find out what hit you. I should have asked immediately, but I was more concerned with getting you to safety. Once you're settled, I'll get one of the other agents to go in and meet with the officers onsite. Now lie back, you're almost home."

A tear trickled down her cheek, and she dashed it away.

"Hey? Are you okay?" He engaged the manual overdrive with a click, and the vehicle veered off the roadway to a verge. Once it came to a stop, he turned, his face a mask of uncertainty. "I can take you back. The doc—"

"No." She bit her lip and shook her head, and another bloom of agony hit. "I want to go home. Please?"

"Dan—Senator, you're hurting, and I'm not sure..." Jonah was clearly overset by emotions, and for a moment a whisper of hope bloomed in her chest, inching its way into the corners of her mind. Her brain refused to categorize the emotion, fearing it would change everything she'd worked for and came so close to achieving.

"No. Take me home. I'll be fine. If I look sick though, contact Dr. Windhower. She'll come once you explain the situation."

Silence.

He was thinking over her words, and she reached out a hand, touched his, and a zap of electricity shot between them. "Oh!"

He tugged away and settled both hands on the steering wheel, looking forward. "If you're sure, senator."

The chill in his voice made her frown. "Dammit, my name is Daniella. Use it when we're alone."

Daniella couldn't control the frustration in her tone. Didn't want to. They'd known each other from the time Michael, her younger brother, had been in the Medical Corps.

"After all these years, I'd think it's at least acceptable in private."

Jonah's laugh was bitter and strung out. "I don't think that would be wise, senator." He turned back to her and speared her with a hot glare. "Anything less than formality would be very, very unwise."

FURY COILED like a snake in Jonah's gut. Daniella should have been safe in the senate chamber. That she'd been injured meant there had been a monumental failure of the assembly's security.

Someone would be held accountable for this.

The sight of the dark blood staining her tunic fed a primal urge within him. One he'd kept leashed, but those boundaries were little more than weak tethers at this point, strained and ready to split.

He stalked back and forth after she'd slowly made her way up the stairs to her room, her hands clutching the rails after she'd refused all offers of assistance. A glance at the clock told him barely ten minutes had passed, yet they dragged like hours. He pulled his hand through his hair, ignoring the post-adrenalin jitters.

His communicator buzzed, and even as he flicked it on, he scanned the caller. "My sister—" Michael's voice boomed, and he exhaled heavily.

"She's fine. Hurt but without any major damage."

"Good. Look, Clarissa and I are heading home—"

"No, Michael. I've got it under control. I've called the team in, and we're going to investigate exactly what happened. Where the failure stems from and find a workable solution for overcoming it. Her personal security team will be beefed up. You've got my word on it."

Michael swore, but Jonah pushed on.

"She'll be fine. Take the opportunity for the downtime, brother, because I seriously doubt we'll get another for a while."

The grunt of agreement had him unclenching the hands he'd fisted. "All right. But if you need me—"

"We'll call. Now go spend some quality time with your bride." On that note, he clicked the communication device off and whirled at the sound of an opening door.

David entered the room, his lips tight, white lines of anger. "Where is she?"

"The senator is bathing. I've got the team meeting her as soon as possible, and I've already apprised your brother of the situation."

"Give me the status of her injuries." David paced, his face set in hard lines of rage.

"The doctor said a mild concussion. She was knocked out, but only momentarily. She'll be sore and needs rest. I haven't yet apprised her of the fact, but she won't be leaving the house until I've re-aligned her security team. She can work from home and only attend the chamber as necessary. I'll be making a direct request to President Yin that the chamber be closed until we've dealt with the issue at hand."

David stopped and scoured him with a glare. "Will it work?"

"Normally I'd say no, but this time I think there's more at play than even we expected. I watched the vision on my way. I'd bet every credit I own that it was staged. The Protocol vote sailed through in spite of the disruption. He looked at her—"

"Who?" David advanced three long, hard steps, and Jonah scowled.

"Delspar. He smiled before handing over the floor, just before the crowd jostled and the item was thrown. They knew the placement of the spy eyes. It feels like a finely tuned instrument, and she was the fucking pluck."

David cocked his head to the side. "You need to sort that out."

He grunted at the barely hidden suggestion of personal involvement. "Wrong time. Wrong place and the wrong woman." Jonah shrugged it off and turned away. "We need extra security. Someone we can trust."

"Who?"

When Jonah turned back, he'd once more dragged the mask of interested outsider onto his face. "McNally. She's bright and can stay closer than the rest of us."

This time David made an angry sound.

Chapter 5

Daniella liked Agent McNally. The woman looked soft and sweet, which was so far from the truth that it always amazed her. Standing a mere five-foot-five and built slightly, if you didn't watch the canny shrewdness in her eyes or the careful way she held herself, it would be easy to think her a piece of fluff.

The woman was an efficient human weapon though. Trained and far more than merely proficient in tools of war, hand-to-hand, and martial arts, she was also a strategizing wonder kid, who'd been raised by the state as an orphan. She kept her red hair short, her nails shorter, and her list of friends to an absolute minimum.

Daniella considered her a friend and now added 'nanny' to her list of roles. The new title didn't sit well.

"How long will you be on my tail?"

The woman handled the vehicle with fluid grace and shocked her with a grin. "Tired of me already? It's a bit late for that, senator. I'm here until we track down the offender and determine that there is no further risk to you. You are, after all, spearheading the Anti-Protocol movement, and that makes you public target number one."

Daniella glanced out the window of the vehicle, biting her lip. How to proceed now with an Anti-Protocol vote left her grasping for ideas and plans. She knew they didn't currently have the support of the community, and even though they'd worked hard to try to outmaneuver the others, they hadn't known the exact situation of the imbalance until now.

So, why had vote skewed the way it had? Was it the will of constituents, interference from the unknown faction, or individual ideology? And how could she stymie the last step?

She pondered the question as they drove. Some of the other senators would vote based on the needs of their voters—she could list them easily. Some would base theirs on the longevity of any political capital, while others appeared invested on a superficial level. For a few, some kind of kickback came into play. It was how it had always been, but working out who sat in which camp presented more of a challenge.

Clicking the tiny communicator she carried in her hand, she spoke softly to her assistant, Kallee. "I need a full list of the senators' votes yesterday. Who voted for, against, and abstained with the 21st Protocol. Also, I'm going to want dossiers on those who are new to the chamber, their platforms, etcetera. How soon can you arrange that?"

The long-suffering sigh that greeted her request left Daniella frowning.

"Kallee?"

"There are more than two hundred new senators in the chamber since the last investiture. Among those, I know hardly any. As to their platforms, it's going to take a while. I can get some of the juniors—"

"No. Play this one close to the chest. Just you, Kallee. Take as long as you need. Delegate everything else. I need this info as soon as you can scrabble it together."

In her mind, Daniella could imagine Kallee pushing the bridge of her glasses up with a single finger, her eyes almost crossed as she thought over the request. "This has to do with yesterday, right? You think—"

Daniella cut her off, feeling guilt at dragging her PA into the mess. "Leave the thoughts and considerations to those who deal with this daily. Right now, delegate your usual tasks and get me whatever you can."

"Got it, senator," said Kallee, then the line clicked off.

"Do you think that was wise?" Agent McNally spoke quietly.

Daniella turned, frustration uppermost in her mind as she peered at the woman driving. "I don't know, but it's information that I think is vital. Once we have that, I can give it to the team to delve deeper." Uncertainty, guilt, and more than a dollop of anger clawed at her.

"Jonah won't be happy with—"

"Jonah will have to suck it up then, won't he? I call the shots. He's a strategist, and with Michael away, effectively the team's second-in-command, but I'm the one that has to front the public." The fury abated somewhat as she considered her words, flushing beet red if the heat of her face was anything to go by.

Daniella tensed in her seat. She counted backward from ten before she was once more in control of her emotions.

"I'm sorry. That's unfair and uncalled for. Jonah is a good agent and exceptional at his work. I need to try to find a way to sell the truth to the public—or at least what we can tell them. Make them understand that the Protocol will be a bad decision all around. I'm just feeling the pressure right now."

The silence from the other side of the vehicle left her feeling decidedly uncomfortable, and the longer it stretched, the worse she felt.

"You know, Jonah feels that he's responsible for the attack."

Upon hearing McNally's words, Daniella felt like a worm. Lower than a worm, because the words were echoing in her mind. She'd effectively suggested he wasn't pulling his weight.

"I'm sorry, McNally."

Silence.

Dammit, she'd made a total mess of her apology and explanation. McNally—did she even have a first name—didn't reprimand her like Daniella roundly deserved. "McNally?"

"Yeah?"

"What's your name?" She turned and stared at the agent

driving, pleased to see the surprise on the woman's face. It was a hundred times better than the anger she richly deserved.

"I, uh... Why do you want to know?"

Daniella wondered why she was hemming and hawing. "Well?"

"It's Wilhemina. But no one calls me that. I'm Mac or McNally. Some call me Erin. It's my middle name."

Daniella stifled the laugh. "Well then, Mac. Let's get into work and see what we need to do next."

The woman eyed her doubtfully. "You aren't going to tell the others, are you?" Suspicion dripped from her voice and painted her face.

"No, Mac. I promise. Your secret is safe with me."

The vehicle came to a stop, and they decamped, Mac depressing the lock and alarm activator as they scurried up the steps.

JONAH'S EYES BURNED, the grittiness harsh and sandpapery on his aching eyeballs. The screen swam in front of him, and he lurched from the desk.

He remembered McNally's admonition to drink more water and grabbed a bottle, twisting the cap decisively before lifting the open bottle to his lips. The water flowed down his throat, soothing the burn as he swallowed. The day and night past were long distant memories as the clock ticked over to yet another mealtime.

He sifted through the list of entries into the chamber, the visitors who completed the full data scan. No one stood out. Women and men—some from the old school group—none of the names triggering further scans.

There was more to this than met the eye though. He knew it instinctively.

The jangle of his communicator split the air. "Yeah?"

"Hey, Jonah. The senator pulled the details of the new members and asked me to shunt it over," McNally informed him. "She reckons it's probably a high priority."

He swore, long and loud, then sighed. Great, now she was

digging around. Might as well paint a bloody huge target on her forehead too. He'd be talking to her the next time they were in the same location about keeping her pretty head down.

"Hey, don't shoot the messenger. Right now, I'm sitting in her office watching her play nicely with the slimiest toad of senators ever."

"We could swap." The exhaustion echoed as the drag pulled once more at his senses.

"Yeah... Nah! Anyway, you should have the file via secure system about now. Anything you want me to do specifically?" McNally sounded hopeful, as if the task of babysitting the senator was arduous, and he grunted.

"Talk with the PA. Get what info you can on who knows the senator's routine, knew she'd be the first to rebut the argument, and anything that seems to trigger a reaction. Anything you learn which may fill in the gaps, contact me immediately. I'm going to farm some of this out to the others in the team."

"'Kay then. Well, I'll leave you with it."

The line buzzed and he dragged himself back to the seat before slumping. Maybe closing his eyes for five minutes would help.

They fluttered closed, and the world melted away. * ***

Daniella's day had been a write-off. Nothing useful, just more of the schmoozing and useless platitudes that these career politicians—with nothing more significant to achieve than re- election—seemed to excel at.

McNally had met with the security officers, and Daniella had seen the woman's face tighten with distaste. Now, as she packed up her desk, ready to retreat home, she felt exhausted; mentally and physically depleted.

"Is that everything?" McNally reached out and retrieved the heavy bag from her hand.

"Yeah. I've got enough work to keep me busy in my home office until I'm needed back again next week. Kallee is going to swing over here tomorrow and pick up the correspondence before heading to the house. We can go."

She followed the agent to the door and waited as she peered through the security glass. "Looks all clear," stated McNally.

The door slid open automatically.

The wail of the security klaxon split the air, the eerie wail stopping them both midstride—McNally beyond the door and Daniella inside.

McNally reacted first. "Get back!"

The shove against Daniella's chest had her sailing backward into the vestibule, and the door slammed shut as she watched McNally's body jerk, scarlet pluming.

The woman fell as Daniella screamed and battered at the door. "No! No! McNally!" Her eyes all but blinded with tears, Daniella scrabbled to find the intercom button. "Officer down! Assistance needed in the western secured entrance."

She slumped as the pool of red spread beneath the agent on the other side of the door. In the distance, she noted people, black-clad, moving forward, and instinct kicked in. She slammed the lockdown button and sat there, watching as the crowd advanced.

They reached for the door, hands grasping the panel, shaking it.

One cocked his rifle and aimed. Daniella closed her eyes, fearing this was her end, her brain screaming at the injustice to the whine of rollers as the clear, reinforced barrier dropped.

The secure inner door clanged shut. The military-grade, ballistic glass shuddered beneath the onslaught from outside—groaning but remaining in place with every blow of rifle against the egress. It blocked their attempts to enter the building even as it shivered and creaked.

Daniella scrunched her eyes tightly for a moment then opened them, looked up and straight into the cold, blue eyes of a young man.

The slap of feet behind her was met with the retreat of the combatants. "Senator! Are you hurt?"

She shook her head. "McNally! She needs assistance."

THEY GATHERED in the hospital room. Michael and Clarissa had cut short their honeymoon and were heading in their direction. They'd argued long and loud about how to keep the senator from joining them. Jonah had been adamant that her home would be the safest place for her. Of course, he'd been overruled by the senator herself.

The news so far had been limited. McNally had taken several life-threatening gunshots to the chest and abdomen. She'd bled copiously, and her likelihood of pulling through was touch- and-go at best.

Slumped on the metal chair, Jonah wanted to snarl. She'd been doing her job. Babysitting the senator. He'd been in charge, and he hated that she'd sustained an injury on his watch.

He'd been sleeping, for heaven's sake. The knowledge ate at him like acid. She could have died while he slept. Once more, he curled his hands into tight fists.

"It wasn't your fault."

He turned blind eyes to the senator who huddled beside him. The pallor of her face and the still constant shaking reminded him that she too struggled with guilt.

"I should have been the one there. It was my job to look after you."

Her eyes widened as she searched his face. "You hadn't had downtime for the best part of two days. There's no way—"

"Save it, senator. I dropped the ball. It won't happen again." The snarl had them all swiveling to gaze at him.

"That's bullshit, Jonah!" Franklin growled. "You know that we're a team. Hell, you know what makes a team better than most. There's no 'I' in the word team, and you aren't the only person who's feeling guilty. We all have to take responsibility for what went wrong today. That you were left with McNally and no one else was available was a mistake on everyone's part. We—all of us—thought that we could take downtime. We need to schedule ourselves, just like in the war, man. You know how to do that, instead of wallowing in mistakes." Franklin delivered his tirade then rose from his seat.

"I'm getting coffee, and not the slop from these machines. Who else?"

They all sat there stunned by the outburst, if the open mouths and wide eyes were an indication, and Franklin shrugged then mooched off.

Silence reigned, and Jonah considered his words. Franklin usually only spoke when he had something to say. This time he'd hit the nail on the head. Jonah was wallowing, lost in his guilt. That led to disaster.

"Okay then. When we leave here, we convene at the senator's house. We'll divide up the shifts. Make a roster. From this point on, we move and work in pairs."

Footsteps, moving fast, drummed up the corridor, and a disheveled man, David, came careening to a halt. "Where is she?"

It didn't take a blind man to realize he meant McNally. "Operating theatre. They're repairing the damage."

He paled, and Daniella rose, laid a hand against her brother's cheek, and bent toward him. She spoke so quietly that no one else in the room could hear, but they saw the glassy, moist look that filled his eyes.

Jonah looked away, the intensity of the quiet conversation far too intimate for him to watch.

Daniella—the senator—urged the ambassadorial security agent, who was her brother, forward and he settled in the seat beside her. Jonah felt her presence as warmth flooded his cold limbs, and he sank, legs slightly apart while elbows balanced on his knees and his hands clasped together.

Time passed, and they waited in silence. Now and then a doctor or nurse would wander by, and heads snapped up, hopeful, but also fearing a negative report.

This time a slower, measured set of steps echoed in the once again silent hallway. Jonah glanced up and rose, seeing the haggard features of the doctor melt away to be replaced with a smile. Professor Venos—he remembered the man from the altercation with the teenager still in their cells—entered the waiting area.

"I have good news. She'll make a full recovery barring anything unforeseen. However, she won't be back in active service for some time. Agent McNally will require extensive physical therapy, but her excellent health and physical condition will help there."

Jonah wanted to drop. He cleared his throat and a garbled, "Thanks, professor," was about all he could manage.

David hovered at his shoulder. "When can I...uh, we, see her?"

He'd wondered for a long time about David's interest in the agent, and this seemed to clarify it. Jonah couldn't hide the grin that grew on his face. "I'm sure we all understand that you want to see her."

The man snarled, but it was pitiful.

The professor gave a tiny laugh. "She's in recovery now. I'd say give us an hour or so. And one at a time is suggested. Her family—"

"That would be us." He heard the mixture of strain and exhaustion in the senator's voice. "She's an orphan, and we're her family."

He nodded. "Fine then. The majority of you should go home, come back tomorrow at about eleven and McNally should be on the ward."

"No. Professor, she's to have a private room. Send the bill to me, and I'll make sure it's covered."

The professor gave a thoughtful look to the senator then nodded. "If that's the way you want it. I'll advise the staff. Now please, go home. You're scaring my staff."

Jonah snickered. "Come on, gang. Let's get out of here."

Those who had remained in seats rose, but Daniella grabbed his arm. "I should stay with David."

Shaking his head, Jonah looked at the man in question, who quirked his eyebrow in response—the question and agreement unspoken. "No, senator. The best thing you can do right now is head home. I'll drive." He turned to the haggard man who'd arrived earlier. "David, I'll apprise you of the decisions once you contact me." With that, he drew the senator close. "Stay with me. The others will flank us, and once we're in the vehicle, they'll disperse."

It wasn't enough of a shield in his mind, but he made a mental note to requisition appropriate armored clothing for her. Until this was settled, he refused to allow any more mistakes.

Chapter 6

Dawn etched its way over the horizon as they turned into the gated property. Daniella couldn't contain the yawn that snapped her jaws.

"Go in and change into something comfortable, senator. I'll meet the others, and you come down when you're ready."

Jonah spoke carefully, and Daniella wanted to grind her teeth. "You're not shutting me out. I need to know what's happening so..."

The enigmatical look he gave her stopped her in her tracks. The intransigence she'd come to know him for was there in the depths of his eyes. "Senator, I'm merely organizing my team. Michael and Clarissa are due here in the next couple of hours, and I need to re-arrange rosters. Unless you're telling me you're better at that kind of strategic organization—"

Daniella squirmed in her seat at the tone he used.

"—let me conduct the planning session, and I'll ensure you're briefed after the fact. I will need your input on the information we have to hand, but we're tired, spread thin, and in need of downtime."

She bit her lip, accepting that perhaps this was the best option, and she craved a shower and clean clothes. The ones she wore were splattered with McNally's blood. Her second set of ruined clothes in two days.

Her head ached viciously, and the hunger for a nap rose. "Perhaps I should take a nap then, and have something to eat."

Jonah nodded. "Excellent, and exactly what I would have suggested under the circumstances. We'll organize an immediate roster, then re-convene in four hours."

She moaned softly. The thought of horizontal rest, even for under four hours hovered like manna from heaven. "Fine. Say two o'clock in my office. Full team?"

His short nod answered her question as they pulled up to the steps.

Her butler-cum-household assistant hurried down the steps, his face etched in lines of worry. "Senator, I'm so pleased you're unharmed. I heard about Agent McNally, and I hope she's..." He gulped, and Daniella patted his hand.

"She'll make a full recovery, but it's going to take time. Jonah has the team assembling in my office. Please ensure that they have whatever they require."

He nodded stiffly. "Of course." He reached into the back and grabbed her bag. "I've had Mrs. Garmy arrange a light meal in your room, and you'll rest, won't you?"

She patted his hand, feeling the aged skin and bones. Weariness washed over her. She should have contacted him so he didn't worry so much. "Yes, Callum. I'll rest. I'm going to shower, eat, then have a nap."

"Good. I've got the temperature set to your favorite, and I'll have your meal brought up in ten minutes?"

"Yes, please. And could you arrange something for Jonah too?"

Callum looked at her solemnly. "I will. Now you go upstairs."

JONAH STRETCHED out on the bed in the room Callum Horsen, Daniella's man about the house, led him to. It was comfortable, with a deep, cushiony mattress. The colors were easy on the eye in mossy green and gray tones. It should have been the perfect place to take a nap, but he was so wired it felt impossible that he'd even close his eyes.

His men had agreed to the pairing of duties. He'd take on full responsibility for guarding the senator and would be aided by one or the other of his people. They'd be thinly spread, but it would allow them to continue their investigations. Not perfect, but do-able. For the short term anyway.

Frustration ate at him, and with a grizzled sigh, he rose, stripping the clothes as he went and opening the door to the compact bathroom. A shower always helped to clear his mind. He stepped within the cubicle, uncaring that he'd left the door to the bedroom open. He'd requested they wake him in three and a half hours after he'd cleaned up and rested.

He demanded his favored temperature of the water, and the jets engaged. Hot water beat down on him, and he bent his head, wondering just what to do about Daniella—the senator, he reminded himself—but the reaction of his body was instantaneous. Everything whirred to life, and he groaned. The woman was the very devil when it came to temptation.

"The senator. Daughter of Gavin and Francine Villede. Senator of A'Garve district. Age thirty-two." He ran through the facts he knew, hoping the dry information would ease the ache that settled down below. Locked legs held him still, but his interest grew. "That was a failure," he muttered, then he growled the demand for water off.

A sound, the creaking of a door, had him stilling, every muscle ready to react. He stepped out of the cubicle, peering into the room beyond. Nothing to see. He exhaled. *Perhaps I'm just overthinking things.* He took another cautious step, then stared. The senator, eyes wide with shock, had entered his room.

He knew the instant she was aware of him as more than an agent. The way her eyes dipped down, scanning his skin, then coming to rest exactly at the jerking erection.

"Well, now that we've ascertained I'm naked, how can I help you, senator?"

She licked her lips, and he felt as if someone had poked him with an electric prod.

"I, uh... I shouldn't have barged in."

The heat he noted in her face, and the interest she showed in him as a man, the movement of her gaze over his skin, set his heart to a slow, viscous cadence. Hunger rose, biting and gnawing at him.

She reached out, her hand touching the bare skin of his chest. The heat of her fingers warmed him.

It was all he could do to will his body not to move closer, to gather her against him and tear the bloody clothes from her magnificent body.

His mouth dried, and his breathing shallowed as the scent of her arousal, musky and potent, teased his senses.

"What do you want?" His deeper-than-usual voice had her glancing at his eyes.

"I want..." Her tongue flicked out again, and stars help him, the groan that tore from his lips was merely the start of a chain reaction.

Jonah grabbed her, fingers digging deep into her soft flesh, and he pulled her body flat against his. The water which still coated his body soaked her light clothes, so they molded to her skin. The jut of her nipples, hard points of pleasure, grazed his pecs.

His lips found hers, devoured and took, the dark sensuality of the kiss unmistakable and ferocious. His body urged for more, and he warred with it. Slowly, the drum beat in his chest eased, the deep hunger banked but certainly not assuaged.

He pulled back, his mind once more in control, and he grunted. "Apologies." Anything more would be a lie, and Jonah prided himself on honesty.

"You kissed me." Her fingers touched her red, bee-stung lips while her eyes betrayed the confusion that he knew threaded itself around her. "Why? Why did you stop?"

She blushed, and he turned and stalked to the bathroom, tugging the thick towel from the rack and slinging it around his hips.

"I don't know, senator. Probably because this is a bad idea." Jonah spoke drily, the affectation hard won, because it wouldn't take much to propel her back into the embrace his body demanded. But more than anything, he was aware that the distance between them was close to insurmountable. She was a senator, and he a lowly agent-cum-soldier. She was far above his paygrade.

A droplet of moisture leaked from her eyes, and fury at himself for making this woman cry shattered him.

"I'm sorry, senator."

"I think, after this, you can call me Daniella."

She hiccupped and swiped at the tears as he tugged her close, enfolding her in his arms and resting his chin on her head. "I don't think that's wise. This here proves the point."

"You think?" Now it was her turn to sound like paper crinkling from age, and he laughed.

"So, how can I help you?" He pulled away, and his body mourned the loss of heat even as he fought to contain himself.

"I could tell you, but you'd regret it afterward." She sighed and shrugged. "Kallee is here with the files I requested yesterday and some other information that I think you'd want to see. I came to ask if you'd pop up to my office straight away."

One moment passed, then another, as he worked hard to decipher the details. "Right. Let me get dressed, and I'll be there."

She waited.

Jonah shrugged and dropped the towel, his eyes on hers, and she fled, the door crashing behind her as she left.

Jonah slumped to the bed and exhaled. "Well now, that went well." He smiled ruefully.

"At least I know she's as hot at kissing as everything else." The memory didn't help as he reached down to gather his clothes, then stood to drag them over his nude body. "She's not for me." *Maybe I should get that tattooed on my butt. Michael and David can kick it every time I think of her.*

Once more fully clothed, he stomped from the bedroom and headed for her office. He smiled, spying her dressed in a dry outfit, similar to the one she'd worn before as she descended the stairs—casual, flowing pants and a light top that winnowed in the breeze.

"You changed?"

She blushed, and he offered her his hand. She blinked. "What? So you can tease me again? I don't think so."

It swiped the smile from his face, replacing it with a deep frown. "I'm not teasing you, senator. We just need space and distance. Otherwise, we'll make a disastrous mistake. One that might cost both of us more than we can afford."

On that, he whirled and opened her office door.

Kallee, her assistant, waited in a chair. Her brows knit closely together as she took in the two of them. Wisely, she kept her own counsel.

"You wanted to see me?" asked Daniella.

"Yes, senator. I brought the correspondence. It was only after I got here, I set to opening it. You're going to want to see this." Kallee passed him a piece of paper. He took it, noting the way her fingers shook.

It took a mere second to understand the dread. A photo. McNally on the ground. Daniella's white face beyond the secure barrier. Five words were inscribed on the image. *We won't miss next time.*

"Where did this come from?"

She shook her head mutely.

He launched into action, tugging the communicator from his pocket and summoning Sevres. He was their guru on all things evidential.

"Yo! How can I help, Jonah?"

"Are you still in the house?"

"I'm in the guest house. What do you need? I'm on my way now."

Adrenaline surged inside Jonah's body as he explained the letter, Kallee's delivery, and the tiny, unmarked envelope. By the time he'd finished, Sevres entered the room, and they hung up.

"You haven't checked for prints?" Middle-aged with thinning, salt-and-pepper hair, Sevres was single and happy, having told Jonah during the search for Clarissa that he didn't have a family because they got in the way of doing his job. Besides, he'd tried it once and didn't like it.

Jonah was sure it was more because they got in the way of his more academic pursuits, such as keeping up with the latest scientific detection methods.

The man tugged a tiny scanner from the baggy jacket he wore, and Jonah wondered just how many other gadgets he had stashed about himself. The light glowed blue, and Sevres grunted. "The prints are unclear. Too many have handled it. Let me see the envelope."

Kallee handed it to him, and he flashed the scanner over it.

"Useless. But to have it printed on paper? That's another kettle of fish. I need to access my full unit and do a fibroid scan to check, then I might be able to pinpoint the supplier. This stuff isn't cheap, you know, and only registered purchasers can obtain these kinds of materials."

Jonah waited, expecting more. The silence drew out. "And?"

"My comp is in the guest house. We should call the entire team together and run through what we have. Perhaps we're missing something. In the meantime, any update on McNally?"

Daniella—the senator—looked stunned then chagrined. "No. I'll contact David and get an update."

THE TEAM SETTLED into the seats Daniella, Kallee, and Jonah had dragged into a circle. Incongruous to see this motley crew of men, clearly uncomfortable in the surroundings, Daniella made a mental note to set up a situation room somewhere else. She tapped a list of requirements on her tiny palm unit as they settled.

"So, what do we have so far?" Daniella demanded.

The men eyed her, clearly wondering if she knew what she was doing. Awareness of their dismay at her taking on effective control of the meeting aside, she knew they required time and space to consider all the information—or lack thereof—so they might find a way forward.

She opened her mouth, about to request Sevres update her on

the letter, when the door crashed open and her brother, Michael, and his new bride, Clarissa, surged into the room.

Daniella watched his eyes flicker left and right. "Where's David?"

"Still at the hospital," Jonah answered and was rewarded with a grunt.

"He's going to have to settle that, soon. She won't stand for it," Daniella said with a smile in her voice. The room erupted in laughter. They all knew David was more than fascinated with the female agent, yet he'd refused to act on it. "Otherwise she'll move on."

Michael strode forward and enfolded Daniella in a bear hug. "Are you okay?"

"Yeah. I've got a hard head," she teased. He laughed, and she grinned. "You've been telling me that for years, and now I have the proof!"

Clarissa bussed her on the cheek as Michael pulled away. "Glad you're in one piece. It took a lot longer than we hoped for getting back. Security with this hardware posed a few issues."

Daniella frowned. Had they been given a hard time because of their bio-cybernetic implants? She opened her mouth to question that when Jonah's communicator blared.

He stood and retreated to the back of the room. "Holy hot fucking damn. I'm on my way."

Her stomach clenched. What could be going on now?

Jonah's gaze met hers. "We've got another kid. More extensive damage this time, but they can clearly see their bio-synth implants. I'm going to need assistance. Michael?"

Her brother nodded. "Count me in." Then they left, the two largest men in the room retreating to deal with yet another emergency.

"Sevres, can you update us on your findings?"

Clarissa sank into the seat Jonah had abandoned, and Daniella wondered how much more could go wrong.

Chapter 7

Jonah and Michael might be here on business, but first, Jonah would take care of their own. Traveling on the escalator, they reached McNally's floor then moved down the hall with swift, long strides.

They'd received an update that she was conscious, and the infusion of the new healing product ZL-2-Tec was working optimally. They'd be releasing her soon, but Michael and Jonah needed to check on her status before she went anywhere. He smiled, knowing David had already made arrangements for her accommodations post-release.

"Reckon he's worked out yet that he's a goner?"

Michael's question left Jonah smiling. "Oh, he knows it. It's more that he's tied up in so many knots that he doesn't know which way to act. See, some of us don't think that the situation we've been handed is as simple as fall in love and do the deed."

"That's an odd way of looking at it, Jonah. It can be that simple and that hard. Look at Clarissa and me."

Jonah couldn't contain the mirth that bubbled inside him. "I do and am. David is afraid McNally won't have him because he's her superior. McNally is a good woman, but she's afraid. She's got no idea how families work because of her history."

"That's all well and good, but what's your problem with Daniella then?"

Poleaxed, Jonah stilled and stared at his friend. "I'm not—"

Michael smiled. "You are. Always have been. It's like a beacon, and she's too caught up in her role and the Protocol business. When this settles though, you're both going to have to think about the situation, because things are getting mighty fraught."

Jonah gritted his teeth. "We need to check on McNally."

He thumped in the direction of the door, which opened to show David, wheeling a chair containing McNally. She might be bruised and in pain—judging from the radiating pain lines on her face—but she was a fighter.

"You're just in time. They're sending me home, or at least I would be going home, but Agent Villede here was insistent I stay with him. He's organized a 'visiting nurse'." She spoke in terms of derision, while David, haggard and worn, shrugged.

"It makes sense. You need your dressings changed regularly and injections twice a day.

The sooner you get them all clear, the sooner you can rehab and be back on deck," David muttered.

If anyone could read the mixture of fear and thankfulness in David's eyes, they didn't comment. An orderly followed them to the door, arms full of flowers and a small case in hand.

"Right, well, we'll leave you to it." Jonah started to turn, then paused and looked at David. "I'll want a daily report so we can stay apprised of her recovery."

It wasn't much, but both David and McNally were left in no doubt as to his concern and worry, but right now he needed to get down to the room on the first floor where their quarry lay.

He and Michael took the escalators to the ground floor, and as it moved, Jonah glanced up into the massive atrium that filled his view. Fourteen levels spanned the building, rooms rimming the edges, while the center glass, encased in shining silver metal, reflected light into the middle of the building.

At the bottom, they checked in with the main reception desk. There, they contacted the professor, then followed the conveyed directions as to where they'd find the patient they were there to discuss and take responsibility for, moving at a rapid clip.

The professor met them at the main doorway and ushered them inside. "She came in this morning, her injuries to chest and abdomen requiring emergency triage, otherwise, I would have contacted you before. Come this way."

He led them up the corridor and into a quieter section of the building.

"If she's older than twelve, I'd be surprised. We took the DNA swab because she was left just inside the doorway and we hoped to find her guardians. As seems to be the way with these kids, we couldn't find any parents. Vision on the eyes in the waiting room is blurry, and we think someone tampered with the feed. My security guys are on it, but they have very little hope of working out who brought the child in. Boys, I don't know what's going on, but these are *children*."

Jonah felt the weight of the professor's words. He knew the older man was assuming these were almost normal kids. Jonah hated to disillusion him. "No. These aren't children, professor. They are machines of death and torture in training."

The professor stopped in his tracks, a sound of distress filling the air, but Jonah had to continue. It was the only way he could impress on the man the gravity of the situation.

"I can't and won't tell you more at this point, but the situation is dangerous. These kids are more than human and yet less. Has she regained consciousness?"

The professor shook his head, and Jonah released the pent-up breath. They might be able to get her out of here quickly then. Whether she'd tell them anything though, depended on what conditioning she'd already received.

"What other information do you have?" Jonah asked.

The professor stopped at a doorway, barring the way with his arm, his face pale under the fluorescent light. "Her age is questionable. She looks and talks like an older child, yet the DNA testing makes me think she's younger. Our best geneticists on staff took a look. We're confused and need something to help us understand what's happening."

That information rocked him. *Younger?* "What do you mean by that?" A dark and deep emotion swirled around him. Fear and something far more basic. Primal.

"Do you know much about DNA and sequencing?"

Jonah shook his head.

"Okay, the DNA strands are like a cookbook. They tell parts of the body what they should look like and the job they do. As we age, different parts of the string turn on, like a light at night. They also turn off when they're no longer needed. We have discovered special markers—epigenetic markers, they're called—give the body the instructions that allow us to age a person, like the rings on a tree. The markers in the girl's body appear to have her much younger than appearances suggest. They've turned on what she should have at say eight or ten, but ones that should have been activated earlier don't appear to have been triggered at all. This information is questionable of course, given the injuries she's sustained, and that we've had only a few hours to consider the information, but if that's the case..."

"They could be speeding up the aging process. That would be catastrophic." Michael's words pealed over his head and dread churned.

If they'd managed to speed up the aging process, how soon could these killers be on the loose? How fast had they managed to speed the process up, and as a result, how stable could these children be?

Glancing at Michael, he saw his fears mirrored. "We need to get her out of here."

"She's going to need a medical doctor to supervise her removal—"

"I'm a qualified doctor. I'll take responsibility for her removal, transport, and ongoing care. Have your team process the documentation." Michael was a force to be reckoned with, and the professor dropped his arm.

"Then go in and I'll get the paperwork. It'll only take a moment."

Jonah opened the door, and they stepped into the quiet room, the beeping of machines telling them that the child's blood pressure and heartbeat were stable.

The little, blonde-haired girl lay there on the bed, eyes closed, her pink, rosebud lips parted enough for breath to whisper in and out.

His gut twisted. She looked sweet and innocent, but potentially could be dangerous to everyone around him. "Got the cuffs?"

Michael nodded and handed them to Jonah, who clipped them into place before he gently slid his hands under the child, wrapping her firmly in the bedclothes then lifting her in readiness to leave. With Michael here, at least he had someone able to defend them should they face any intervention.

An orderly entered the room. "Hey, watcha doing to the kid?"

Jonah stepped forward. "She's being moved to another hospital."

The orderly frowned, his shoulders tensing. "Then you need a gurney and—" The words were a growl.

The professor appeared at his side. "It's okay. I've authorized it. Her situation is stable now, Manuel, so we're doing this in the least invasive and quickest manner possible." He pushed past the startled orderly. "The paperwork." He shoved some papers at Jonah.

"You can't let them take her," the orderly ground out, feeding Jonah's suspicions.

Jonah's blood pressure spiked. "We're duly authorized, as the professor just told you."

It could have been the glint of the orderly's eyes or the suddenly vicious way he pushed the professor aside. The professor thudded to the floor as alarms rang in Jonah's head. He turned as Michael reached for his pistol, moving quick as lightning, the *pzzt* of sound indicating he'd chosen to stun the now disabled man who lay on the ground.

Jonah stood there, looking down. "We'll need him in custody." He shifted the child in his arms and withdrew his communicator and arranged for his people to collect him as the professor groaned on the floor.

"What... What have you done?" His voice edged with groggy fear.

"We've only disabled him. Your security guys should be here in a minute. We'll have them hold him until my people arrive."

"But he was just protecting the girl." The professor pushed to his feet, protesting the orderly's innocence, but Jonah pierced him with an angry frown.

"Maybe, and maybe he knew more. We'll look into it. Whatever it takes to sort this mess out. Meanwhile, we'll get this girl out of here before she wakes." Michael took the girl from Jonah's grasp.

Two guards ran to the door and peered inside. "Professor? What the hell happened here?"

Jonah dragged out his identification and thrust it at the security officers. "The orderly pushed him to the floor as we were preparing to transfer the child. His attack was unprovoked, and my people are en route to collect him for questioning."

One of the guards peered at his identification tag. "You're Special Forces?"

Jonah nodded. "Yes. This man is to be kept away from others." He indicated to the orderly still unconscious on the floor. "No matter what he says, don't contact anyone regarding this matter. Don't discuss it with him. Agent Sevres—middle-aged with salt-and-pepper hair— will be here soon to take him into custody. Check his ID and only release this man to him."

Michael handed the girl over, and they marched from the room with the girl in Jonah's arms. They'd done all they could so far.

Once in the vehicle, with the girl carefully strapped in, Jonah stepped on the gas. He wanted her contained and in a safe location with all due speed. The longer they took, the greater the chances that things would go wrong.

Even as they sped into the night, a niggle took wing in his mind. On impulse, he clicked on his comm and contacted the security services and identified himself. "Get the professor to go home."

"What?" He'd shocked the person who answered the phone.

Hell, he didn't know why he was doing this, but for some reason, he felt it was imperative. "Send him home. Now."

The man muttered but agreed to contact Jonah once the request was fulfilled. Within moments a text appeared on the communicator, letting them know the professor had left the building.

The vehicle descended into silence as they drove on. Almost ten minutes later, a flare filled the sky behind them, and Jonah braked, scanning the scene in the rearview mirror. "What the hell is that?"

Michael turned in his seat and swore volubly.

Jonah clicked on the scanner, alert to the chatter of police.

"Explosion at Velspar Community Care. All units to respond immediately. Casualty status unknown."

His heart stopped, stomach congealing to a cold blob in the center of his gut. "What the fuck?"

Michael looked at him, gaze wide. "I don't know how you knew, but I think you just saved the professor. That is if he got out."

The groan from the back seat alerted him that the child wasn't far from waking. "We need to get her contained now." Jonah pressed the accelerator, and the vehicle jerked forward.

DANIELLA HAD SETTLED behind her desk, wondering what the hell she was going to do about the Protocol. There was no facility to appeal the decision. She'd been injured, and if Jonah's words were correct, it was with the sole intention of getting her out of the chamber so she couldn't lead the charge. The others who'd followed had sections of the argument, but none of them were in the position to be able to focus all the varied points.

She was still seething about it.

The best she could come up with was to craft a bill meant to soften it. There had to be some way to contain the worst excesses, although even that would be hamstrung by the legalities that surrounded the children. They didn't know how many there were, and they couldn't argue for their rights, because, to be honest, she wasn't sure that they weren't vicious killers without remorse.

The situation rattled around in her head, making her dizzy.

She reached for the glass on the edge of her desk and sipped the water as the door smacked open. "There's been an explosion at Velspar Community Care."

Fear bloomed. "Isn't that where..." Completing the words was an impossibility. If she gave it voice, acknowledged it in any way, then she'd have to accept that perhaps they'd been hurt. To lose David, Michael, McNally, and Jonah...

Nausea clamped her in its greasy fist.

Her communicator blared, and she hunted blindly through her pockets, grabbing its cold case and pressing the button.

"Hello?"

"Did they get out?" *David.* She sent a silent 'thank you' into the heavens. He was safe. That meant McNally was too, because he'd contacted her to warn her that he'd engaged a specialist nurse.

"I don't know. I haven't heard from Michael or Jonah. Have you?"

"We met as they were releasing McNally into my care. They were busy, and I sincerely doubt it was to check on us. Was it?"

Moisture pooled at the corner of her eyes. "No. There was a child, and they were going to retrieve her. Take her to their offices in the hopes they'd be able to get information. I believe she was badly injured. I haven't heard from them since they arrived."

"Are you going to call?"

Therein lay the crux now. If she called and got them, she might be interrupting. If they didn't answer, that could mean anything from their communicators were out of range, the battery empty, or...

The last possibility was one she emotionally clamped down on. *Don't focus on the worst- case scenario, Daniella.*

"No. They'll check in when they can." The bravado cost her dearly.

"Fine. When you know something, let me know." He clicked off, and she exhaled, but Kallee hovered.

"You aren't going to ring?"

"No. They're professionals. And grown-ups. They don't need me checking on them every five seconds." The words didn't settle the see-saw motion going on in her stomach though.

She bit her lip and concentrated hard. A semblance of normality settled in, thin though it was.

"Now, I was wondering if we were to craft a bill, one that softens the effects of the Protocol? What do you think? Let's get President Yin on the line."

Chapter 8

Shunting the girl into the room had taken both Jonah and Michael's combined efforts. She'd woken just as they arrived at the building, and Michael asked Fairburn to assist them. He'd hooked up the medical equipment so they could monitor her health, found the hand scanner, and arranged the small room which was carefully reinforced to withstand the children they'd so far gathered.

Dr. Aros peered around the corner. "Gentlemen, another one?"

Jonah didn't like Aros, even though he'd single-handedly petitioned as to the suitability of both Clarissa and Michael to be released into the general populace. "Yeah. Picked her up at the Community Center moments before it blew."

A moment of pleasure trickled as Aros absorbed his words, but even as they left his mouth, he regretted it, given the way Aros paled and shook. He remembered after the fact that Michael, Aros, and Sara Windhower, Michael's personal physician and long-time friend, had all studied and worked there. Shame filled Jonah, and he sighed.

"What? The Community Center is gone?" Aros uttered the disbelieving words.

"Give it a rest, Jonah. The Community Center was the scene of an explosion this evening. Don't know any more except they mobilized all official units." Michael worked efficiently, checking the few charts and notations Venos had given them before they left.

Aros gaped like a fish out of water. "Will they need—"

"Let's wait and see," Jonah grunted. "In the short term, we have a child, likely about twelve years old, in custody. There's some question about her maturational age. Her DNA is showing signs of tampering. The epigenetic markers appear to have been altered. We hypothesize that she could be younger."

Aros stared at them both as if they'd gone mad. "That's not possible. The effects of that would render the child unstable, without the moral indicators and..."

"And without the experience of knowing how to deal with their emotions. Yes." Michael's addition finished the sentence effectively.

"How long do I have to make an initial assessment?"

Hearing the bone-deep weariness in Aros's voice, Jonah shifted uncomfortably, unsure exactly what all the information meant, though he was able to extract the important aspects.

Their situation right now was dire. They had little information, there were uncounted children somewhere out there in the clutches of a mad and evil genius, things were being blown up, leaving people dead, and members of his team had been injured.

The strands of the case tangled unmistakably, but trying to find the origination point was proving to be a puzzle. He was also aware that the political turmoil—which was totally out of his control—was a further distraction for the multi-disciplined team.

"Her file isn't very thick, but it's a jumble of terms and information," grumped Aros.

Michael groaned. "I haven't had time to fully read it yet."

Therein lay part of the issue. No one had time because they were all trying to sort and sift through the leads they'd discovered, spread thin offering security to the senator.

Jonah speared his fingers into his hair. "What if we call Windhower in to consult? She can take over the medical assessment, and with her knowledge of bio-cybernetic implantation therapy, she's best placed to understand what's been done? We've retrieved copies of the IVF clinic where Colvert was working and the implantation routines. She'd be able to understand that, right?"

Michael's brow knit tightly. "Yeah, but to bring another civilian in who—"

"If I may, Michael? I would agree with Jonah. She'd be a good choice, and we're going to need a physician on hand. These children also require a female presence. We don't know how they've been raised as none are willing to share, but I feel that we need to provide something softer than the situation we have so far." Aros spoke quietly but with a force that had Jonah rocking back on his heels with a sigh.

"Okay then. Let's bring her in. But we're going to need more troops to ensure everyone's safety. Jonah? Can you suggest—"

"I know a few. Let me talk to David and the senator. We'll fix it."

He stepped away, digging out the tiny device, and contacted the senator.

"Jonah?" Her voice whispered over the line, and his hackles rose.

"What's wrong? Are you safe?" He heard a sniffle and frowned.

"Yes. We heard about the Community Center and didn't know if you were okay. I'm glad you called in. Is Michael safe too?"

He rubbed his aching brow. They should have called in, but first, they'd needed to transport the girl, then she'd woken, and their unofficial planning meeting with Aros had pushed that from his mind. He cursed the case and himself. It wasn't how he usually worked.

"Yeah, he's good. I'll have him contact Clarissa too. Ease her mind. But we have a problem, or several. We're going to have to pull in Windhower, but we need staff here to oversee the situation. So far, we have two kids, with strength levels we haven't managed to plumb. Our team is stretched too thin because we need a guard here. I know of a few others who'd be trustworthy, but we need a reason and the funding. Can you make it happen?"

It was a huge risk. She'd have to find a way to hide the cost of expanding a covert investigation team. Then they'd need to co-opt the people he had in mind, which meant the creation of a paper trail—dangerous in these current times—and he'd need to house them, drag them from anyone that could be pinned to the situation.

"How many do you need?"

"Four to six is a start. Can you make this happen?"

"Yes, but I need time—"

"Which is in limited supply, senator. I'll have the names to you in the next couple of hours. I'll make contact first, check where they're stationed and their availability. Report on your desk in about four hours. We need to talk to the kid first. She's woken, and there's a whole heap more mess to do with the clinic than even we thought." He rubbed the back of his neck.

"Jonah? Be safe."

The line clicked off, and he stared into space, wondering how the hell he was going to deal with that mess. Later. He didn't have time now, and it would keep.

<hr>

THE BEEP of Daniella's computer alerted her to the incoming message. She and Kallee had hunted and picked through their files, searching for ways to bring at least six more into their team.

The call from President Yin had helped. He'd offered her a small force to deal with the province she'd recently taken responsibility for.

Daniella printed out the report, feeling the polymer substance under her fingers and wishing—not for the first time—that paper hadn't been phased out for all but the most important communications. The polymer just didn't have the same tactile qualities.

With a groan, she returned to the task at hand, waiting for Jonah and Michael to return when a thought occurred to her. "Kallee? Can you find Clarissa for me? I've got a question and idea in mind."

Kallee's head popped up from behind the seat. "Sure. What is it?"

Daniella smiled. "Wait and see. Ask her how quick she can get over here."

With that, Daniella made a further notation in her files, then turned to the stack of reports she needed to scan and understand. Even with the crises, her day-to-day oversight didn't just melt away. She couldn't delegate these responsibilities if she wanted any hope of moving up the political ranks, though she honestly questioned if that was her choice or that of others.

Shrugging aside the introspection, she made her way through budget reports, noting questions and theories. Seeking out documents that she'd seen before to marry up with what she hypothesized. Just as Daniella opened the third file, a rap came at the door.

"Come in."

Clarissa, her sister-in-law, entered the room. Tall and slight with blonde hair and blue eyes, she'd captured her brother Michael's attention with her good nature and high cheekbones, he'd said. When they'd first met, Clarissa had been scarecrow thin with sunken cheeks from malnutrition. She'd been Colvert's experiment, along with a few others, of course, but the first to survive his plans.

"Clarissa, you were a nanny, weren't you?" She gestured with her hand, silently inviting the woman to settle on the chair opposite her.

Clarissa's eyes narrowed. "Yes, why?"

"We have a problem. So far, two children have come into our care, and Michael and Jonah are suggesting that we need a female on hand. We've got Dr. Windhower attending as a physician, but we're going to need someone with experience of children. Out of our team, you're it. What if we placed you and Michael at the center as a backup physician, guard, and—"

"Babysitter?" Clarissa finished the sentence with a dry voice. "I'm capable of more than that."

Daniella blushed. "You are, and Dr. Aros will need someone who understands the behaviors of children, age-appropriate behavior in order to find a way to reach them. What do you think?"

Clarissa blinked. "I guess it might work. And the fact that Michael and I are both—"

She gave a decisive nod to Clarissa. "Exactly. Well?"

"Has Jonah—"

"I haven't raised it with him yet, but I plan to as soon as he returns. I'll let him and Michael know you're here, and when they arrive, we can discuss this."

Clarissa rose. "Okay. Anyway, right now we should be thinking about a meal. Have you spoken to Mrs. Garmy?"

Daniella inspected her chrono, amazed to realize meal times had come and gone. "Kallee, are you heading home?"

Her assistant glanced around the corner and shook her head. "I thought it best if I stayed for the duration. I've got a bag in my car. I'll grab it. Then we can keep working if you prefer?"

Daniella pinched the bridge of her nose. So many people she was assuming responsibility for. But Kallee had been with her for over four years, working by her side through good and bad. "All right, then. Take the floral bedroom on the third floor. Let Mrs. Garmy know, and she'll grab linens for you."

Clarissa smiled. "Let's go to the kitchen and see what's cooking."

Stretching, Daniella felt the tug of muscles that had been locked into position for hours releasing. "Sure."

It had been a long time since she'd had someone to remind her to take a break, and it felt good.

THE LIGHT HAD FADED to an inky night by the time Jonah arrived at Daniella's house. Michael slumped back in his seat, eyes closed, as they rounded the corner.

Hidden behind high walls covered with green vines, it was a far cry from Jonah's home as a child. His parents had been grunts—laborers who'd been paid a living wage but not much more. Their lack of education had been overshadowed by the depressive years in the lead up to the wars.

His father had worked in a smelting factory and his mother cooked at the local school he'd attended; long hours and back-breaking work, yet they'd cheerfully accepted their lot in life and hoped for more for him. They weren't poor, but luxuries were few and far between. An only child, his parents had given him as many opportunities as they could manage, but the factory fire that had killed his father had been the beginning of the end for his family.

With the main breadwinner of the family gone, Jonah had chosen to join the combat forces. They'd trained him, honed him, and paid handsomely. He'd met Franklin and Michael there, and he'd learned so much, taking on every opportunity offered. His mother had given up though, and she passed within twelve months.

As the only child of two only children, it fascinated him the way Michael's family had opened their arms to admit those around them. They'd somehow formed this ragtag family of misfits: himself, McNally, Sevres, a loner, and Fairburn, who tried to keep a distance but occasionally forgot and dropped the barriers. They'd gravitated to the three at the center— Michael, David, and Daniella—like moths to a flame.

"Why? Why do you mingle with us instead of keeping your distance?" He silently swore; he hadn't intended to say the words out loud.

"Us? Clarissa and I?" Michael turned his head, opened one eye, and spoke with a surprised tone.

"No. Ah, don't worry. I don't know why I asked." He shrugged and waited for the gates to open, then drove up the long, sweeping track.

They pulled up, and he clambered out, headed for the steps, when a heavy hand descended on his shoulder. The physical show of solidarity grounded him, soothed the ragged edges of his psyche.

"You said Clarissa was here?" Jonah asked.

"Yeah. She and Daniella have been talking and may have some ideas on how we organize the team effectively," Michael offered.

Jonah shrugged, more than happy to welcome input if it made the team stronger and more efficient.

Callum opened the door. "They're in the dining room, Mr. Michael. Let me take your coats."

"Thanks," Jonah said as he shrugged out of the jacket he'd been wearing for the best part of four days and let the older man take it. He'd grown used to this kind of treatment over the years, but always thanked those who offered such a service, the grounding of his early years reminding him constantly of the thanklessness of such menial tasks.

Daniella and Clarissa were perched at the table along with Kallee, filling three of the five places set for a meal.

"Sit down, Jonah, Michael. Mrs. Garmy asked us to wait for you before serving ourselves."

The dishes circled the table, and they dug deep, piling food on their plates. It smelled good; spicy and colorful with specks of red and orange dotted through the clotted, light cream- colored sauce.

"What is it?" Jonah sniffed at the rich aromas, and his stomach growled.

"It's a chicken curry with saffron carrots and beets on a bed of rice." Kallee grinned. "Mrs. Garmy's specialty, which I only get here."

He settled into the seat beside Daniella, wondering if the fates were plotting. The first forkful exploded in his mouth as flavor after flavor emerged.

The table turned quiet as they ate. Only when Mrs. Garmy returned to clear away did they sit back and begin their discussion.

"Today, while I was working through my files, I had a thought," Daniella said. "We've got children who may or may not be the age we think they are. We need guards on them, and while in their current quarters, physicians and psychotherapists, right? But to achieve that, we're going to need at least four to six people. Bodies we can't fund under normal circumstances. Is that right, Jonah?"

He grunted, waiting to see how Daniella had managed to reorganize things to make the situation more workable.

"Michael is both guard and physician. With Sara Windhower, we'd have a medical team with expertise and knowledge of bio-cybernetics as much as general ailments. Dr. Aros is a specialist at therapy, though he's currently available to us without cost because he wants to know more about what the motivation is, according to Michael."

Daniella looked at her brother, and he nodded.

"Then we have Clarissa, with her knowledge of children and maturational behavior and markers. If we place Clarissa and

Michael full time with Sara and Dr. Aros, I believe it's workable. That would free the team with the extra agents that Jonah requested available to undertake the investigation, which has been funded privately through the province income stream. That swells our ranks as little as possible but places suitable staff in the areas they are best capable of handling."

Daniella looked pleased with herself, the tiny smile and the shine in her eyes warming him. He couldn't argue with anything she'd said. It was basic, but she was right. The right people for the job would make it easier.

On a nod, Jonah added, "Okay then. I'm good with that. Clarissa? Michael?"

They both nodded, and he didn't miss the way they briefly touched hands in an intimate form of communion.

"You two head over there tomorrow. That will give you time to make arrangements. In the meantime, we need to arrange to house—"

"Use our place. It's only a block away and big enough to house those left. I'll warn Mrs. Hudson and Clarrie that there will be others in the house for the short term. They'll look after them." Michael plugged yet another gap for the team, and the tension seeped out of Jonah's shoulders.

"Fine. I vote we finish here then turn in for the night. Tomorrow is going to be a busy day, and I want you and Clarissa here no later than 0700."

Mrs. Garmy, with her impeccable timing, emerged through the doorway carrying an enormous, silver tray dotted with five bowls. "My creme caramel," she announced before serving them, and once again, silence filled the room.

Chapter 9

Jonah settled on the bed, watching the play of shadows on the ceiling. He'd showered, crawled into the pajamas he'd gathered sometime yesterday from his sparse apartment, and waited for sleep.

Memories and plans filled his mind as he attempted to weigh up what they'd managed to learn, how they'd talk to the children, and what information they needed to know. Aros had been clear that the children may know nothing useful, given the dichotomous situation with their maturational ages, lack of formal education, and the way they'd lived, secluded from the world.

The girl had been key so far. She'd trembled every time a man came near her, and the possibilities of why made Jonah's gut ache. Were they training her to be a tool of war, or was there more to her rearing? A sinister, secondary use?

He rose and stalked to the small computer desk in the corner. He called up the files he'd accessed earlier in the night, including the interviews.

The girl huddled in the corner, her face pale, and strands of greasy, blonde hair hung limply.
Jonah placed both hands on the table, in full view, understanding she

feared him. "What's your name?"

She shook her head, eyes open wide and her pupils dilated.

"Do you know why you're here?"

Again she shook her head, hair whipping back and forward.

He sighed and stood. Someone knocked on the door, the interruption welcome since the interview was stymied by her refusal to speak.

Jonah opened the door to find Aros on the other side, holding a plate.

"This is for the girl. If she doesn't eat, you might need to show her it's okay by picking a bit of everything."

Jonah closed his eyes, the fury replaced with horror and understanding. She thought the food might be drugged, or worse. With a curse, he opened his eyes again.

Carrying the plate to the table, he watched as her eyes settled on the food, her nostrils flaring. Hunger flashed, then she hid it.

"This is for you." He pushed it closer, and she flicked her gaze in his direction, then back to the food.

He sighed, tore a piece of chicken meat from the leg and chewed. Then he swallowed, the whole time staring at the girl. Willing her to eat. She watched with wary eyes. He picked up a potato, broke the chunk in half, and ate that too. Did the same with the carrot and beans.

Silence.

"Would you like this?" Once more, he pushed the plate toward the end of the table.

She trembled, and he rose. The girl flinched. Striding to the door, he exited the room.

The vision didn't show the way he'd slumped against the wall, waiting. Knowing that if he entered, she'd be trying to swallow as much as possible.

"Why? Why are these children so afraid? The boy isn't." Indeed, the boy they'd retrieved earlier in the week from the Community Center was brash and loud, demanding to be turned free. So why the difference?

His mind whirred, looking at two more children they'd retrieved during the last few days. The girl was quieter; coloring her reaction.

He tapped out a note to Aros.

Girl B exhibits a high level of fear, unlike boy B. He's brash and loud, and yet boy A is quieter, as is girl A. Subdued but willing enough to make decisions, and their actions don't have the constraints. Is this a symptom of their treatment or caused by their treatment and bio- cybernetic implants?

He knew Aros would have settled in for the night and didn't expect an answer. So he moved away from the screen and headed for the door that led to a patio. Opening the large, glass panels, he stepped into the night.

The scents of honeysuckle and rose mingled in the moonlight. Jonah gripped the balustrade and glanced into the garden. A pale form moved, and his eyes narrowed, muscles tensing, ready to react to a threat. On silent feet he moved to the end of the balcony, took the four steps down into the garden, and waited in the shadows.

Long strands of golden hair shone under the light of a stray moonbeam, and he exhaled then moved without a thought in the direction of Daniella.

"A late-night walk, senator?"

She jumped, startled, and whirled around. "You frightened me. Why would you do that?" Her voice was wispy and as insubstantial as the thin robe she wore belted at the waist. A hint of lace peeked above the neck and drew his gaze.

"I saw movement and came to make sure it wasn't a threat."

"Oh. I'm sorry, Jonah. I needed air and time to think. It's been a hectic and upside-down kind of few days, and I don't, umm... Well, I don't like feeling like I'm not in control."

The smile that spread over his face belied the heat that suffused him. "I worked that out."

Daniella swallowed, the movement of her throat drawing his eye back to the lace; delicate and pale, like her.

"You shouldn't be out here."

She cocked her head. "It's my garden, and I like to think in the open air."

"Perhaps, but we aren't sure of anyone's safety right now, including yours."

She ducked her head, and he felt like a heel.

He reached out to her, his hand extended palm up. "Come on."

When she glanced back up at him, he saw sadness on her face. "If only it were that easy." Then she stepped closer, placing her hands on his shoulders, bare because he only wore sleep shorts and a light button-up shirt, which was currently open. Her fingers molded around the joints, warm and silken, as fire streaked. Nerves jumped and pulsed, and his breath quickened.

"Don't—"

Daniella stopped his words with her glossy lips slanting across his, her tongue demanding entry, and God help him, he couldn't contain the moan that rose in his throat.

He jerked his arms around her waist, tugging her closer, so their bodies touched every possible way except for the barrier of thin fabric. She squirmed, and reality intruded. He pulled away, heaving for breath, his body aching for the release he refused to allow.

"My apologies, senator. I didn't mean to overstep the mark."

Her face turned crimson, a slash of beet-red coloring staining her cheeks as her lips wobbled. "The error in judgment, it seems, was all mine. Goodnight, Jonah McDowell."

Now it was his turn to flinch at the touch of frost in her tone.

She flounced away, head high, though her shoulders hunched, and he stood watching her go, feeling lower than a snake's belly.

I did her a favor. Stopped her from making a huge mistake. But the thoughts didn't quell the internal dialogue that reprimanded him for the hurtful fool who'd made a mistake.

On a sigh, Jonah headed back to his room, to shower, once again in frigid water.

***

DANIELLA ROSE, feeling rumpled and unrested. "Tossing and turning for hours will do that to you." Her actions the night before had been unwise and not in the least bit thought out. "But I'll be damned if I let him see how much it hurt." Nope, she'd dress for success. It wasn't uncommon that she'd dress up to work, even if at home.

She glanced through her wardrobe, mourning the loss of her

favorite white pantsuit. Her gaze settled on a pale blue, lacey blouse, and she tugged it from the wardrobe and tossed it on the bed, knowing the matching camisole was in one of her drawers. Then she turned her attention to a pair of black lounging pants.

With low-heeled shoes, she'd feel comfortable. A long line jacket in the same tones would complete her ensemble, and if for some reason she needed to leave the house, she'd appear put together.

A sudden sense of urgency sent her dashing to the bathroom. Daniella unbound her hair and tugged off the nightgown, gave the voice command for the water to flow, and stepped beneath the spray. It sluiced over her body, and she let the sensual feel release endorphins. She leaned against the wall.

"Not as good as sex, but it'll have to do. Water off." At her command, the flow ceased, and she staggered from the enclosure, scooping up the towel and drying vigorously. It wasn't nearly enough, and her body ached for release.

She shook her head and rammed her legs together, feeling the pulse deep within.

Hanging the towel back on the rail, she headed to the bedroom, seeking underwear, and while she had a choice of the rainbow of lingerie, she chose a daring, little balconette bra in silver threaded sky blue and matching thong. He wouldn't see it, but it suited her mood.

The material of the bra cupped her breasts, rasping over straining nipples, and she gasped. The thong settled against her sensitive skin and another sound, this time a moan, erupted.

"I need to sort this out, otherwise I'm going to be a mess soon." But of course, she wouldn't sort it with Jonah. He'd made it brutally evident that he wasn't interested in her that way.

Raking the brush through her hair brought tears to her eyes and set the mood she wore like a cape wrapped around her. Kallee had finished breakfast and was settled in the office when Daniella stomped in and dropped into her chair. "Any further news or developments?"

Kallee stared at her. "Uh, no. Are you okay, boss?"

"Of course I am. Now, let's take another look at those planning documents for the Protocol Amendment Bill."

Kallee found the file and placed it on the desk in front of her. "Okay, so we've got a range of ways we can tackle this. Financial, moral, and rights."

Daniella peered at the information, bit her lip, and re-read their concepts from the day before. "Who do we have that could head up each of these sections?"

Kallee rattled off names, and Daniella vetoed most of them. "That doesn't give us a lot of options."

Most of the senators she could rely on were long term, and Daniella wondered if the influx of those were among the supporters of the Protocol.

"Kallee, can you search through the list of new and incoming members who voted for the bill? I'm wondering if we need to look at their backgrounds more closely and see how they're aligned."

Kallee cocked her head. "That's going to take some time."

Daniella reclined back in her chair. "Yeah, but since the implementation of the 'One Planet, One Rule, One Senate' Policy, we should be able to get cross-border support. Contact the province security force. I know you'll come up with a suitable reason, just let me know what when the task is complete in case someone asks me!" She laughed and swung the chair around, stopping as her gaze settled on the garden, and the hard-won good mood melted away again.

A SMALL MEETING room at the end of the hallway overflowed with agents who'd been working the covert investigation since the start. It now swelled with the inclusion of the newly drafted members. Jonah knew every face in the room. Could account for their affiliations and skills.

He stepped up to the front of the room, and the sound of voices died away. "Good morning, team. Before I begin, I'll run through some of the background, so you'll have a greater understanding of the dynamics and pitfalls of this mission. The team was originally under the leadership of Michael Villede, intending to track down Clarissa after her abduction. As you're aware, both Clarissa and Michael are bio-cybernetically enhanced. Since then, under the auspices of Senator Daniella Villede, the team has increased to what we currently are. Agent David Villede, Agents McNally, Fairburn, and Sevres, myself, and Franklin Mann, Dr. Aros as our psych consultant, Dr. Sara Windhower as our bio-tech consultant, and now six new members."

He cleared his throat and waited as they glanced around the room, sizing each other up.

"I took on leadership when Michael left on his honeymoon, and since then, I was requested to take on the full leadership effective immediately."

Michael nodded, and Jonah checked all those in the room were following. They all sat straight in the old, metal chairs, the newest six with folders balanced on their laps.

"What you probably don't know is that we currently have four children in custody."

The movement of feet and shifting in chairs signaled the new members were unhappy with that disclosure, and he hurried to explain the situation.

"Some of you were on hand at the point of discovery of the laboratories of Dr. Jeremy Colvert. Since then, we've ascertained that he used the in vitro fertilization clinics he owned to not only fund but also to further his research of bio-cybernetic implantation and the evolution, in direct contravention of the No Harm Oath. We discovered that for eleven years he tampered with the embryos and began a system of implantation of an organic form of cybernetic material. Side effects for the children born with these abnormalities include psychological impairment, an inability to control anger and react to external triggers, increased strength, and so on. However, we've also discovered that the manipulation may have triggered accelerated growth and damaged their ability to empathize as well. In other words, many of these children are weapons."

Horror showed on the latest recruits' faces, and he forged on, needing to get the last of the information to them. It was imperative that they understood the scope at this point.

"We believe that the 21st Testing Protocol currently making its way through the assembly chamber is directly related to our discoveries and the planning of this combined assault on our system of government. It encapsulates medical, political, and other areas. Our mission is to find and neutralize these threats, to seek and rehabilitate the children, and shut down any further experimentation. In the folders you've received are details of what we know so far. There's not a lot. We've hunted up desks, down in the basement. They must be set up and ready for use later by midday, so there's no rest. We'll reconvene at 1300 to organize working partnerships. I want those who've been working the case paired with those new to our team. Any questions?"

Silence. Not a single hand raised. Jonah narrowed his gaze, checked the face of every member of the team. He read commitment and eagerness on the newer faces. He just hoped they'd be able to deal with what they'd learn.

"Okay then. Michael and Clarissa, can you meet me in my office in fifteen minutes? The rest of you follow Franklin. He's going to show you where everything is stashed and the location of the work areas. Get onto it."

He left the room and headed to his office, only dimly aware of the muted sounds of voices and feet as his team scattered. In the small room he'd commandeered for his work area, he made a coffee and settled into his chair. Piles of files waited for his attention, electronic mail overflowed his inbox, and message slips littered his desk.

He sifted through the piles, trying to gauge the most time-sensitive issues, and placed them to the left so he'd deal with them in order.

As he sipped the beverage, he scanned the messages and found one from Professor Venos. *Ring him back* was scribbled along with a communication number, and he sighed, picking up his unit and dialing.

"Venos."

"It's Jonah McDowell, returning your call."

"What the hell happened, McDowell?" Fury spurted at him from the professor, and Jonah waited for the man to stop talking. "Did you have anything to do with..." Quiet from the other side of the call urged Jonah to answer the rest of the question.

"No. Call it a gut feeling, but the problem I'm working on has, I think, spilled over to your hospital. I'm wondering though, would you be interested in consulting on our case? I have three very talented medical staff, but we may need to present a case yet to the courts, and your availability might assist us."

The silence drew out. "I... Perhaps." The man was waiting for more information, caution infusing his voice, and Jonah didn't repress his grin. He'd be wanting to know more too before committing.

"Fine. I can't tell you much at this point, but I'm going to keep your details on file. This case is..." Jonah hunted for the right words to explain the intricacies without sharing any more than necessary. "There are difficulties involving the No Harm Oath and questions about the legalities of genetics if you will. I must caution you though, if anyone approaches you, contact me immediately. Don't engage with these people. They're dangerous."

The professor grunted, "I'm not in my dotage yet, but I'll be cautious."

Jonah waited, knowing—sure deep in his bones—the professor was expecting more. Details he couldn't and wouldn't disclose at this point.

"Fine, you'll tell me more when you can. Keep in touch, McDowell, because I need to know exactly what we're dealing with."

Thank heavens the man didn't push for more details than I can share. He placed the communicator on the desk and prepared for the next meeting. The professor had been of tremendous help, and Jonah hated to lie to him.

The door opened, and Michael and Clarissa entered the room.

"Shut the door and sit down." Jonah indicated the two small modular chairs opposite his crowded desk. "Did you discuss the arrangement I suggested?"

Michael nodded. "I have spoken with Clarissa, and we agree this would be the best outcome for all involved."

For a moment, Jonah waited, sure something had to go wrong, but as the seconds ticked by, he cocked his head to the side and smiled. "Good. Then what comes next is finding a way to set up accommodation for you. Head up to the next level and see what rooms would suit you. I'll need a plan for alterations. We also need to find someone to cater—"

"Already done. I've asked our cook, Mrs. Hudson, to prepare the meals. We'll arrange for a delivery every day, including all three meals and snacks." Michael settled back in his chair, a self-satisfied air curling around him.

Clarissa snorted. "I saw what the children have been eating, and it's not healthy. I'll arrange a meal plan with Mrs. Hudson to meet their nutritional needs. I'm also going to head down to the cells to meet with the children. It's not a perfect situation meeting them in the enclosed location, but until we have a room customized and reinforced, I feel this is the best I can do. I've given Michael some plans already and chosen a room I believe would fit the bill."

Jonah steepled his fingers, considered her suggestions and plans. They all made sense to him, and he shrugged after scribbling them down. "We'll need to access the funding, but I think the senator will go to bat for that right now. Anything else?"

Clarissa pursed her lips. "I understand the necessity for placing the kids in cells, but to be honest, the best outcome is never to make them feel caged. I want to check their accommodations and assess how we might soften them without compromising the necessary security."

Michael ran his fingers through his hair, no doubt considering his next suggestion. "Reinforced plasglass fronting might be an improvement on the bars?"

Jonah squinted. "That might be do-able. I'd need to check the glass ratings, but would that help remove some of the institutional feel, Clarissa?"

"Perhaps. The other thing is the children need an education."

He stilled. "I agree, but right now, these are combatants. We need to attend to the most urgent—"

"If you want them to be anything else, you're going to have to consider their long-term needs, Jonah. If we don't get started now, we're going to be dealing with this into the future, and it won't be easy."

Clarissa clasped her hands together, and Jonah's stomach squeezed painfully. He understood she'd been in a similar situation, held against her wishes. Used as a lab rat.

"We need to normalize them as much as we can now, to make the future..." She shook her head, eyes screwed up tight like she was searching for the right term. "...easier?"

Jonah scrubbed his hands over his face, releasing some of the knotted tension that bunched up inside him. "I'll see what we can do. They won't be suitable to release into a school, but perhaps we could access a teaching program that will allow us to ascertain what educational skills they have."

She nodded. "Fine. That's all I've got right now."

Jonah scanned Michael's face. "Anything?"

His friend shook his head, and Jonah exhaled.

"Okay then. You go do your thing, and I'll..." Jonah waved his hand over the stacks and piles, watching them leave, as Michael flung, 'rather you than me,' over his shoulder.

Now that it was silent in his office, he sat back, focused on his breathing, and settled his mind. In the corner was his intrigue with the senator, but that wouldn't help him. It wouldn't give him any extra power to deal with the danger that lay ahead, and he certainly wasn't going to travel down that path.

With a grunt, he pushed forward in his chair, snapped up the messages, and started prioritizing.

DANIELLA HOVERED IN THE DOORWAY. She'd had her security team bring her to the building so she could inspect the premises, observe the children, and bring herself some hint of equilibrium with the situation. Locking children into cells revolted her, yet they were dangerous. The whole situation was precarious, and until they could find a solution, it would only get worse. Visions of half-grown children armed with guns, roaming the streets, kept her awake nightly.

Indecision slashed at her. President Yin promised more funds, hidden monies that would help them to fight the encroaching evil.

Daniella clattered up the metal staircase from the front heavy doorway and glanced around. It was a hive of activity, with office furnishings carted here and there, boxes of items and files, and the din of chatter filling the air. These were the men and women that would be their front-line defense against the unknown enemy.

"Hey, Daniella, what are you doing here?" Michael called to her, and she turned swiftly, a box scraping over her jacket, and she shied away.

"I'm here to inspect the setup and talk to Jonah about what's needed."

"That's great timing, because I gave him the details earlier today. Clarissa and I are moving into the top level, leaving this one for the office space, and the basement level as the containment area."

She frowned. "Let me check in with Jonah first, then I'll take a look. Will Clarissa join us?"

Michael shrugged. "Depends on what Jonah wants, I guess. I'm merely a doctor."

A bubble of laughter erupted. "Just a doctor my foot. These days you're just as much a strategist too. Show me the way to his office, and I'll catch up with you later."

He indicated the room at the far end, then picked up a box and retreated. The hallway wasn't long, though dotted with scattered detritus, and she had to inch forward, turning this way and that before she reached the scarred, wooden door.

Two quick knocks were met with a called out, "Come."

Jonah sat hunched at a desk, a protein bar in hand, sleeves rolled up, squinting at the data screen before him. When he looked up, his face bloomed with surprise.

"Senator." He pushed back from the desk, dumping the bar, and she moved quickly, shutting the door behind her.

"I've come to see how much you've achieved. I see a lot of people and movement."

Jonah cleared his throat, a slight tinge of crimson slashing his cheeks. "We're getting organized. More bodies mean more desks and office space."

Cocking her head to the side, Daniella wondered if he was embarrassed. "I'm not questioning what's happening, just stating that there's a lot of movement." She stepped closer so that only the desk separated them. "Mind if I sit?"

"Sure. I mean, please do. I needed to talk to you about arrangements for the children and—"

"I've spoken to the president. He's helped me locate some extra funds, which we'll tag as government infrastructure. It's not a huge amount, and we'll need to be careful, but it should allow us to reinforce, rebuild, and hire as necessary. I've also arranged for another half dozen pool vehicles to be made available. The placement of the new team members we plan to absorb as mid-range development officers. It's the best I could do without alerting anyone to what we're attempting to achieve." Daniella bit her lip. "We can only hold those positions for a short while though, possibly six to twelve months, before there will be questions asked. I've also appropriated other funding from my office. The entire fit-out cost is being absorbed within my budget, but if there are questions asked..." She gazed at him, willing him to understand what she wasn't saying.

"I understand, senator." The gravity of his voice told her clearly that he knew she was between a rock and a hard place.

"I'm trying to find ways, but there's only so much careful naming I can put in place." The seat was hard, but she perched on the edge of the chair, the bite of sharp edges cutting into the back of her thighs. "What needs to be done to make this a workable space for you and your crew?"

She waited, her gaze eating him up. The play of light from the dirty window accentuated the harsh planes of his face. The strength of his chin and the shine in his eyes gave him a dangerous and sexy air. Not for the first time, her breath fled as visions of running her hands over his skin, bared for her touch, overlaid her thought processes.

"Senator?"

She jumped at his question. "Oh, uh sorry. I was thinking about something."

When his eyebrow rose in question, she blinked, and her hands shook where she clasped them together on her lap.

"It's not important," she said. "And I... My inattention was unprofessional."

His smile heated her internally, and she stifled the moan that rose in her throat. "It's been a long morning and a couple of weeks. We can postpone this meeting if it's better for you."

Shaking her head, strands of hair whipping around her, she negated his suggestion. "No, we need to get this going and now. If we put it off much longer, we won't be able to make the modifications. Give me the precis, and we can work from there."

He turned the screen, blunt fingers firm on the frame. "Speaking with my people, we have several factors. The children have some specific needs, and Michael suggested a re- enforced plas-glass screening. Clarissa feels that the children would probably benefit from a less cell-like environment. While they may be combatants with a range of training, she's also raised the fact that they might not have received any education. We can't release them to a traditional school, but I've made some inquiries, and we can institute a screen-based tutor system. It's not ideal, but at least we might be able to ignite their minds. We'll need some hardware, but I've spoken to someone I know who may be able to make some school-obsolete units available."

"School-obsolete?" She blinked at his terminology.

"With the 'New Tech, New School' Policy, units can only be used for the first twelve months after release. These are ones that we'd ship to mining and other low-value enterprises, so there's no material loss to the schools. Given they're already compensated, they're fiscally accounted for. We can employ basic testing systems and get an accurate idea of what the children know."

Daniella pondered his words, wondering just how he'd managed to accomplish so much in a matter of hours. "You've been busy. McNally is keen to get back to work. I know she's been authorized for light duties, but if you have some work…"

He raked his hands through his short hair. "To be honest, I could use her here right now. McNally's a fine researcher and would be an efficient backup to Clarissa and Michael, keeping an eye on the security cameras while everything else is happening. Plus, she can do some of the scut work, so long as she's been passed as capable by the doctors."

Daniella nodded then sighed. She probably should inform him of the latest development regarding Agent McNally and her brother. "I'll let David know. He's taken her back to his place."

Jonah got the look on his face again, all concentration and concern, lines crinkling around his eyes and mouth. "Is that wise?"

"Maybe, maybe not, but David and McNally are adults and need to resolve whatever is between them." She held up her hand as he opened his mouth. "So long as it doesn't get in the way of the mission."

She stilled for a moment and pondered what she'd just said. *So long as it doesn't get in the way of the mission.* That said it all. It encapsulated her issues with Jonah too.

"Fine. Come on upstairs, I'll show you the wing Michael and Clarissa intend to make into their living area."

He rose, and so did she. As he moved around the desk with his usual fluid grace, the blood in her veins pumped slowly, like the viscosity somehow changed to syrup.

He might be courteous and gentlemanly with her, but beneath the exterior was a warrior—primal, and dangerous. She gulped, and he caught her gaze, eyes becoming smoky with a hedonistic intensity.

"Senator?" The tone warned her that he felt the emotional pull, the arousal that ribboned between them.

"No. I won't." Lifting her chin, she stared at him. "Business. This is all about business."

———————————————

Chapter 10

———————————————

Slumping into his seat was about all Jonah could manage after the senator left. The look she'd given him in this very office tore at him, the utter refusal in her gaze burning deep into his psyche. Clearly, the inability to move or think when the heat descended didn't affect her. That knowledge burned him just as much, if not more.

He spun the chair, staring out the window at the gray city that unfolded to his view. The office sat atop a small hill in the middle of the industrial district. Defensible and reinforced, its construction had taken place at the height of the war. Like most of the buildings constructed at that time, the structure had been prepared off-site then raised into position. Every anchor point and fastener made of high-grade liquid titanium, speeding up the process of completion.

Now it felt like a prison. He snorted at the thought, shook his head, and turned back to the screen. "You're reaching, buddy. She's beyond your pay grade, and while you can fool yourself, you'll never be more than what you are."

Tapping the screen woke it from the screen saving process, and his gaze settled on an image. The communication came from a friend of his in arson services. It was a grainy still of the outside of the hospital with three children carrying a package.

"Fucking bingo!" Jonah launched from his seat, stepping lightly around the mounds of files on the floor as he grabbed his jacket. His flicked his communicator on and it beeped loudly, then he demanded to connect to Senna Reed.

"Senna? Jonah McDowell. I see you sent me a pic of the hospital." He slammed his office door shut and strode down the hallway.

"Just like you requested. What I don't get is—"

"Not now, Senna. Meet me at the coffee shop down the road from your place. I'll fill you in." He descended the steps and reached for the door.

Senna had been a commander in the combat forces during his time. The woman was rough and tough with an eye for detail. She'd come from a firefighter family, and her goal had been to return to her birthright. She'd intended for the combat training to kick her up a gear when she finally applied to the fire academy, and once she completed her basic training, they made her an arson investigator.

The door slammed shut behind him, and Jonah reached the car as the ground rumbled beneath his feet. The shockwave punched him back against the wall. "Oomph!"

Heat rose like a wall around him, and he shoved his hands up, protecting his face. Heat singed the hairs on his hands as he hunched down. As quickly as it came, it fled.

Carefully, he peered around the protection of his hands. His vehicle was a charred mess. Tiny dots of flame flickered and danced in the street, and he scanned the view. No one loitered— not a single body.

They got close enough to lay some kind of incendiary device. Jonah planned to check the security feeds, but first, he had to get to Senna. He stomped inside, stepping over the remains of his communicator, which he'd dropped in the explosion.

Reaching for the door, he tugged his hand away and hissed. Spasms of pain ricocheted from his palm, and he glanced down at his hands. They'd welted, abraded and reddened from the heat of the explosion and flying shrapnel. "Fuck it!"

He inhaled deeply, holding the oxygen for the count of five, then slowly exhaled. This time he was prepared for the shock of pain as he wound his hand around the knob and tugged. Slamming the door shut, he took the stairs at a run and was met at the top by Clarissa, her eyes wide, face pale.

"You're okay, Jonah? I saw it on the screen. I came as soon as I could."

"Yeah. But I need a vehicle."

She shook her head. "You need first aid before you can go anywhere."

He grunted. "I had to be somewhere five minutes ago. If I can't drive, then someone will need to take me. Where's Franklin?"

Clarissa bit her lip, lifted her communicator, and punched in the call button. "Franklin? I need you at the front steps now."

Within seconds, the hulking frame of Franklin, one of his closest friends, appeared at his side. "What happened?"

"Not entirely sure, but I'm meeting with Senna."

Franklin frowned. "That explains some of the ash and stuff. But how did you get hold of her so quickly?"

"I'll explain in the car. Let's go." He turned, knowing that Franklin would follow. They hurried down the steps, the clatter loud, and he reached for the door and hissed as the pain exploded again. "You still got your first aid case in your car?"

Franklin glanced at his hand and winced. "Yeah. Get in, and I'll pass it over." He clicked the unlock button and tugged the door open for Jonah then strode to the other side and got in himself.

Jonah didn't look back as they drove off. He rummaged through the medical box Franklin had passed him. Cleaning the skin was painful, the stinging followed by the spray of adhesive skin replacement, then he applied the patches and bandaged them.

"Better let Mike take a look at that once we get back to base."

He couldn't fault Franklin, but while it hurt, it was only going to increase his ire if he wasted more time. Even as he opened his mouth, Franklin pulled up to the nearest available parking space close to the coffee shop, and instead, he grunted, "You better come in and hear this so I don't need to repeat it." He reached for the door, but the layers of gauze were too thick, and he snarled.

Franklin depressed the remote which opened Jonah's door then climbed out himself.

Jonah heard the *chick-schnick* as Franklin locked the car.

Their strides ate up the pavement, and they entered the café, Jonah scanning to look for the woman he'd come to meet. In the corner sat Senna. She looked about twenty-one but was in her mid-thirties with brown hair and eyes. It was up close that you'd catch sight of her pale, flawless skin and careful makeup application. Even on the battleground, she'd taken pains to present a professional image.

She stood, her gaze focused on his hands, the narrowing and tightening of her mouth the only indication that she wasn't happy. "What happened?"

"Someone decided my car had outlived its usefulness. What's left is outside my office. A ruin."

"And of course, you called it in?" Senna settled back into her seat, raising a hand, and before he could answer a young girl strode up to the table, requesting their order.

He waited until she was gone and followed Senna's lead, sitting on the seat. "No. I believe it's connected to the case we're working through. The one you sent me the image of."

She tugged a communicator from her pocket, clicked on something, and video played on the screen. Three children, hurrying across the parking zone, in dark clothing, baggy enough to hide their gender and yet somehow resembling military cut. A bag was slung over the oldest child's shoulder.

"They get to the door and dump it. I'm sure these two are lookouts. Watch the way they stand against this one's back and watch." She pointed at the one who'd carried the bag. "Now, my friend. What the hell is going on?"

Jonah scowled, wondering just how much he could safely share with this woman. "They're not quite what they seem."

She opened her mouth, and he raised a hand, stopping her.

"Yes, they're children as we know them, but there's more. They have..." He cleared his throat as the young server returned, coffees on a tray, and placed them on the table.

They waited until the server had left, then Senna said, "Jonah, I need to know, otherwise things could get far messier than they already are."

Senna steepled her fingers, and a cold chill of premonition whipped through him. They'd been like this before, at the beginning of the war, not long after they'd signed up. Coffee on the table and Senna's eyes taking on the dark, flat look he associated with entering battle.

"We think the kids are genetically enhanced using bio-cybernetic formulations. They were implanted in an IVF clinic. They're dangerous because they're weapons. Raised to kill and without empathy."

With each word, her eyes grew bigger. "You're kidding me."

He shook his head. "Nope. These kids are dangerous. They set that explosion."

She wriggled in her seat. "I don't know, Jonah. I mean, dropped the bag, sure, but set the charges?"

"Have you determined what kind of device it was?"

Now she paled. "There was more than one." The words were strangled, and he covered his face with his gauze-covered hands, eyes closed for a moment.

"We've got problems. Big ones." Then he sighed, uncovered his face, and pinned her with his gaze. "I need to know what you're aware of, but there's another problem. We can't do this officially. I can't tell you much more at this point. Just that you're going to have to deal directly with me."

"I tried to ring you back—"

He grunted, and Franklin laughed. "Yeah, well, he's going to need a new communicator."

Jonah stared at the big man who grinned.

"I saw it on the ground, J. Near your car, which was still smoldering when we left."

Senna turned, her voice now dry. "That's really inconvenient."

"They blew up his car, that's more so." Franklin's smile melted away, and a gleam took up residence. "But have no fear, they won't get away with it. J and Mike will find the kids."

"Tell me more..."

———

DANIELLA SLID the last folder into the carrier, ready for collection the next day. Kallee had insisted they use a certified carrier, and she'd agreed. "But I feel like a prisoner in my own home." The only time she'd left had been to go to the mission office for the inspection. Even her housekeeper was adhering to the rigid restrictions her brothers and Jonah had set in place.

Jonah. A problem she didn't want to deal with. Her attraction was the elephant in the room though.

Her gaze settled on the small, marble statue in the corner of her office. The remainder of her hopes and dreams and how easily they could be dashed.

"No. I won't do this." She stood abruptly, the chair pushing out from under her, and she smoothed down the ecru lace and silk lounge suit she wore.

Daniella gathered up the bundle of files and shoved them into the bag, frowning when they didn't fit in all the way. On a sigh, she tugged them out and shoved her hand into the opening, fishing around.

Fingertips quested until she felt an obstruction, and she stilled. "What?" Peering into the bag showed a piece of card, the same color as the bag. She pulled, surprise warring with anxiety. *What did I miss?*

The card was an envelope, no writing on the cover, and she flipped it open. Inside was a note. Her insides froze and horror mixed with nausea that burned her throat as she scanned the words.

Clutching the missive in nerveless hands, Daniella dropped to her chair, gazing sightlessly forward.

The door to her office clattered open. "Senator, what did you want—"

In the dim recesses of her brain, she recognized the woman's voice. Kallee.

"Senator?"

Kallee stepped forward, and shaking off some of the fugue surrounding her, Daniella shook her head. "Stay out there and contact Jonah McDowell. Tell him I need to see him. Urgently."

Kallee took another step. "Can I do—"

"Ring him, Kallee. Ring him now."

JONAH TOOK the stairs at a dead run. The call from Kallee had left his insides a quivering, slushy mass of terror. Kallee had been adamant that he hurry.

Franklin had rushed, and he was sure their arrival was reasonably close to record time. The door slid open, and Kallee peered around the corner, her face white, eyes wide open. "Come in. She won't come out and won't let me in. I tried to—" Her babbling indicated a level of fear she hadn't even exhibited after the attack on the senator.

His fury ratcheted up. "You did what you needed to do. Let me handle this." Franklin made to follow him, but he raised a hand. "Stay here with Kallee."

The woman nodded then glanced down at his hands, swallowing hard. "What... What happened?"

He'd already turned to the office door. "Nothing that will stop me."

Jonah slid into the room, his eyes roaming and taking stock before settling on Daniella— the senator, he reminded himself firmly—hunched over her chair.

"I came as soon as I could," he said.

She lifted her head, and tracks shone on her cheeks. "I swear to God, I've never been more furious or more frightened in my life, Jonah. These bastards sent me a note."

The fluttering of his heart ceased, then resumed a faster rhythm. "Did they? Where is it?"

Daniella fluttered her hands over her desk. "There. You need to read it. They know what we're doing, or at least parts of it. They know we've got the children. They want them back."

He reached for his pocket and swore as the ache reminded him of the injury to his hands.

"What... What did you do?" Her voice shook, and he gazed at her.

"They blew up my car."

Her complexion took on the tinge of fresh mid-winter snow as every ounce of blood fled from her face. "What?"

"It's nothing."

She rose, visibly shaking. "It's not nothing. They've tried to kill you, me, Agent McNally. They've turned these kids into weapons. How much worse can it get?"

He didn't want to tell her about the hospital, but she was effectively the head of the organization. She needed to know, but to share that now? It surely couldn't be helpful.

"Jonah? What are you hiding from me?"

Closing his eyes, he inhaled deeply, taking in the essence of woman as he fought to unscramble his emotions. "Senator—"

"No. I need to know what's going on. Tell me."

"They were also instrumental in the destruction of the hospital, according to my sources. We have vision of the incident."

"Oh Lord."

She staggered, thrust out a hand seeking support, and he stepped forward and reached for her. His hand glanced against her, the searing pain from his burns ignored as he tugged her close. He needed to support her, and she needed him.

"I need to see the note, senator."

Her eyes were pools of moisture as she looked at him. "But you're hurt."

"It won't stop me from doing my job. Tell me how you found it."

Her breath shuddered, then she tugged away. He let go, realizing that this—interludes of physical support—made the situation harder for them both.

"I was preparing to put my files into the courier sack. Since we agreed we wouldn't go into the office, Kallee made arrangements for a company we sometimes use to transport sensitive documents. They delivered the files. I took control of them, worked through the documents, and was about to put them into the sack to send back. They didn't fit, and that made no sense. I put my hand in, checked, and found the note."

He frowned. "You didn't think it was unusual?"

"We sometimes get notes like that. It's not unusual, so I didn't think twice."

"Where is it?"

"On my desk." She pointed to the bulky wood furnishing, and he moved forward. He leaned down and read the text.

You might have some of the children, but we have more. By the time we're through, you and your team won't even be postscripts in the history of humanity.
We know where you are and intend to take back what's ours.

No chance they wouldn't understand that message, he thought. The danger was clear, the threat direct. A haze of red descended, and it took more than a dozen breaths to beat it back.

"I'll need a team here. Go out and get Kallee to call for David and tell Franklin I need him. I'll also need details of the courier company, the delivery person. I need a recorder. Mine was in the vehicle." He didn't look up, just stared at the note, processing the heavy cardboard. He was sure he had seen some like it before, but where?

The door squeaked open, and he looked up. "Tell Franklin I'll also need an evidence kit."

Her nod was short, then she was gone. He settled in the seat and tugged out the replacement communicator he'd purchased after coffee with Senna as the sting and tug of his skin bit deep.

"Michael?" He didn't wait for the man to respond. "They sent your sister a note. I need you here, because I've seen this cardstock before, but I can't place where. And make sure you bump up the security on the building. They've already destroyed my car, and they know we've got the kids."

"I'll be there as soon as I can, and yes, I'll beef it up."

The communicator clicked off as the door opened again.

Daniella—it was getting harder to think of her as the senator—stood in the doorway. "Do you need anything else?"

A loaded question in his mind. "Not at this time. As soon as Michael, David, and Franklin arrive, we'll arrange for the removal of the evidence."

"Will you also let Michael take a look at your hands?" She spoke so quietly he almost missed her question.

"Why?"

"Because I'm asking." The soft plea in her tone warred with the primal male. The entreaty won.

"All right. I'll let him look at them."

The tremulous smile she gave him warmed the coldness in his chest. "Thank you."

DANIELLA STOOD on the balcony of her room. The night closed in, the scent of rose and jasmine filling the air. The garden lay in shadow. She could go down. He might join her again.

Memories of the last time wound around her. Magic tingles danced under her skin as hope surged.

She's squashed it time and again, but it was getting harder to remember why she shouldn't give in to the hunger and need that rose within her. Warmth flooded her belly.

On impulse, Daniella turned and headed for the dressing table against the wall and opened the tiny, middle drawer. Gazing down at the ring she'd hidden away, long-ago memories tugged.

She danced on the pavement, her face wreathed in smiles at the promise the tiny ring Luis had shoved into her hand represented.

Her parents wouldn't understand, thought the fifteen-year-old girl. Luis might be the son of an itinerant worker, but he got her. Realized that she chafed at the restrictions they'd put in place.

Sneaking out to meet him tonight, she'd known something was going to happen.

The kiss in the park had spread warmth through her. His careful touches and shy, stumbling-over words were evidence of his love for her. "He wants me. Daniella Villede the woman, not the daughter of my parents. He doesn't care about my background, and I don't care about his." She spoke to the night, sure that everything she felt and knew had to be true.

Anything else was unacceptable in her mind.

The sound of a truck lumbering down her street distracted her from her thoughts, and she stepped into the shadows of the large trees hiding the security wall of her parents' property. It wasn't that she was a snob, she told herself firmly, but there shouldn't be any trucks on this street. This was an exclusive suburb, and those who drove trucks didn't live here.

Why would they even be here at one in the morning?

The tiny, hidden gate was just ahead, and instinctively, Daniella hurried her steps. No one knew about it, except herself and Luis.

That stopped her dead. Maybe Luis had come to make sure she'd gotten home safely. Maybe.

She stepped deeper in the bushes as uncertainty gnawed at her mind. What if it wasn't Luis?

Come on, Daniella, who else would it be?

The ingrained wariness her parents' guards had instilled in her rose, and she automatically followed the teachings of years.

The truck lurched to a stop by the gate, and she crouched down to make as small a target as possible. More than one person climbed down as she watched.

"Has she arrived yet?" Luis's older brother whispered loudly as he waited beside the truck.

"The tracker says she's nearby. Unless she ran, and to be honest, she was practically dancing on air after I kissed her, so I doubt that would be the case. It's not like she was going home to tell her folks." The distaste in Luis's words hit her like a hammer.

"We should..." Luis's brother's voice was cut off by the rattle of the massive double gates.

"Shit! They've detected there's someone out there. We need to get away before they find us." Fear colored Luis's voice.

"But we haven't completed the mission. Luis, you need to find a way in, to neutralize the guards. If we're caught, the mission is screwed."

They waited too long though, and her parents' guards bellowed. Luis and his brother piled back into the truck, the engine sputtering before they rumbled off.

While the commotion kept the armed personnel busy, Daniella snuck to the gate, entered the security code, and hurried into the compound.

"Miss Daniella, you know better than to sneak out at night." Minster, her parents' senior security expert, towered over her, his face the usual calm facade.

His words scared her, and she bit her lip hard enough to draw blood. "I..."

"Come on, Miss Daniella. You look like you need a friend right about now. I'll make you a coffee, and you can tell me what's going on."

Daniella swiped her shaking hand over her brow. She'd trusted the wrong boy once before.

Minster had informed her days afterward that Luis had been part of a plot to abduct her parents. Their connections and finances had been the primary reason, and she'd merely been the pawn. He'd been kind and considerate of her feelings. Or so she thought.

Daniella had never told her parents. Even now, she remained unsure of what Minster had shared with them about the situation. Michael and David were unaware. She'd pleaded with Minster to keep her secret, and he'd agreed.

What it had done, though, was dent her ability to trust a man on that level again. It didn't matter that nearly twenty years had passed; she'd endangered her family foolishly.

"But Jonah isn't like that." She tested the words, examined them. No, he wasn't. But what if she made another mistake?

Confusion filled her. Anger warred as she tried to throw off its mantle.

On a whim, she pulled the ring from the drawer and turned it over to see where Minster had found and removed the tiny tracking device. The war had much to answer for. It made everyone question his or her safety and choices.

"The war is over."

She scrubbed at her tired eyes and dropped the ring onto the bed, watching as it bounced on the coverlet.

Daniella reached for her wrap, tugged it around herself, and walked to the door. She needed fresh air and time to think, where she wasn't cooped up.

If Jonah just happened to be out there, then he was. Life had to go on.

Chapter 11

The night air settled around Jonah, darkness welcome after the manic day. Michael had dressed his hands after applying an antibiotic ointment that would also speed the healing. He could now move his fingers and grasp something without the burst of pain.

"At least tomorrow I'll be unhampered."

"What was that?"

The voice surprised him, and he turned on the seat, almost toppling. "Senator." He sat up straighter, some need deep within him rising to the surface. His psyche demanding she see him as more than just her protector.

It didn't make any sense, his brain reasoned.

But it made perfect sense on a far deeper, more emotional level.

The rustle of her wrap dried his mouth. Beneath flimsy layers of silk were miles of silken flesh. He couldn't see it but knew it was there. Hell, he'd smelled the lilac cream she applied to her skin, touched her hands, and felt the suppleness.

She was trim, and always impeccably groomed. Daniella took care of herself. While she rarely shared her emotions with the public —the press regularly referred to her as the 'Ice Queen' as did sections of political circles—he'd glimpsed the woman beneath the facade. Knew her to be caring, affectionate, and passionate about things she believed in.

"I'm sure I told you to call me Daniella when we're alone."

He gulped. Something was different about her tonight. As if she'd cast off restraints, and it made being rational a whole lot harder. Along with other parts of his body.

She placed her hand on his shoulder as she rounded the bench. He burned from the touch.

"Senator, I don't think…" The words died away at the sneaky smile she shot at him.

His heart nearly gave out as she crouched beside him. "Then don't think, Jonah. Only feel." The whisper of her breath played on his skin, tormenting him as nerves rippled and quivered.

He closed his eyes and surrendered to her innate sensuality as she pushed her lips against his. Her tongue flicked at the seam of his mouth, and he groaned. Gave in to the onslaught as sensation after sensation crashed down.

He reached out and pulled her close, every nerve screaming for more. He felt the tension in her shoulders, dug in for a moment, then soothed the area as he let his fingers splay and caress. His tongue surging deep into her mouth, he tasted her essence, womanly and hot, while the molten flow of blood rose in his veins. Hunger roared, but she tugged away from him, leaving him suddenly adrift.

"Come with me, Jonah." She reached out a hand, and he took it, noting the shake as adrenalin pounded.

He stood and followed her beneath the trees.

"I've wanted to kiss you for a long time. But I've been afraid. I'm a bad pick of men."

Confusion filled him at her words. She'd urged a connection between them, then ended it abruptly. She pulled him into a darkened garden redolent with scents of romance but wanted to tell him she was terrible at picking men?

"Daniella? You don't need—"

"Actually, I do. See, a long time ago, I ignored every sensible thought. I met a guy—well, a boy, now that I think back. He gave me a ring, and I thought, rather naively, that it meant he loved me."

"What happened?"

"He had a tracker put in the ring he gave me. He was looking for a way into my parents' compound. I snuck out after dark to meet him. It was part of the plan. He made sure it was a public location, so I'd be seen. Then he planned to kidnap me and use it as leverage to grab my parents and use their political connection. It was just before the war. He was a Surdanista Rebel. I was the girl with connections who thought the world was her oyster."

"He was captured?"

"Oh, yes. My parents' security service had a very wise man heading it up. Minster kept my secret, found him and his brother. Made a deal that kept my name out of things."

Unable to help himself, Jonah reached out and cupped her cheek, caressed the skin with his thumb. "It wasn't your fault. How old were you?"

"Fifteen."

"Not yet fully grown. Daniella, we all make missteps. It's the ones we don't learn from that are the biggest problem."

"You're very wise, Jonah McDowell. How did that happen?"

"It must have rubbed off on me."

He tugged her close so that their lips met and clung. The gentle kiss ignited the roaring flames of hunger, but he banked them. She needed to learn to trust herself, and pushing too hard and too fast wasn't the way to achieve that.

DANIELLA FELT THE SWAMPING PASSION, and it swirled and eddied, sucking at her senses. It stole her ability to reason, and she wasn't sure she was capable of pushing it back. Didn't want to. Not if she were honest with herself.

Covering his hand with hers, Daniella kept Jonah close. She leaned in and whispered, "Jonah, I don't know if this is wise or not, but I want to trust my instincts. I feel the need to step into the heat with you and dance in the flames until I'm burned away. I just don't know how."

Baring her soul was difficult after all these years of control and repression. She'd enjoyed the odd encounter here and there, but she'd never allowed anything more than a shallow connection, fearing another mistake.

Now, she craved more. So damned much more that it was almost a compulsion.

"We can take whatever time you need, Daniella. There's no rush."

She bit her lip hard, felt the sting, and tasted copper. Maybe she was vacillating for no good reason, yet there was also an awareness that things would get worse before they got better. How much worse she couldn't say, but the odds were, terrible. They'd lived through a war, lost friends and comrades. Watched relationships implode, and grieved with those who'd lost the other half of their souls. There was the potential for that again.

"Jonah, I know what I want. You. But I don't know how to do that. Hell, I'm not even sure it——"

The hunger in the kiss he initiated blew her mind.

When he ended it, they were both breathless, her hands wound around his neck, and his hands under her wrap and kneading her skin through the single layer covering her body. Flutters of sensation in her belly joined with the balled heat of desire pooling between her legs.

His eyes were half-closed, yet she could see the smoky fires of sexual hunger ablaze in his gaze.

She shivered.

"Cold?" His word echoed through her entire body.

"No. Hungry. For you." She stepped back, captured his gaze with her eyes, and reached up, shedding her wrap, so she stood before him in the thin, silk chemise.

"You're incredibly beautiful, Daniella. But you deserve better than me, and better than this. You should have candlelight, champagne, and romance."

The words hit her solar plexus. "You don't want me?"

"Oh, I do. I want to fuck the *Ice Queen* until she melts in my arms. I need you to scream my name as you come. I would kiss and lick every inch of you. Just think of how you'd squirm, soaked with sweat and naked. With me."

He was withdrawing from her, and it hurt. Dammit, it was like a savage slash to her heart.

"I'm so sorry I've inconvenienced you." She turned, stiff and angry. Hurt and devastated.

He grabbed her arm. She tugged, wanting nothing more than to escape, but he held her still, and when she looked at him, his face was a hard mask. "Not so fast. I didn't say I didn't want you or that you inconvenienced me. I'm rock-hard for you right now, so don't get fucking angry. I'm telling you I want you so badly it's messing with my mind that I want so much more than to be a convenient outlet for your sexual hunger. If I do this, if we make love—and don't get me wrong, because that's exactly what it will be—I'm going to demand everything you've got, Daniella. Then I'll demand more."

The fury melted. "I want you too. I know things are strained, and that we've got a lot to deal with, but this isn't a passing fancy, Jonah. I'm not interested in that either. I want a partner. A lover." She bit back the word *husband*. Neither was ready for that yet, if they ever got there.

"Then let's go to your room. I won't treat you like a rutting animal."

She grinned and held out her hand. "Fine then, follow me."

Moments later, they reached her room, the lights dimmed, and the door clicking closed behind them echoed loudly. Jonah folded Daniella in his arms, tugging her close. The kiss was soft, fluttering like a butterfly over her lips and awakening senses she barely knew existed.

"Kiss me back," he murmured, and she opened her mouth, met the thrust of his tongue, and tasted the manly essence of him.

Her hands curled over his shoulders, feeling the ligaments and muscles hidden beneath the light sleep shirt he wore.

The hunger to run her hands over the heated skin concealed below rode her hard, and she pulled away. "Take it off." The voice she used didn't sound like her own. Instead, it was a raspy, sensual version.

He gave a tight laugh. "Only if you lose the wrap."

"Tit-for-tat?"

His laugh echoed through her, grazing her nerve endings so that her nipples, already tight and hard, became stiff peaks of arousal. She blushed, but reached up and shed the wrap, then gloried in the way his gaze narrowed on the beaded flesh of her nipples.

Jonah grabbed the bottom edge of his shirt and tugged upward, so miles of skin emerged. Reaching out was instinctual, and Daniella ran her fingertip over his chest, feeling the play of nerves beneath her careful caress. His skin was marred, but totally masculine, and he let her toy with the naked flesh for a moment, then captured her wrist.

"I'll be honest. I'm not going to be able to take a lot of that."

Shock rippled, and she checked his face, finding it hard and tight with lust.

Her grin had him rocking back. "That's okay, because I don't want you to." Daniella shoved the straps of her gown over her shoulder and felt it slide down her body, a caress of silk on highly aroused skin. She moaned as the air caressed her skin and stood back, curved her finger, and retreated for the bed.

"I don't—" He sounded strangled even as he shucked the boxers and she gaped at the hard erection that jutted from his body.

"Well, if that can't do the job, then we're in trouble."

The confusion was replaced by surprise as he looked down. "Oh, it'll do the job, but we don't have any protection."

"Yes, we do. In the drawer beside the bed, so stop coming up with excuses and get over here."

He advanced like a lion on its prey. "Don't say you weren't warned."

Climbing onto the bed, he caged her, arms beside her head, and dipped down, his lips capturing hers and devouring. The banked craving exploded within her. Now he feasted, his mouth moving so that it traced the curve of her jaw, then slid down the sensitized flesh of her neck.

She arched and writhed, lost in the shadowy world of sensation that dragged at her. His mouth found her nipples and tugged gently, at first with teeth and lips, then increased pressure, and she moaned her arousal.

Her hands twined in the coverlet before releasing and negotiating the planes of his body, her body moving and searching for release.

When he positioned his cock at the entry of her body, her pleading echoed in the fresh night air, "Please, Jonah. Fill me up."

One tremendous slide was all it took, and she arched as the invasion filled and stretched. He stilled, arms shaking. "Is that enough?" The laser blue of his eyes seemed to search inside her psyche.

"Not nearly enough. Love me, Jonah."

He smiled and complied, moving in a swift rhythm that offered a glimpse of heaven.

Winding her legs around his waist, she met every thrust, kissed the skin she could reach and tasted the saltiness of the sweat on his skin until the fine wire that wound tight inside her snapped.

The orgasm cataclysmic, she arched, screaming his name as she gloried in the intense sensations, milking him. He heaved and slammed into her a final time and jetted deeply within her body.

Reality intruded. "Jonah?"

"Hmm?"

"We didn't use the protection." She waited for fear to grow and wondered at its absence.

"What?" He lifted his head, and she smiled, hoping he too wasn't concerned.

"We didn't—"

He frowned. "I heard you." He pulled her into the shelter of his arms. "Is this a problem?" His tone was careful, as if gauging her response.

"It's not ideal, but to be honest, I'm not exactly devastated. Jonah, I'm not looking for a fling. You spelled it out downstairs, and my thoughts align with yours. I'm an all-or-nothing kind of girl these days."

Jonah nodded. "Okay then. So, there's no issue. That's good."

Glancing at his wrist, he sighed. "But it is nearly two AM, so we do need to get some sleep." He started to disentangle himself.

"Where are you going?" She raised up on an elbow as he swung to the side of the bed.

"Back to my room."

Sensations feathered inside her belly. "You could stay here. If you want."

His gaze was hooded. "I could. If you want."

With a quick move, Daniella jumped off the bed and lifted the covers. "I want."

He joined her under the bedding, pulling her close against his hard body so they spooned. "I don't have any clothes here, and I'll need to get some in the morning. People will talk."

"They will. I don't care. I'm not embarrassed or ashamed of what we did. Are you?" She waited, breath held.

"Hell no." There was so much disgust in his answer that she laughed.

"Good, then let's get some sleep." She snuggled down and closed her eyes, focused on her breathing until she finally dropped off.

Chapter 12

Jonah woke, disoriented by the warmth of a body snuggled against his, and the strands of hair on his face. He brushed them away carefully and opened his eyes as memories of the night before rose.

Staying still seemed the best option, so he held Daniella close and accepted the heat and desire that rose in him for what it was. Lust and love for the woman in his arms. The generous but infinitely fragile creature who didn't trust herself to make another mistake.

Daniella stirred as if attuned to his thoughts. "Uhh, who..." The confusion in her voice was amusingly endearing. She turned in his embrace. "Jonah."

Grinning and tugging her close, he leaned in. "Good morning, senator."

She groaned. "I thought we were past that nonsense."

His kiss was gentle. "We are, but I couldn't help myself."

She giggled.

"We need to get up." He started to pull away, but she clung to him.

"Won't happen anywhere else today."

Quirking his brow at her naughty words, he attempted a glower, and her laugh was infectious.

Her hand reached for his cheek. "You need to shave."

"And dress." The last two words were regretful, but he tugged away. "I also need to get moving. I need to catch up with Senna, the arson investigator, and check on—"

Her eyes gleamed. "I know, and I have lots to do too."

He stilled, a bloom of panic filling his chest. "Be careful. The courier last night said nothing had been tampered with. I've sent the note to the team, but until we have some specifics as to how it got on your desk, be wary. And if you get any more notes, let me know."

"I will. Jonah? Take care out there. Things are getting dangerous, and I don't intend to lose you."

He leaned in one more time, kissed her hard and quick. "I have to go." Then he turned, gathered his shirt and boxers, pulled them over his nakedness, and slid the door open. "Ring me if you're leaving here. Where you go from now on, I go."

Reassured by her agreement, he left her and made his way down the corridor and staircase, hoping for some privacy for them both.

That hope shattered when Kallee met him at the bottom of the steps, her gaze narrowed. Her head cocked to the side as attitude flowed. "What were you doing up there?"

Frustration shimmered. Jonah balled his fists, aware he couldn't just tell her to back off. "Private business, Kallee."

Shaking her head, the little woman showed that the answer wasn't satisfactory to her. "The senator's rooms are up there."

He thinned his lips as the sharp edges of temper bit deep. "That so?"

"The senator's business is my business." She thrust out her chin, and Jonah sighed.

He scratched his head, then muttered, "Bloody meddling women." He inhaled and held that breath while she waited with a mulish expression on her face. "Look, Kallee, if the senator wants to tell you, she will. But what happens between the senator and me is..." Hunting for the best word, he shrugged. "It's complicated. I'll tell you what you need to know—only that. Now, if you don't mind, I need to shower and dress. I have a long day ahead of me."

On that, he turned and headed to his room. It was quiet, and he took a moment to ponder the lightning change in his life. The sex had been mind-blowing; the best he'd experienced in his life.

Was it enough to forge a future? That remained to be seen, as did how they'd overcome the disparity in their upbringing, and how his 'brothers' would react. They all weighed on him, but right now, he was riding the high. He sighed. Not everything was going to be so simple.

The case they were investigating was a minefield, and Daniella was firmly entrenched in the middle of the mess.

"One step at a time, Jonah. Shower, shave, and dress, then formulate the plan for the day. Meet with Senna. You've already got enough going on. Don't ask for trouble."

A quick shower refreshed him, then he removed the stubble and dressed in a suit.

As he was exiting the room, his communicator beeped, and he answered with a curt, "Jonah McDowell."

"I don't know what's going on, Jonah, but you only told me part of the story." Senna's voice echoed, overlaid with fury and what he thought sounded a whole heap like fear.

"Senna?"

"They busted my arse, Jonah. I'm on suspension for sharing details of an investigation outside acceptable parameters. What the hell is going on?"

He hurried down the hall, rounded the corner, and pulled up short as Kallee put out a hand to stop him. "Just a minute, Senna."

"The senator needs to see you," Kallee said. "She says it's not urgent but—"

"I'm onto something right now. Tell her I'll be back as soon as I can, and I'm bringing in a new team asset. Someone who can help us understand other facets of the case."

The tightening of Kallee's face made it clear his words weren't what she wanted to hear, but right now, time was short.

He turned his attention back to the phone call. "Where are you right now, Senna?"

"Outside my office, because they took my car as well as my codes." Fury of the frigid variety colored her tone.

He swore. "Stay there, in view of people. I'm on my way."

Galloping down the steps, he headed for the replacement car that sat in the drive, just as he'd directed. Jonah frowned. "What's this?"

Waving his hand over the door, it slid open, and he peered in. The scent of lemon assaulted his senses as he slid into the driver's seat.

A note sat on the passenger seat, and he scooped it up.

The car's a classic, so take care of her. Given the circumstances, I thought you'd need something with both grunt and speed. You can return it when you get your new car sorted.
M.

He grinned. Michael had organized this beauty. He punched the ignition start button as he glanced down at the key port. The growl filled the air, vibrating through him. "Holy jeez, that man knows vehicles."

"What?" Senna spoke through the tiny communicator, and he laughed.

"I'm on my way, Senna. Just look out for a classic black car that's extraordinarily loud."

"Huh. Be quick."

He accelerated, and the vehicle flowed down the driveway.

DANIELLA STRUGGLED to settle to anything. Her mind was overwhelmed by tumultuous emotions. How the hell were they going to find any way of getting to the bottom of this mess?

She bit her lip and read through the message she'd already

skimmed four times so far today. The door opened, and Kallee entered the room, looking flustered and wild-eyed.

"Jonah?" Daniella started to rise from her chair, but Kallee shook her head.

"He had to go. He had a call and said to tell you he was bringing back an asset. Senator, I don't exactly know what happened last night, but this isn't wise. I mean, what with the work you're doing for President Yin, the attacks on you, and the mess of this mission, plus the increased workload."

Daniella reached for the coffee carafe. Those were among the topics that rolled around in her head continuously.

"Pass me the Record of Assembly then. I want to take another look at those who were voting on the day I was attacked."

Kallee slid a small memory stick into the reader, and Daniella engaged the vision. The records were dry, filled with the banter and repetition that they'd tossed around the house that day.

She got to Delspar's speech and read it in full using the screen's text writer so as not to miss anything, teeth gritted as he made grandiose statements about safety, the security of the planet. "He's a lying bastard."

The record ended, and she leaned back into her chair, letting her mind mull over everything he'd said and done.

"Kallee, I don't suppose he's admitted to any mentoring program? Any new members who he's taken under his wing?"

Her PA scrunched up her face. "No. If anything, he's distanced himself, so that he can become 'the man they want to be,' aloof and guarded."

Daniella nodded. She too had noticed that he'd rarely been in the news, his wife curiously absent from the fashion tabloids. "You know what? They've almost disappeared from the eye of the public. Why is that? You've got contacts, so use them. Find out what's going on in his camp, but do it quietly. I don't want blowback. Now, let's have a look at the province figures. I think there's some room to trim back more expenses."

Daniella reached for the green financial folder on her desk. If they were going to grow the team, they needed funds. Not so much that every dollar was stripped from the province, but more than they currently had access to. That was unacceptable, given it too required assistance.

The work was tedious, scrolling through figures, checking every possible outcome of expenditure. Most senators handed this work over to their advisors. But Daniella refused to do so, understanding the complexities of the mostly agrarian region. She totted up a final calculation on her desk comp when Kallee cleared her throat. Glancing up, she read worry on Kallee's face.

"You've been invited to address their local assembly concerning what you plan to do for the region in two weeks. Can you manage it?" Kallee asked.

Daniella rubbed her now aching head. "I'll need to check with Jonah, because he's asked me not to leave here without him. If he clears it—"

"They need an answer today, senator."

Daniella sighed. "Buy me an hour or two, and I'll let you know."

THE VEHICLE SLOWED, traffic crawling to a near-stop as Jonah approached the building where Senna worked. Glancing into the distance, he noted an argument between drivers, windows open as they gesticulated, arms waving. He groaned. "I didn't miss this at all in the corps."

An itch settled at the back of his neck, and he narrowed his gaze, seeking the cause beyond the vehicle. He'd experienced this kind of warning before, during the war. It always served him well.

Whatever the holdup, it finally cleared, and cars started rolling again, the itch becoming more like the grate of a razor on his mind. He was two blocks from Senna's office, but something felt off.

Jonah lifted his communicator and dialed. Senna picked up with a breathy, "Yes?"

Something was wrong with the scenario. He rolled forward a few more buildings, thinking furiously. "Senna, are you occupied?"

"Uhh, no. But I think someone is about to be. Tell me you're on your way."

"Nearly there. Why?"

"I don't know, J. Something feels foul, and I don't think I want to be here."

He grunted and read the sign for the street ahead. "Walk down to Vale and meet me. I'm in a black classic car."

The communicator clicked off, and he rolled to the corner and pulled to the side, his eyes on the rearview mirror.

Moments later, Senna emerged from the throngs of people, moving to their place of employment, a lone woman against a tide of humanity. He wound down the window and motioned her forward as a gaggle of school children wandered down the road.

She climbed in, breathing more heavily. "Get the window up now, J." Then she hunched down in the seat. "We can't stay here."

"What's wrong?"

She speared him, and in her eyes, he read terror. "There's something about those kids. Look at the way they hold themselves, their grip on their satchels. Watch their eyes."

"Holy Christ!" He accelerated, punching his way into traffic, ignoring the blasting horns and screams of anger.

"What are they, Jonah? Who are they?"

"They're the fucking weapons I was talking about, and it's a damn good thing you had your wits about you. What gave it away?"

"After I spoke to you, I noticed the first one, on the footpath. It wasn't any one thing to begin with, but then another turned up. They didn't laugh and joke, as kids do. They just stood there, watching. A third joined them, and they were still, almost at parade rest. It was unnerving. By the time the fourth arrived, I knew I was in trouble. I've never been so damned pleased to see you in my life."

She breathed in short, choppy pants, swiping an unsteady hand over her sweaty brow. "If that's the super-soldiers you've alluded to, then there's really bad shit going down, and I'm not sure who's going to survive it."

He pressed the button on his communicator and winced when he heard McNally on the line. "What's up, Jonah?"

"I have a body of combatants down near Vale Street. Seven or eight on the loose. They followed a package, which I've secured. Get someone down there to follow them, but use extreme caution. We don't want them to know we're following."

"I'll send Francis down there. He's an excellent sniffer."

"McNally?"

"Yeah?"

"Healing?"

"Getting there. So long as I don't go running any mile-long sprints, I'll last the distance." He grunted. "Fine. I'll be in later today. Urgent messages re-route to my comm."

The car ate up the miles while the engine roared.

"Nice ride. Yours?" Senna quirked her eye at him, and he blinked.

"No. Michael's actually. He thought I needed something a bit more grunty to get me by."

"Ha! The only problem is it's flashy, and those kids will know that you've got me. That's if they're as well trained as we expect."

Jonah gripped the steering wheel, feeling the bite of metal cased in leather. "They're blunt weapons. I'm not sure they're trained to think about the various parameters of strategy. I'm of the opinion right now that they only have one objective, and that's to destroy." Even though he tried hard to cast off her comments, they stayed, lodged in his brain for him to tumble over again and again.

He turned into the estate, noting the completion of the reinforcing of the walls and gateway. The security guards he'd personally chosen were waiting behind the bullet and projectile proof glass of the sentry booths.

"Your work, I take it?"

"I'm good at it, and the senator needs protection."

Senna smiled. "It probably doesn't hurt that she's a leggy blonde too, right?"

He settled cold eyes on the woman in the seat beside her, watching as her grin melted away. "She's more than that, Senna."

"Oh, crap! You too? I swear all the good men are being snapped up."

Jonah squinted as the glare of sunlight beat down on the windscreen, advancing as the gates slid open. "Good women are a treasure. Don't worry, Senna. Someday your knight in shining armor will come down off the mountain, wherever that may be."

Her laugh choked. "I think I might be his knight. Good thing I'm not looking though."

Chapter 13

Daniella wasn't sure what to make of the woman settled in the seat opposite her. The dark blue uniform, medals, and medallions covered her chest, and the steely look of determination she'd read on Jonah, Franklin, and even Michael's face betrayed her military background.

"So, you knew Michael and Jonah from the corps?" Daniella asked.

"We served together. Your brother is an excellent medic and officer. Jonah was wasted as his guard. He's an amazing strategist. You're lucky to have him."

Daniella almost choked on her tea. "I'm lucky to have him?"

The woman was seeking confirmation of something more profound, but Daniella refused to be drawn in. Instead, she settled back and waited for Jonah to re-join them.

"You were in the same battalion?"

"Yeah. Same intake too. I was assigned as Michael's guard when he worked at the triage center."

"Interesting choice for someone with your skills, Senna."

"I wanted to be a paramedic. It was a stepping stone to help me enter the fire department, but when I was accepted and finished my time at the academy, they suggested arson investigation. It appeals to me because I want to know how things happen. You're a bit like that too though, senator. From what I understand, you've been involved in a range of humanitarian projects."

Daniella sipped the hot drink slowly, then nodded. "I have. Everyone is deserving of a chance at a better future."

"You also championed the rights of the elderly to receive free accommodation and healthcare. I read your speech to the assembly. Rousing stuff."

Daniella wasn't sure if it embarrassed her or just seemed a little odd that this woman sat across from her detailing the things she did, not as a senator, but as a woman who felt the changes were necessary to ensure everyone had the future they deserved.

"And you were instrumental in the formulation of the project to populate the other planets. I seem to remember you were touted as a possible Deputy President at some point."

Daniella shrugged. "I can do more useful things behind the scenes. President Yin is relying on me to focus on the A'Garve Province right now and ensure the farming sector is as vibrant as we can make it."

Senna cocked her head. "Yeah, but he also gave you the leadership of Jonah's mission. To track down and find those who are creating these monsters. He trusts you to do what's right. That's a big call for a woman in her thirties."

The door opened, and Jonah entered the room, then stopped, gazing from one woman to the next. "What?"

"Just chatting." Senna waved her hands, and his brows drew together tightly.

"Any success in finding the children?" Daniella asked.

Jonah advanced and took the seat beside her, raked his hand through his hair, and for a moment, a memory of gripping him close rose, stealing Daniella's breath.

"Not exactly. We've patched into the security net around the city, but we lost them in the direction of Eastcliffe. The uniforms they're wearing are the old, private school before it closed."

Daniella scrubbed her forehead, trying to remember everything.

"The school was demolished three years ago, and replaced with a mall, wasn't it?" Michael had returned from the war, and she'd been knee-deep in Yin's promotion to president. "I only vaguely remember the protests. The school didn't meet any academic guidelines in the last couple of years. There was some talk about arresting the headmaster but..." She shrugged. "Didn't he die in a car accident or something?"

"Yeah. He was taken to the hospital on—" His gaze took on a harsh attitude. "The hospital where Jeremy Colvert was a consultant. The answer was there all the time, and we didn't see the connection. I'll bet it was about the same time Colvert was finalizing his plans for the children."

He leaped up, punched the button on her desk comms system, and when the call was answered, he captured her gaze with his.

"I need records and dates of the hospitalization of the Eastcliffe headmaster and Jeremy Colvert's consultancy. I'll bet he consulted on the case."

He grunted to whoever he spoke to.

"Get me the info as quickly as you can. It's time sensitive and confidential." Jonah grunted, clearly hearing something he didn't like. "I don't care. Break the fucking files if that's what it takes, but get me the information." He hung up and grinned. "You're a bloody genius, senator."

"I could be wrong. I mean, to go from thinking about the headmaster to Jeremy Colvert is..."

Senna cleared her throat. "No such thing as coincidences, senator. Jonah and I learned that one during our time in the corps. I'll bet the same goes for politics."

Daniella inclined her head. "True, Senna. By the way, Jonah. I've received an invitation to a local assembly meeting. I need to attend, but I promised you I'd—"

"You have to?"

His voice was deep and troubled, and she almost sighed, knowing that he desperately wanted to keep her safe. Hell, she wasn't keen on taking chances herself, but... "Yes, Jonah. I can't hide away because there's danger. I have to be seen. It's one of the things I've already noticed with Delspar. He and his wife have become hermits. The kids have been sent back to his parents, and the family estate has beefed up their security too."

His mouth took on a sour moue as if he'd sucked a lemon. "I want to know more about that later." He pointed to Senna. "Right now you and I need to head into the office. I've got an idea I need to pass by Clarissa and Michael."

"Oh, goody! I finally get to meet the wifey. You know, I'm still put out that I wasn't invited to the ceremony." Senna pushed up from her seat and extended her hand to Daniella who accepted it. "It was great to meet you, senator, and I'm sure it'll happen again soon."

With a mischievous smile, the woman left the room, while Jonah hung back, apology shining in his eyes. "Daniella, I'm sorry, she's not exactly the most politically appropriate person, but she'll be an excellent addition to the team."

Daniella stood and placed her hands on his shoulders. "It's okay, Jonah. She's refreshing in a full-on, if slightly exhausting, kind of way." She tugged him closer, rose to her tiptoes, and kissed him. The touch was soft and full of promise. "But take care. I'm kind of hopeful for a re- run of last night, later on."

He looked dazed as she released him and stepped back with a tiny laugh. "You bet."

Then he snaked his arm around her waist and pulled; she tumbled against his chest, breath fleeing. His kiss scorched her, body flaring as heat and hunger swept through her like a cyclone.

"Stay safe, senator."

Then he was gone, and she wavered.

"Wow! That was hot!"

Daniella was shaken from the sensual haze when she realized Kallee had entered the room sometime during the interlude.

"Umm. We need to work." Daniella whirled away, not wanting to see Kallee's reaction, but she couldn't ignore the laugh.

"Sure thing, senator. Sure thing."

THE HIVE of activity didn't surprise Jonah as he entered the building with Senna at his heels. "This is your headquarters?" she asked.

He heard the disdain in her voice.

"Best we can afford as it's covert. Now follow me up to the top level, where Michael and Clarissa's office and private quarters are."

At the top of the first flight, he turned right and headed to a reinforced door, removing the old-fashioned key from around his neck and inserting it.

"You're keeping them behind a locked door?"

"No, this is added security in case the kids escape their cells. They live on-premises right now, and when they sleep I want to know they'll be safe."

"But they're cybes, aren't they?"

He scowled at her words. "They have bio-cybernetic componentry, but it doesn't make them invulnerable."

He caught a flash of concern, but she nodded. "Good call. What about emergency exits?"

Jonah blinked. "Emergency exits?"

She sighed heavily. "Jonah, I've been with the fire department long enough to know that emergency exits can save lives. What have you done to ensure your people can escape?"

"Uh, we're supposed to be reinforcing, not making exits that could allow the bad guys in, Senna."

"Not every exit has to be an entrance. Tell me more and we'll see how we can make it work."

"You're going to remind me constantly until you get your way, aren't you? I've got some ideas and I'll shoot it to you." At the top of the stairs, he turned. "If you can come up with a cost-efficient, secure option, get it to me asap, and I'll have it included in the works. Now, this way." Jonah gestured toward a small office. "Michael said they'd be in here."

He turned the knob and opened the door. Clarissa sat behind a desk, a pile of reports before her, and Michael sat in a chair beside his wife.

"Jonah, I'm glad you're here. I want to discuss the initial testing results with you, because I see something odd."

He blinked at Clarissa's greeting. "Odd? What kind of odd?"

He noted that Senna moved behind him and embraced Michael in a quick hug as he peered over Clarissa's desk.

"The children have been tested at a range of ages. DV-1 for example," she said, referencing their oldest genetically enhanced prisoner, "is testing out with an empathetic age of about ten, yet his academic scores are lower than a five year old. Basic literacy only and the same with numeracy. His understanding of citizenship, history, and so on, is so low they don't even rate. But when we get to technology concepts, he's off the charts. Like tertiary level. I see similar results from the other children in a range of areas. These kids have received some education, but it's patchy."

He scratched the top of his head, considering her early findings. "That works with a theory I'm investigating right now."

"Theory?" Michael asked.

"Yeah. Colvert consulting at a hospital at the same time the headmaster of Eastcliffe's private school, Albert Torr, was interred. Then, we have the kids last known sighting in the vicinity of East-cliffe. I'm wondering if the connection between Torr and Colvert was of longer standing and there's the connection to the children. It could be where they went after they were abandoned. The early families who used Colvert's IVF clinic broke down usually within months of the birth."

He turned a slow circle, mentally surveying the facts as he knew them while considering how to best describe the situation.

"Trying to track them down continues to cause us issues, leaving me to wonder if they were real patients or combatants chosen to incubate the children. Given the regulations for such therapeutic implantation required recognized unions..."

Senna's response was to turn green at his ponderings, and he shrugged.

"The theory works, but we need to be sure. I want to check

Torr's hospital records. I've assigned McNally to track them down. Michael, I want you to go through them with a magnifying glass. Find anything you can. I need connections to Colvert, and if they lead back to Delspar, then all the better, because he's knee-deep in this muck too."

He settled into the chair opposite Clarissa and introduced the two women to each other.

"So, what else have you managed to pry out of the children?" Jonah asked.

Michael sighed. "Their healing factors are astronomical. I've drawn blood from all of them, and there are a couple of anomalies. One thing I'm going to do is sequence the children's DNA, to see if any are related. It's a long shot, but given what you've just suggested, I don't think it's out of order to question it. LV-1, our youngest, is also a carrier for HLT, a genetic disease that compromises the liver and kidneys, which has been kept at bay with injections of rGQ-12 Serum. RMN-3 is healthy and disease-free, as is TRQ-9."

"Who the hell named these kids?" Senna's eyes almost extended out of her head.

"That's what they call themselves," Clarissa whispered. "I think it's their designation with the numbers about their—I don't know—place in conception order? I managed to find out from LV that three others answer to that name only with a different call number." She appeared haunted by that information, and while it sat poorly with Jonah, he shrugged.

"Has Aros indicated if they are suitable for rehabilitation?" Jonah steepled his fingers and waited.

Michael shrugged. "He said it's early days yet."

Jonah rose. "Right then. Clarissa, can you prepare a report for the senator? I'll discuss it with her tonight. I need to see if we've got any connections yet, and Michael, I need to hear from you as soon as you've gone over the files and sequences. Senna? Questions?"

The arson investigator shook her head, stood, and followed him to the door. As it closed behind them, she asked, "How the hell do you cope with this? I mean, what I'm hearing is downright inhuman. We saw some weird shit on the battlefield, but nothing like this."

The tiny box in his psyche where he stashed his reaction to the mission shook. "I cope with it by knowing I'm going to get the bastards. I'll crush them, because anything less isn't good enough."

He turned and headed for the stairs.

Chapter 14

"Senator, I have President Yin on the line."

Daniella raised her head and smiled at Kallee, but the look of sheer panic on her PA's face stole any well-being she might be holding close. "What's happened?"

Kallee shook her head and handed over the handset that she used for emergency communications with the president.

"Sir?"

"Senator Villede, Delspar has just moved against the government. He's raised an emergency sitting to overthrow us, and he's stacked the house. None of our people are in attendance. No one saw this coming, Daniella. Why didn't we know this was in the cards?" His voice carried the defeat that suddenly crashed down on her.

Her stomach congealed like day-old cooking fat, and the pallor on Kallee's face was no doubt mirrored on her own. "Sir, are you secure?" Her mind whirred, and she reached for her communicator. *Jonah.* He'd know what to do in the circumstances.

"My people are already attending to my evacuation. They're destroying all the documentation regarding your team and mission, but you need to alert your team members. Make sure they're secure and those they're holding too."

Frost settled in her chest as she calculated what could be abandoned, how she could lock resources down, and where to send them. Her hands flew over the keyboard, as if independent of conscious thought on her part.

Yin was overwhelmingly popular with the citizens, but Delspar had the numbers in the chamber right now. Might versus people never ended in anything other than anarchy.

"I've enacted the Core Principle, Daniella. It's all I can do."

She gulped at his words. The Core Principle allowed every man and woman to take all precautions in the event of the destruction of civilization. It also allowed members of the corps to disband to protect their own. Michael, Franklin, and Jonah had contacts. They'd need them in the days ahead.

"What about the hardware? Guns and so on?" It required a lot of effort to force the words out.

"Under the Core Principle, whoever has access takes what they need for protection, but the military are with us. Daniella, with an armed populace, the situation is fraught at best."

"I understand. I'll communicate those orders to my team, sir." It didn't seem anywhere near enough, but she whispered, "Thank you for alerting me. God speed, and may we meet again."

"And you, senator."

The line clicked off. Daniella sat there, hazed with a terror of the future they were about to live through. At sea and without a rudder, she shook as the reality crashed down.

"Kallee, turn on the viewer. I need to see exactly who's involved."

Daniella tapped the button on her communicator and waited for Jonah, except his number didn't answer. She left a message for him to ring her as Delspar's voice echoed through the chamber.

"Yin, for all his popularity, hasn't done anything to curb the excesses of a government off the rails. We still have homelessness, vice, and health concerns. Those who have come from privileged backgrounds continue to amass fortunes and look to their own needs, ignoring those who have lost everything. We can no longer afford to wait for change. We must be the change ourselves. Today, my team and I propose to remove the legislative constraints that shackle the government. We will take control and bring order and peace."

Wild cheers erupted as tears dribbled down Daniella's face, watching a madman dismantle the very essence of their civilization. She swiped the tears away as her gaze remained glued to the scene unfolding before her.

"Today is the first day of the future of our world. Today, the 21st Testing Protocol is to be enacted immediately as the first order of this house. This is the time for action and firm leadership. This is my first edict as Prime Senator. Long live our republic!"

The communicator blared, and she saw it was Jonah. "What the fuck just happened, Daniella?"

"Delspar overthrew Yin, named himself Prime Senator, and Yin's being evacuated. He enacted the Core Principle before Delspar took office by force."

Silence.

"Jonah?"

"I'm... I'm here." He sounded distracted, and she grabbed a lock of hair and twirled it around her finger, a tangible tingle of pain breaking through the ice of restraint as she tugged hard with her concern. She gasped. "Daniella?"

"I've started to sequester funds, Jonah. Channeling them to an off-planet resource holding facility. We need to move the team, or at least the children and those most at risk. I have a place—"

"Don't tell me on the line. I'm on my way."

The line clicked off, and Daniella rose. "Contact my parents. Have them moved to the country house in lockdown. No one gets in or out without my authorization. Arrange for your family to join them, and you too if you want."

Kallee straightened up before her. "I'll arrange transport for my family, but my place is here right now, as long as I'm of service. I've seen what Delspar is doing, and there's nothing good in his actions. The Protocol is evil, and he's tied to these children. We need to fight it before we are over-run, and I refuse to turn tail and run away because I'm frightened, senator."

"Daniella. My name is Daniella. I'm not a senator anymore."

"You are a senator. You earned the right to be called that, despite the best efforts of some jumped-up joke who now calls himself the Prime Senator. The people chose you. We honor them by using your title."

Warmth filtered at Kallee's impassioned words. "Call me senator in public then, but privately, I'm Daniella. Our government is gone, and we need to work together if we're going to salvage anything."

Kallee opened her mouth to argue, but Daniella held up a hand. "That's an order, Kallee."

The woman nodded. "So, what do we do first, Daniella?"

"We hide the records pertaining to the team. We bury them so deep no one will be able to find them."

THE ROADS WERE CHOKED. People had got the news, heard about the actions of Delspar and the Core Principle, and acted accordingly, fleeing.

Jonah arrived at Daniella's estate on the edge of town, teeth gritted, anger coiled in his belly like a writhing snake. The gates opened, and he hurtled up the driveway, skidding to a screeching halt at the steps.

She stood there, dressed in black pants that molded to her legs, a dark gray shirt, and sensible-heeled boots. Her hair was in a coil twisted on top of her head.

Jonah climbed out of the vehicle and steadily advanced up the stairs, taking in the wan features of the woman. He opened his arms, and she ducked into his embrace.

"I'm so scared, Jonah. What he's done...it terrifies me."

The pounding of her heart both frightened and reassured him at the same time.

"Dark days are ahead, Daniella. I'm not sure if we'll even win, but right now, if we give in to the fear, it'll be worse for everyone. Let's go inside and make some plans. I want you safely away from here."

Daniella tugged out of his embrace, her face hard. "No. Yin needs me here to carry on, to lead my team, and I won't let Delspar strip what's left of our government without a fight."

"And that will be exactly what he's hoping for. That will allow him to strip you of status and—"

"I don't care. Kallee reminded me today that I was put here by the people. My job is to protect their interests and to make decisions and laws for their future."

He closed his eyes, wondering how he could change her mind. Get her to safety. "Your family?"

"Already on transports and heading for the country house. They'll arrive in an hour or so. And you aren't packing me off to them, so get that out of your mind straight away."

He slid his arm around her, and they entered the house together.

Kallee waited in the entryway, wringing her hands. "Uh, Daniella? I'm sorry." Kallee handed over a tablet, and his heart sank.

"Yin's plane was shot down. There are no survivors." Daniella turned the color of cold, white marble, and he took her in his arms. She didn't respond, and he swore.

"Get Daniella a tea. Sweet. Lots of sugar. We'll be through to the kitchen in a moment." He waited as Kallee scurried away, just holding Daniella close.

"I asked him if he was safe. He was a good man, and they killed him. I can barely accept that he's gone. His whole family too."

There wasn't much he could say, so he waited until she wriggled in his embrace, then steered her toward the room at the back of the house.

Her housekeeper, Mrs. Garmy, stood in front of a viewer, her hands tightly clasped, and

McNally stood beside her. "I saw what happened, senator," Mrs. Garmy said. "It's wrong. I've spoken to my family, told them I'm staying where you are and—"

Daniella shook her head. "No, Mrs. G. I'm sending you to my parents. Right now, worrying about your safety is one thing too many. For me, please go."

Jonah understood the woman felt she needed to be near Daniella, but he added his weight to the argument. "I agree with Daniella. I'll be looking after the senator and Kallee. I will do everything within my power to keep them safe."

The door crashed open, and Michael, Clarissa, and David surged in. "We heard the news. Daniella, you need to go to our parents." David spoke forcefully.

Daniella stepped back, Jonah placing his hands on her shoulders to steady her.

"No, David. I'm staying. Yin's dead, and Gravely will need me. I need to brief him and—"

Michael shook his head. "He sided with Delspar, Daniella. Handed over the government offices ten minutes ago. He's with them. We're on our own now."

At hearing that, she collapsed, sagging with a weak cry, and Jonah caught her in his arms. "You didn't have to break it like that, Michael."

His friend frowned. "What's going on?"

Kallee sighed. "They're sleeping together. She's had a lot of shocks, and you two are thoughtless asses the way you slammed in here, dropped the bombshell, and demanded she give up."

Clarissa balled her fist and whacked her husband in the arm. "I told you. You should have let me tell her, and now you've upset your sister and Jonah."

Jonah glowered at the man, but Michael laughed. "About bloody time. Fine, we can discuss this rationally in a moment." He reached out to the counter where a range of snacks sat, but Mrs. Garmy smacked his hand.

Michael frowned at her. "What?"

"You know better than that. Now go sit at the table before I ring Mrs. Hudson and tell her not to cook your favorite meals."

He retreated to the table with Clarissa and David, Kallee

hovered, and Daniella shook her head. "I'm okay now. Really." She sniffled and wiped at her eyes which were still moist.

She wasn't, but Jonah admired the way she rallied. "Okay then. What we need to do is make sure everything is as secure as we can make it. We need to arrange for a lockdown of the office and containment areas. We need a lead on the children."

Michael narrowed his gaze. "That's a big list, and I'm not sure it's immediately achievable."

"Our biggest problem is securing our offices and the children. We need an alternative, secure location to send any others to."

"That splits the resources though, Jonah. We don't have the people to police both properly and track down whoever is behind what's going on."

David was earnest, and Jonah understood and agreed with his thoughts, but the children had already found their office once. He rubbed his brow as he and Daniella sat down. "I know, but realistically they know where we are. We can defend it under most circumstances, but if more of the children are involved, I'm not sure it will be enough. If we could just—"

"Jonah? Before Yin died, he enacted the Core Principle, right?" Senna asked as she entered the room. "We've got loyal people—well-trained soldiers. We connect with them, explain what we know. It means we have more to fight, more to hunt them down."

He sat up straight at Senna's words. "Yeah, but we're also a bigger target."

"Then we go underground. We're good at that. Always have been. We move our families into the military compound, for their protection, send them off once things are ready, and we fight to get our planet back."

"You also need to have someone who's politically capable, someone to front the fight publicly," Daniella added. "That would be me."

Terror clawed at Jonah as he turned to face Daniella. "No. You need to be—"

"I'm no princess. I may not be able to fight, but I can talk, and you need my skills. I can present the arguments to the people. Yin was popular, and I was one of his team. They know me. They *trust* me, Jonah. The people need someone who will fight for them, but they need to be reminded of what they deserve."

His heart squeezed. They did need public support and assistance, but if Daniella did this, the target on her forehead could almost be painted in neon.

Daniella reached out and covered his hand with hers. "I know this is hard for you to accept, but I can do this. I need to do something useful."

David and Michael exchanged glances. "Daniella, you'd be a target." David spoke forcefully, and she smiled.

"I know that. I won't be the only one though, because all of you will be too. It's my duty. I never shirk my duty. Don't ask me to do that."

The steel in her voice almost had Jonah cheering. Almost.

Clarissa cleared her throat. "Okay, so we have a public face, being Daniella. Jonah leads the resistance, and Michael and I have the kids. Agent McNally goes back to working with Daniella and Kallee, and who else? Franklin?"

Jonah turned to meet the gaze of his best friend's wife. "He's a hell of a guard and someone we trust, so we need to use him appropriately. Guarding the kids and hospital perhaps. Senna?"

"We could do with another female, so she looks like a soft target," Clarissa said.

Heat suffused Senna's face at the words, but Clarissa raised a hand.

"I'm not saying she is, just that she looks like it. We work in teams and create a new base. Somewhere no one would think to look. Something that is easily defensible. Somewhere central..."

"The military base. They're loyal, and everything we need is there." McNally's words were quiet but exploded into the silence around the table.

"The base?" The only one that came to mind was the corps base, on the other side of the river, divided from the town by chain-link fences, extensive laser scanners, and who knew what else. "But..."

Senna grinned. "I like this woman. She thinks quickly. I know the head of the base well, his brother is my boss and contacted me last night after he heard of my suspension. I can—"

"Ring him. If he's on our side and his apparent loyalty, based on what we've seen so far, is indicative of the majority of those remaining on the base, then we might have hope. Make it quick, and share as little information as possible. We can fill him in once we secure the location."

The thumbs-up from Senna as she rose and tugged the communicator from her pocket brought a smile to his lips.

They waited, drinking the coffees and tea Mrs. Garmy slid onto the scarred table, along with the sweet bites.

"We'll need to pack then, won't we?" Callum's voice dripped with disdain.

"Yes, Callum. I want you and Mrs. Garmy to go to my parents when we leave. I need you safe and away from here." Daniella reached out and patted the older man on the hand. "What's more, I won't accept any argument. You're like my family. You've been with me for a long time, and I won't put you in a position of danger. I need to know that you and my parents will be safe so I can do my job. Please?"

The man stiffened at her words, but while he seemed to open his mouth to remonstrate, he stopped, stared for a moment, then nodded. "If you insist."

"I do." Daniella sniffed and smiled tremulously. "So, go pack and get Mrs. Garmy to do so as well."

"Wait." Clarissa stood. "I want you to take Clarrie and Mrs. Hudson with you." She turned and crouched before Michael. "You know that's for the best, Michael. They should all go and be safe."

"I agree, and I'm pleased you thought about it. I would have, in time. But it's better to move them immediately."

Senna re-entered the room. "Well, he's pissed but agrees with us. He's got about fifty men with families he wants moved to the base. Can we manage that?"

Jonah sighed and scratched his head, wondering how much

more difficult this could be. "We'll have to make it work, won't we? But they'll need guards posted."

"Already fixed, Jonah. General DuSaint has started to pick men. It's almost as if he expected something like this." Senna slumped into a chair.

"He probably did," Daniella said. "He's a member of the Military Assembly. In my experience, they talk as much as old women do."

Jonah swiveled in his chair and stared at Daniella.

She shrugged. "Experience. I was a junior senator to the Defense Minister for a year. I was in on their deliberations several times, and I can honestly say they didn't stop talking at all."

"All right then, so we send out the call, get as many of our people in place as soon as possible. We'll want to close access to the base swiftly. Michael, you take care of talking to the others you know, we vet them though...carefully. We need to know who's coming into the ranks. David, you take care of the transportation of families and placement once the base is available to us. Do whatever it takes to get the base management on the same side as us, and keep them working. Senna, you become our liaison with the corps base and General DuSaint. McNally, round up Franklin, and you're on Daniella."

The room became silent as they mulled over their assigned roles.

"It's not going to be easy. There will be some who'll refuse." Clarissa sighed. "Clarrie won't want to go."

Michael wrapped his hand around Clarissa's. "No, but we appeal to his protective self. We need those who can assist in the protection of the base. The men and women. The children."

Jonah nodded at the sentiment. "Good. If we're all ready then? Let's get moving." He rose to call an end to the meeting.

The others followed his lead, chairs scraping on the ceramic tiles and the thudding of feet. He waited until just the two of them stood there, and Daniella rounded the table.

"You handled that very well." She cupped his cheek, pulled him closer, and kissed him.

He shuddered, for a moment letting the chink in his emotional defenses show. "I'm scared, Daniella. You're in the front line, and this could all go badly. We could roll over and accept the change." Then he sighed, lowered his head so that their foreheads touched.

"You could, but that would be wrong. The children are just that. They shouldn't be weapons. That's not what humanity is about. We're doing the right thing."

He wound his arms around her. "I know. I'm just not certain we'll all survive to see the better world."

Chapter 15

Daniella watched the taillights of the vehicle taking Mrs. Garmy and Callum to safety fade away through the gate that shut firmly behind them. Tears dribbled down her cheeks, but she swiped them away.

She remembered the war vividly. She'd watched friends and lovers departing on the viewscreen daily. Saw the effects on families, those who lost husbands and partners. Brothers and sisters.

For the first time as an adult, she understood the fear that came with letting those she cared for deeply leave. It wasn't that she hadn't felt Michael's going, but she'd still been young, with the enthusiasm of youth, and had been so damned sure that Michael would survive. This time, she couldn't rely on wishing and hoping.

Jonah waited inside the house. She'd asked him for the privacy to say goodbye—needing to do this on her own and test her internal strength.

She turned and headed to the house, which was almost empty. Jonah had suggested sending anything of value to the estate, and she'd agreed. The house was now a target because it was hers. Once she became the face of the resistance, they'd come at her with everything.

With slow steps, she ascended to the door, then reached out, but it opened before she could turn the handle. He knew, understood, and had given her the time and space she'd needed.

Jonah spread his arms, and she moved in, needing the reassurance for a moment before pulling away. "We need to get out of here."

Piles of bags mounded in the entranceway, Kallee joined them and stood in the shadows.

"We should. Do you want to..."

Did she want to say goodbye to the house? She'd bought it when she'd become a senator, aware she needed her own space. It was nice. Comfortable. But everything of importance to her had already been shipped out. It was a shell.

"No. Let's get everything together and go."

"I'll get the van then." Jonah left them alone, and Kallee looked at the pile of bags.

They'd agreed to use a small van and added bogus signage to the side using magnetic holders. Anonymous and otherwise unmarked, she and Jonah would remain in the back with the luggage. No one expected a senator to hide in a delivery vehicle, it would fit their belongings, and they'd be able to travel to the corps base incognito.

"It's going to take a while to load up," Kallee remarked.

Daniella smiled. "Well, if you didn't insist on me taking so many clothes." She covered her fears with light talk, hoping Kallee would join her.

"You're still the senator, and for the appearances in the media, you're going to need to look the part. Who would believe a wind-blown woman with messy hair and no makeup?"

She grinned. "Only you would consider that."

Footsteps echoed, and she waited for Jonah. He came in through the doorway. "Ready?"

They each reached for bags and headed to the kitchen, piling them by the boxes and files, comp-units, and armaments. The food in the kitchen had already been sent ahead to base so nothing was wasted.

They stacked everything into the vehicle, creating a small crouch way for both of them, just in case the combatants stopped the car. Then Daniella headed to the oversized pantry, searching the uniform cupboard hidden in it, and tugged out a plain black uniform of a courier company.

Kallee waited by the door and accepted the uniform with a sniff. "Do I have to?"

Daniella chuckled at Kallee's derision to the clothing. "Yes, you do. Now hurry, before we get caught."

Kallee slid into the pantry, closing the sliding door. Barely a moment later, she opened the door a crack and handed her pants and top to Daniella. "Here. Take them. I'll be putting them back on once it's safe."

She stepped out, the uniform in place and her hair wound up. It made her look far different from the Kallee that Daniella was used to.

Jonah paced in the kitchen and glanced at them as soon as they entered the room. "We have to move. I've heard the children are moving en masse. We don't want to get caught."

He ushered them to the vehicle, helping Daniella inside then following her and re- arranging the boxes as he moved. They sat on the floor, looking through the tiny peepholes Jonah had fashioned as Kallee slammed her door shut, started the engine, and the van rolled down the driveway.

At the gate, the guard waved them through. As far as they knew, Jonah and Daniella remained in the house. If arrested, they'd have no information to provide.

Jonah had promised he would give the evacuation order once they were clear. He kept his words, as at the five-minute mark he beeped them. "Evacuate immediately. The house is compromised, and we're away."

They didn't respond, and Daniella fought off nausea that rose. "Jonah, are we..."

"Look ahead, Daniella. See that wall of children? They're heading for your house. We escaped just in time."

Her fingers itched to form a ball. Instead, she splayed them on the floor of the vehicle, welcoming the pulse of the engine as the crowd of children parted for them.

She held her breath as Kallee slowed, then stopped, winding down the window. "What's going on?"

"Continue on your way, woman. We're not here for you."

The thud of feet echoed, and Kallee moved the van forward once again. "We're through."

"That was far too close, Jonah. They'll know Kallee's face now too, if they put it together. I don't understand why they didn't check the van. We came in the direction of—"

"Because they're untrained. They don't understand about planning and strategy because they're simply weapons. Now if we could just lay our hands on one. Get them to switch sides." He inhaled deeply.

"What?"

"That's the key." He grabbed his communicator. "Get LV to the corps base, Sevres, I have an idea."

They rolled forward, the base looming before them. It felt too easy. No one had stopped them, and Daniella's belly settled with a hard knot of worry in her gut.

Jonah pushed out of their hidey-hole and scrambled into the front seat beside Kallee. At the gate, the van rolled to a stop.

Guards in tactical suits lifted weapons, snub-nosed rifles trained on them, the intention to kill should they attack clear, while large, hulking tanks were stationed at various points along the fence.

Daniella's mouth dried, and she moved up to her knees.

"Sir, you've been authorized to move through with your team. Go up that path. Second building on the right. I'll alert the general that you and the senator and her assistant have arrived."

The boom gate rose, and once they cleared the first line of defense, Daniella drew a full breath. "I think this is going to be quite different from anything else I've ever experienced."

Kallee and Jonah remained quiet as the vehicle swung into a slow arc and came to a standstill outside a squat, red brick building.

"I'll let you out." Jonah climbed from the vehicle, and Daniella listened to the screech of the door as it shut.

The thud of the rear opening and the shuffle of boxes alerted her that Jonah had joined her. When the last items were cleared away, he held out a hand, his gaze dark and unreadable. She accepted his assistance, moved through the piles, and followed him down to the ground.

"I'm not sure that's my favorite way to travel, Jonah."

He barked a laugh at her dry words. "Maybe not, but it did the job. Come on, let's get inside."

JONAH WAITED in the corner as the lights lit up the desk Daniella and Kallee decided met their needs. The team had removed every other identifying feature from the viewing area. Daniella fiddled, the movement of her hands the only give away of her nerves.

Her senatorial robes and the makeup she and Kallee had applied hid the pallor of her skin. They'd decided the first broadcast had to be impactful—a blow to the newly formed republic.

Kallee moved behind the camera, her fingers twiddling and refining until she called, "Good to go."

Daniella smoothed her hands over her hair, settled them in her lap, and attained an attitude of 'we'll get through this together' as she settled in.

Kallee indicated *three, two, one* with her fingers.

"Good evening. I am Senator Daniella Villede. You would be aware by now that President Yin's government was overturned less than twenty-four hours ago. Since then, his plane was attacked and brought down with a total loss of life. His successor handed over the government to Senator Delspar after locking the majority of the senators from the chamber of government. This so-called government is illegal. Before his death, President Yin enacted the Core Principle. This means that you and everyone you know should prepare for and defend what is yours in any way you deem necessary. Be that property or members of your family. We, the legitimate government, have done so as well. As of now, we have control of the Armed Corps, the Air Defenses, and Water Guardians. But we need your help. Without you, without the things you know and the people you have connections with, we are sightless. We call on all citizens to make a difference. Since the enaction of the 21st Testing Protocol, armies of children—bio- cybernetically enhanced warrior children —have taken to roaming the streets. These children are dangerous. Your children are in as much in danger as we are. Hold them close. Keep them near, do not let them wander, because citizens who do not know them may take action as the incursions grow worse. Be aware, citizens. We are now at war. We are all facing extreme danger. Prepare yourselves, and know that we, your rightful government, are taking steps to address the situation. It may take a long time, resolve will be tested, and you may question the rightness of our actions. We don't take them lightly. We don't take them unlawfully."

For a moment, she waited. A heartbeat in time allowing the words to sink in.

"We will leave no stone unturned, and we will resume control. Life will return to normal, but right now, we must fight what is thrust upon us. We do this to honor those who came before. To protect those who are yet to be, and to ensure the freedom of all. Until then, I'm here. I'm watching and working with our forces."

The light flicked off, and Daniella slumped, breathing hard.

"Did it tape? I don't think I can do that again." She tugged at the robes as Kallee moved to the desk, extending a glass of water.

"It was better than I expected. You looked strong and in control, and damn it if I didn't get a little girlie-crush right then and there."

Daniella smiled, a weak shadow, as Jonah strode up to her. "Come on. Let's wash off the gunk and get you settled in something more comfortable." He could tell she needed a moment, in the way she twisted her fingers.

She nodded and rose, and he slid his hand around her waist. "Did LV arrive?"

He nodded. "She did, and we have the girl firmly contained in the brig right now. Clarissa isn't overly happy, but until we can work with her, it's the safest location for everyone."

"Will they check for an implant? We found one in Clarissa after Jeremy..."

"Sara Windhower is looking at her scans. If there is one, we'll find it and neutralize the threat. Right now, though, you need some downtime."

Daniella grunted. "I'm not an invalid. What I should be doing is drilling with everyone else, for safety."

He cocked his head. "You want to drill?"

Her bark was dry. "Not really, but I'm neither tame nor easy to take even if they do get near me. You did listen to what I said, right? We're all responsible. Me, as much as anyone else on this base. Give me a gun and teach me to use it. Teach me how to fight." Her face hardened, driving away the softness she regularly wore around him, lips tight, and eyes cold and flat. Now she was a warrior, and this was the attitude she'd worn in the chamber the day they'd attacked her.

"All right, McNally can drill you on the basics. If I think it's safe, you can then join the other recruits."

She opened her mouth to speak, but he stopped her with a soft finger to her lips.

"You're a key target. I will take every precaution, senator. You are the face of our resistance. If we lose you, then the heart leaves our campaign. And I will not lose you."

Did she understand what he was saying? The profession he'd buried in the words.

Blinking, Daniella glanced away. "Kallee, can I have a moment?"

The other woman scurried from the room, and Daniella turned back to face Jonah.

"I'm not a weakling, Jonah. I know exactly what I am to the resistance."

A sudden flare of anger erupted. "Dammit, you're more than the sum total of the fucking resistance. You mean a whole heap more than that to me, but I won't put you in a position that could be dangerous. Understand?"

When she cocked her head in silence and glared at him, he stepped back. "Jonah, do you trust me?"

That stopped him more effectively than a brick to the back of the head. "Yes, I trust you."

"Did you trust me when I addressed the people and called them to our defense?"

Shaky ground here, he thought. "Yes."

"Then why don't you trust me to train with the others? The men and women who've come to the base to help us?"

"Because I refuse to lose you like I've lost almost everyone else I care about. Dammit, Daniella, don't ask me to put you in a position where I can't control your safety."

She grinned like the cat who ate the cream. "Ahh, I knew it. See, I don't want you taking chances either. You're the heart of the combat arm of this new resistance. I could ask that you stay here, be safe and move the chess pieces on the board, but I wouldn't, and I won't. I care about you too."

She reached out, captured his head between the palms of her hands.

"I trust you. You'll stay safe because there's a whole lot more we want to explore together. I want the same. I'll be safe. I'll follow McNally's orders, and each night we'll come together, share a bed, and talk about our day. But Jonah, in war, things happen. Bad things."

He sighed. "I know. I just... I don't like feeling like I'm not in control and your safety..."

They kissed, a soft sigh that whispered over their lips. Gradually, the tension in his muscles released. He pulled her against his body, let her rest against him.

MORNING LIGHT FILTERED through the blinds, and Daniella moved, trying to twist, but a warm and substantial something stopped her. She cracked open her eyes. *Jonah.*

The banging on the door had her jerking, and Jonah came

awake, sitting bolt upright in the bed, his arm already tunneling beneath the pillow where he'd stashed a handgun.

"Senator? You've got a delivery."

She started to climb out of bed, but Jonah slung out his arm. "Wait. We don't know what it is, so we need to be cautious. We'll meet them in the secure zone, so get dressed." As Jonah moved away from the bed, she was treated to a view of his naked back, and she sighed, clearing the haze from her mind.

"Leave it at the main building," Daniella called out. "We'll come to you in a few minutes."

Now she rose, glancing around for clothing, and spied the black leather pants and tight, form-fitting shirt she'd laid out the night before.

Gathering up her hair in front of the mirror, Daniella frowned. "I think the hair has to go."

Jonah stepped up to her, his hands fastening over her hips. "Why?"

"Because I don't have time to fuss with it, and in a fight, it'll only get in the way."

Tension filled his body, and she waited for the recommencement of yesterday's argument. When he remained silent, Daniella spun in his arms.

"Nothing to say?" she asked.

"I like your hair, but it's your decision. Whatever you choose will be right with me."

Warmth tingled, spreading to every nerve ending in her body, and she kissed him. "Urgh, I haven't even had time to brush my teeth!"

He laughed. "I'm sure five minutes more won't kill anyone."

He released her, and she hurried to the bathroom, took care of the basics, and was back in record time.

Jonah grabbed her hand, and they moved through the door, up the hallway and past other tiny units. They'd squeezed as many into the accommodation sector as possible. The night before the general had informed them that the number of people on base had nearly doubled.

They stepped lightly up the roadway, passing cadets running in groups, others loading into vehicles to attend what she guessed was armament training and a range of other exercises she didn't have a clue about.

At the main building, they moved through the security portal and settled in the small office that had been set aside for their use, the desks pockmarked and the chairs screeching, but it gave them some privacy to conduct their work.

The door slid open, and General Armand DuSaint stepped inside, a packet in his hands.

"What's wrong, general?" Jonah peered at the man.

He shook his head. "Our scanners couldn't tell if there was anything dangerous in it, but I've got a secura-tent on the way."

Daniella screwed up her face. "I'm not sure I know—"

"A secure tactical container. Explosives, dangerous powders, and compounds can be secured. There's also a remote system for handling the item."

She made an 'O' with her mouth. "Fine then, we should wait, I guess. General, did LV have a comfortable night?"

The general had to be in his sixth decade with sharp, gray eyes that could turn frosty in an instant. His hair was closely cropped in shades of salt-and-pepper, while his frame was wiry. "I don't know much about the children, but the guards said she didn't eat anything. We're wondering if she's got a port device. Didn't sleep, spent part of the night howling she didn't like the dark or separation. The rest of the time, she was like a robot, sitting in her cell."

Daniella bit her lip. "Maybe McNally could see what's going on?"

"Fine. I'll have her swing by before you begin your training," grunted Jonah, as if his mind was on something else.

A knock at the door surprised Daniella, and she jumped. When both sets of eyes settled on her, she blushed. "I'm a little out of my league here, gentlemen."

"Enter," Jonah bellowed, and a younger woman entered the room carrying a clear box with metallic hands inside.

From her pocket, she retrieved a set of heavy gloves. "The

remote gloves allow you to activate and use the item. The left glove palm has the device unlock and lock remotely. Slip it on, press the button, and the door opens at the top. Pop your package in and press the button. The box is then locked and will allow you to manipulate the hands using the gloves. The concept is simple. Once you see what's inside the package, you can run a diagnostic on the item. So long as whatever you're checking is in our database, we'll have an almost instantaneous idea of what it is. If we can't work it out, the box will not re-open without a hard override."

The woman assumed parade rest once Daniella tugged on the gloves. "Left hand, you said?"

"Yes, ma'am."

She pressed the small, red point, and the box opened with a whoosh.

The general placed the packet inside, and she pressed the button once more. The box locked with a click, and the general stepped back.

Feeling foolish, Daniella moved her hands, and the tiny remote pair in the box mirrored her moves. The brown paper slid away as she tugged on it.

The item before her had her stomach roiling. A charred digit, the nail bed blue and purple. A ring. One she knew.

"It's Yin's."

Jonah swore and made to cover it. The general and the woman both stayed absolutely still.

"Leave it, Jonah. They want me to give in and cave to their demands. I won't let the bastards make me. Who delivered this?"

The general frowned. "We found it in the vehicle the child, LV, was transported in. We thought it was from one of your people. It has your name on it."

Daniella pressed the button to release the locking mechanism, but it beeped and glowed red.

"Uh, senator. There's a threat. Let me check." The soldier dragged a tiny computer from her rear pocket and pressed buttons in a quick sequence, then sighed. "It's Geronica-B."

When Daniella looked at the solider, confused, the woman shook her head.

"It's a dangerous compound and causes extreme pain followed by a swift death. The digit is coated in it. The paper is now compromised. I'll take it back to the lab. We'll take a print of the writing and return it to you, sir." She turned to Jonah with an efficient movement. "For handwriting analysis."

The soldier gathered the box and hurried from the room, followed by the general.

"How did you know it was Yin's finger?"

"The ring was one his wife gave him when he became president. The mix of silver, platinum, and gold was set into waves. It served to remind him that time and decision making creates a ripple effect. He told me about it when I became the senator for A'Garve Province."

A knock on the door signaled the end of their conversation, and she called, "Enter," the way he'd done before.

McNally peered in. "Senator, I wondered if you'd like to come with me to meet with LV? I mean..." Her gaze moved between them both.

"No, the timing is perfect. Then we can train immediately afterward." Daniella rose and trailed her hand gently over Jonah's shoulder as she passed him. "I'll be back afterward. I've got my communicator."

He grunted, "I'll contact you if you're needed."

It wasn't much, but he wasn't stopping her. She'd take that as the first step. She followed McNally into the hall, the door sliding closed behind her.

"The child didn't have a good night, according to the general. It's going to take a bit to gain her trust," McNally informed her.

"Maybe, but Dr. Windhower says there's no tracker, unlike the others. I'm wondering what that means." Daniella bit her lip, the worst of scenarios passing through her mind.

They left the building and headed to the secure holding area they called The Brig. The construction was stone and metal, substantial and imposing even in the midst of the corps base.

They submitted to the security procedures, handing over their hastily arranged official identification. The deference in the soldier's action annoyed Daniella.

"Don't worry. You're an asset, and they'll treat you like spun glass until you prove you can protect yourself." McNally's words confirmed Daniella's understanding of how the military world worked.

They were ushered down a set of steps, the atmosphere closing in as a large chain-link gate opened before them. After passing through another checkpoint, a barred door stood between them and the cells.

"For your safety, senator, we've restrained the child."

Daniella quirked an eyebrow. "How did that go?"

The guard stared, and McNally rolled her eyes. "The senator needs to know if there were any casualties."

He cleared his throat and raised his left hand, which was covered in gauze. "I came out best, three bites. Doms took a blow to the leg, and it's broken. Figgers has a concussion."

Daniella couldn't understand how one small child, especially the angelic and slight- looking child they knew as LV-1, had almost taken them out. She opened her mouth, but McNally shook her head, quieting Daniella. "So, we'll be careful then."

McNally secured her pistol in the lockbox, and Daniella submitted her communicator and the tiny stun device Jonah had given her. She then waited through the pat-down in silence and watched as they followed suit with McNally. She hissed as they touched the sites where she'd been injured.

Finally satisfied, the guard rolled back the gate. He instructed another guard to take them to the cell where the child huddled, attached to a metal desk.

She looked so small, and Daniella almost forgot the danger. She stepped within, but McNally grabbed her. "Sit down, senator."

Daniella took the first seat and lowered herself into it while McNally rounded the table and settled beside Daniella, hands clasped on the metal tabletop.

"Advise your designation."

"I'm LV-1. The first of the LV designation." The child answered with a sullen growl, and Daniella couldn't control the curl of dismay at McNally's questioning techniques.

This wasn't the charming child she remembered from the other day, and she started to rise.

Once more, McNally shook her head, and with a tiny hiss of impatience, she resettled in her uncomfortable metal chair.

"LV-1, you are being held as part of an investigation into the subversion of the senate, the murder of President Yin, subsequent attacks on—"

"I didn't do anything. That's not my job!" The child tugged at her restraints, and Daniella stared at McNally, her face a cold mask of indifference.

"McN—"

"Not now, senator. Allow me to do my job."

Her teeth gritted together, nearly grinding down with fury, Daniella waited.

"What is your job, LV-1?"

"I'm to collect intelligence to relay back. Once I'm able, my body sufficiently matured, I'm scheduled for impregnation and will carry more of my kind."

Hot lava-like bile rose in Daniella's throat, scouring her with bitterness.

A hand clamped on hers. Daniella turned with a jerk of her head toward McNally who radiated both understanding and weariness.

"Is that what you want, LV-1?" McNally turned back to the child, her tone remote.

"It's what I was made for."

The child's total acceptance was too much, and Daniella couldn't keep silent any longer. "But you weren't, LV. You're a child. You're—"

"You're overly emotional. Just like they warned us. Human women rely on emotions and fears. We're stronger. Faster. We're the fighters and protectors. Your weaknesses make you a target." Rote words rolled off the child's tongue, and they left Daniella reeling.

"When are you due to reach maturity, LV?"

"Two years three months is the estimated time to total physical maturity, making me suitable for the first round of genetic implantation." The tiny tremor in the girl's final words was the trigger, it seemed, for McNally to sigh, slump back in her chair, and shake her head.

"Is that what you want though? I mean, if you had the choice, wouldn't you rather be someone other than a designation maturational container?" McNally sneered, and Daniella frowned. This wasn't the McNally she'd seen in action. Where were the empathy and understanding?

Wisely, she remained quiet as the girl shot up in her seat. "That's what I was bred for. It's what they've prepared me for over the last years. I don't have the choices—"

"Bullshit!" McNally's bellow echoed, and the child stilled, eyes growing round as her mouth dropped open. "You can be more than what they told you. You can have choices and options like the rest of our people."

The girl leaned forward. "No. Because I'm cyber-enhanced. Cybes don't get to choose. They don't—"

Unable to listen anymore, Daniella cleared her throat. "That's not true. My brother, Michael—the doctor at the holding facility—he and his wife, Clarissa, are both cybes. They have options and choices. They earned that right, and so can you."

The way the young girl wrinkled her brow betrayed her skepticism.

Daniella plowed on. "You children don't just have to buy into the future that someone pre-determined for you. You can have choices too. You can make your future."

Deep emotional hunger flared in the girl's eyes. A flash that lasted for seconds then guttered out. "No. The others will have to pay. I won't leave them to that." She set her lips tight, eyes narrowed.

McNally took her hand. "We're going to go. You need to follow the instructions given to you by the men. You're a prisoner of war and have certain entitlements and responsibilities."

Under the lights, the girl's eyes glinted. "Oh, yes."

McNally bared her teeth. "Not talking about escape. They'll return you to your cell."

The girl grimaced. "Nothing to do there."

Daniella cocked her head. "What would you like to do?" The minute she'd spoken, she regretted the action.

"School. I want an education." The words, spoken quietly, ricocheted.

"Fine. I can arrange that for you."

LV's mouth dropped open, shock creeping over her features. "You can do that?"

"I'm a senator. I can make many things happen."

At McNally's signal, she rose and left the cell, clamping down on her reactions until they were beyond the building.

"You did well, senator. There was a lot of information that wasn't palatable, but you handled yourself nicely."

Daniella didn't reply. She thought she'd seen it all when Clarissa had appeared on the scene. Obviously, she hadn't. The knowledge continued to gnaw at her as they hurried to the offices where Jonah waited.

Chapter 16

Jonah watched as Daniella tottered from the building, her face a stark and icy white. He slid out of the vehicle, but Michael stopped him before he could reach the woman slowly making her way in his direction.

"No. She needs to hold her own in front of the men and women here."

Jonah growled deep in his throat but stopped and waited. He knew the minute she saw him, the glassy look in her eyes melting into distress.

She reached out, then curled her hands into fists. "Jonah?"

The tightness in his gut turned to concrete. "What happened?"

"They're using them. The girls are meant to be walking, talking incubators for their next generation of warriors. That's after they serve their purpose as fighters. How can they do that?"

He sucked in a shuddering breath, feeling the emotional turmoil that rolled off her in thick waves. It didn't surprise him. Perhaps on some intuitive level, he'd already guessed that the children were dispensable, and that through the genetic manipulation, they could be replaced in short order, an army of replaceable drones, completely lacking in empathy.

"Jonah?" Her voice faltered.

"I guess I already worked that out, senator."

"But they're children." A tiny, diamond-like tear fell from her lashes and rolled down her cheek. She didn't wipe it away. Instead, she let him see the level of horror and disgust that wove itself around her.

"Not to them. The ones running this plot placed orders for a mass delivery of emotionless warriors. We need to stop thinking of them as children, because they won't be thinking of us as humans, only as combatants."

Daniella reared away from his harsh reminder. "I can't—"

"If you don't, the war is won by them before we even began taking up arms. They kill. You've already seen their handiwork, senator. We have to be strong." He allowed his voice to harden, becoming an effective weapon, like a hammer. The words slammed into her, and she stepped back, her arms winding around her body.

Daniella bit her lip, blinked once, then again. "I'm not sure I can." She shuddered and exhaled, but she steadied, sliding her arms down so that they lay at her sides, fists curled tight then released.

He grunted, and she reached out to him, gripped onto his wrist. "This is who I am, Jonah. I may be a senator, but I'm also a woman. I feel things deeply, and this... It hits me hard, right here!" She hit her chest, and he couldn't fault the emotions she shared.

Michael sighed. "Daniella, war is never simple. So few things we do or see are black and white, and the tones are even harder to read in this kind of situation. Jonah is trying to explain that we have to think differently. It doesn't make us wrong or bad. Just aware and realistic. Millions of people will rely on us to protect them, our way of life, and the democracy you swore to uphold. We can't do that if we aren't able to separate ourselves from these emotions, no matter how unpalatable it is. He's not a monster by acting the way he is, and neither are you."

Daniella glared at her brother, her bottom lip quivering. "I'll try. But it's still wrong. Morally and ethically."

Jonah couldn't disagree with her. He understood the internal tussle that gnawed at her, but there wasn't an option. "We need to debrief and find out what else you managed to——"

"The senator handled herself well in there, Jonah."

Jonah concentrated on Agent McNally who'd sidled up beside Daniella, her gaze steady, as if she willed him to cut the senator some slack. He couldn't. Not yet, and not here. Michael was right. She had to be seen as reliable, because she was effectively the head of the democratically elected senate now. She hadn't merely rolled over and handed control like Gravely. So, she'd have to suck it up and soldier on. He needed her strength to create a united front. A rallying point. They all had a job to do, and none was simple or straightforward now.

"I understand that. The senator needs to debrief, then you're taking her out for practice, yes?"

A dangerous glint appeared in McNally's eyes. One he knew well. She was about to raise objections. That couldn't happen. Not here in front of anyone to see. He'd talk to her about this, he promised himself. Settle the anger that brewed and bubbled.

Jonah slid his hand down, so he held the senator's, and turned to her. Willed her to understand. "We need to get the information. From both of you. It could make a difference in how we go forward. The truth is, we know so little, and that's only what the team has gleaned so far."

Daniella's nod had the tension that had wound tight inside him releasing. "I understand. McNally, we should head back to..." Her gaze wavered from the woman back to him. "...the office?"

"It seems the most logical place. I'm having people set up debriefing rooms as we speak, but they won't be ready for a day or two. And it's probably better that we do it in the most secure location. Come on. We'll drive over there."

He urged Daniella forward, and she climbed into the back of the vehicle, folding her hands in her lap, head high, and the spunk he'd previously admired was in full force. He mastered the smile and climbed into the vehicle beside her as McNally took the other front seat.

Chapter 17

The day passed into the night, the reds and oranges covering the sky like paint on a canvas. The glass of water Daniella held in her hand was a far cry from the chilled white wine she craved, along with the scents and tranquility of her home.

Given the way the children had destroyed the hospital, Daniella seriously doubted there'd be much left of her house, and a tug of sadness weighed her down.

"So much lost already, and this war has barely begun." The words flittered away on the breeze as she looked out over the base.

The plastic chair bit into the skin of her thighs, and Daniella shifted as the door to the accommodation unit swung open with a squeak. Unable to help herself, she spun to see Jonah wander out of their room.

"I wanted to see if you'd like a cup of tea."

He'd walked wide circles around her since this morning after the debriefing and session with LV-1.

"I'd prefer a cold, white chardonnay or similar."

He grinned. "None here. I could maybe head over to the Officer's Club and see what they have on hand..."

Daniella shook her head. "While it would be nice, I guess I need to get my head cleared and in the game. I'm just trying to come to terms with what I've seen and heard in the last forty- eight hours."

He advanced. "Mind if I sit with you?"

Daniella waved her hand. "Please." They needed to clear the air and find some kind of balance if they could hope for any sort of long-term relationship, and she couldn't help the tiny shimmer of hope that what lay between them might have some permanence attached.

"Thanks." He hunkered down onto the step and settled beside the chair, staring out over the carpark below. Empty now as the members of the unit had retired to eat in the mess. "I know this morning was difficult."

She shrugged. "I understood, you know, after we talked. I can't afford the luxury of feeling hurt or..." No word came to mind to describe the emotions she'd felt. "I guess I need to harden up if I'm going to assume the mantle of authority. It's just Yin never involved me in that stuff. He always said there was time. Now he's gone, and I have to step up. It's a huge thing, Jonah. It frightens me. So much responsibility, and what if I mess it up?"

"Then you admit it, and we move on. There aren't a lot of options now. They're relying on you. On us, senator." He turned and captured her gaze.

She laughed, even though she felt amazed at the ability to deal with what he said with mirth. "Which us, Jonah? Me and the army? Me and the unit? Me and..." She gulped then dove into the question that had played with her thoughts for hours. "Me and you?"

Trepidation and hunger burned inside her, warring for supremacy. She knew they both were dealing with heavy loads. He would be heading up the team in control of hunting down information and dealing with the threat as well as coordinating their army. And she needed to begin cobbling together some semblance of a senate in waiting.

Daniella would become the face of the resistance, find the right people to assume critical positions when this war was over, and when the time to rebuild came they would move into place. And yet...

Jonah slid a soft hand onto her knee, anchoring her and offering support when she most needed it, keeping her grounded. "All of them. But the last one? That's the one I want to work most. Right now, though, we need to focus on the big picture. But when we finally get through this—"

"*If*, Jonah. There are no guarantees, as you keep reminding me." The words tasted sour in her mouth, but shying away from reality wouldn't help anyone survive.

He cocked his head. "That's true, but we also need to do more than just hope. We need to keep our nerve, to believe in what we're doing, otherwise we've let them win before we start."

She sighed and looked back out over the carpark. "I hope we can defeat them. I feel like they've had time to prepare, time to build their defenses, and we're just playing catch up. Things are grim to my way of thinking."

He grunted. "Perhaps, but we've got the people on our side. During the war, I was always amazed at what everyday people are capable of when called to defend what they hold dear. They'll come together again because they believe in what they're doing. It's just going to take time. We need to present the truth, let the people realize that they've been duped. We need time and commitment. Belief. That's what you bring to the table first off. The rest will fall into place."

She hoped so. Daniella pushed out of the chair and rose, turning back to give him her full attention as a seed of devilry bloomed.

"We should head inside. The heads of the armed services will be here soon, and we need to be ready to meet with them and begin formulating a plan." She brushed off her khaki pants and snagged his hand, pulling him closer, and grinning at the small sound of surprise that he gave. "But there's time for a kiss."

Swooping in, Daniella pressed her mouth to his, inhaling the musky taste of him—the hot, firm heat of his kiss. Before it could turn wild, she tugged away.

"That should see us through until we retire." With a small laugh, she skated around him and went inside.

THE MEN in full military regalia sat opposite Daniella, taciturn but steady as they unfurled the map. "This, Madam Senator, is the most likely location of their base."

General Armand DuSaint embodied the spirit of the army. Jonah had served under him during the border skirmishes before DuSaint had taken on the role of Chief of the Army. It seemed surreal that he now found himself a peer or equal to the man before him.

General DuSaint thudded a blunt finger onto a site near the old school. "It's an abandoned pharmaceuticals lab. We received some intelligence about it in the week leading up to the coup."

Unease slithered through Jonah's gut. "What kind of intelligence?"

"Strangely, not the kind I think you're expecting. It caught our attention due to the number of children in the carpark, pitching tents. Initially, we thought some youth organizations had made arrangements until we got the news they were seen up at dawn, forming up and entering the building. One of my men is a long-distance runner. He was scouting out new locations to run and just happened upon it. He raised the concern, and I sent a couple of operatives out to take a look. Yin had privately contacted me with details of your team, senator, and their task."

Daniella peered over the map. "You're sure?"

He grunted and shrugged. "Nothing in war is sure, senator. But we need to look closer at the location, see what's there and what opportunities might come for taking down their base." "General, if I may? Senator?" The grizzled man in the corner, Admiral Daffyd Clwyn, stood and pored over the map. "While there is a case for bolstering the army's defenses, I feel that it should be recognized that the docks are also at risk. In consultation with Fleet Admiral Constantine, we'll move all vessels into deeper water. The naval bases are well-fortified, but we believe further urgent fortification is wise."

Daniella bit her lip as she gazed at the naval officer. "I'm not sure we have the resources. Jonah? What are your thoughts?"

He scratched his head, uncomfortable with this level of responsibility. It had never been his intention to be setting the direction of government and offering military advice.

"With all due respect, senator, I hardly think McDowell is in the position to—"

"General, while you might be the most senior officer in the army, Jonah is the one with the most knowledge on the subject of the warrior children. His people have been the ones who collected the intelligence that saved my life and many others. His team followed through on the activities of this threat. They worked out the children were behind the bombing of the hospital, and he now heads my task force, dealing with the investigation of the plot against the government. That is why I trust his expertise and knowledge." Red flags brightened her cheeks, and her eyes sparkled as she made her reason clear to the men in the room.

Embarrassment washed through him like a burning hot wave. "Uh, senator, I agree with the admiral. We should also actively take steps to secure our other military bases. I'm not so sure it's beyond the realm of possibility that they've trained these children to run the ships and planes and cause us greater issues." He shrugged, then turned back to the general. "I think that, at this stage, we need more information before we can assemble strike forces. We don't know how many bases or children there are. While Colvert was undoubtedly using the in vitro clinic as a front, we don't know that there weren't more. It's one of the many aspects I want to investigate, but we're spread too thinly at this point, in terms of manpower."

The general harrumphed at his answer, and the admiral peered again at the map. "If we take the force out into deep water and form a flotilla, it would make it hard for anyone to ambush us and take our ships. We can keep a single force at the main base, and that's the one we reinforce." He tapped the port at Weir Point. "It's next to the Air Force and Space Base. We pool resources. Move our land-based people there."

Daniella chewed her lip. "How many can you call up to help reinforce the base, Admiral?"

"If I move the ships to full complement, I can spare three thousand or thereabouts for the base. Then we take down the fencing between the other bases. Erect another corridor or two for access. Mine the surrounding areas, so we only have minimal incursion points."

Land mines. Antiquated yet still effective barriers. Jonah knew Daniella wouldn't be comfortable with that, but it made sense to protect the base and those within it. Increase the defensibility meant they'd get more returning soldiers. It increased the chances of survival of their people, including the civilians who now called this place home. However, it brought with it other unintended side issues —how to house and feed so many soldiers and their families. He'd work on that issue later though.

"We add to that, set up a further perimeter. Surface-to-air armaments and machine artillery within the base proper and increase the watch. It's doable, but it will require extensive scheduling and organization." Jonah swiped a hand over his forehead as he gazed at the map.

Daniella tottered to the chair, her gaze on the table. "I wish it hadn't come to this. Get it in place as quickly as you can. I want an update in the morning, gentleman. I want to be assured our people will have the best chance to strike when the opportunity arises."

The general and admiral both read the dismissal in her words and saluted then left the room.

She sighed heavily. "I don't know, Jonah. I mean, our position is weak without the intelligence. We need to defend the most strategic locations and ensure we have the resources, food, and medical access, but how the hell do we do that when we're boxing at shadows? We need more information. We need it quickly."

He nodded his agreement. Right now, things looked increasingly grim.

DANIELLA LAY IN THE DARK, mulling over the consequences of the decisions she'd made. Jonah lay on his side, asleep, and for a moment she wondered how that could be.

Her nerves were taut, stretched like an elastic band about to snap. She could call it all off. Surrender herself, but that wasn't a choice. Too many had already returned, families swarming through the gates.

The men who'd taken on the role of gate security had increased the checks, ensuring only those who were supposed to be there were granted access. Professor Venos would arrive tomorrow with a small group of handpicked medical staff who'd survived the explosion at the hospital, and their families. Michael, Clarissa, and their captives had already transferred in, with the secured accommodation under immense scrutiny.

All these lives in her hands. "How do I do it, Yin? How do I live up to the responsibilities? Make sure my decisions are the best ones for everyone?"

No answer was forthcoming. She hadn't expected one.

The dim glow of the clock above the foot of the bed showed two AM. With a sigh, she snuggled down in the bed, determined to get some rest. Tomorrow would be another busy day.

It took a long time to descend into sleep.

Chapter 18

Jonah ran his gaze over the staffing models, read the health report on the children in the cells, and worried. They'd have to do something soon. Something visible to draw out the combatants.

In the last two weeks, there'd only been a minor skirmish. Everyone was tense and on edge. It felt like a grinder chewed at his brain.

The door opened, and Michael entered. "Why is Daniella meeting with LV-1 again? When we spoke a few days ago, she said she'd refrain from going to the secure zone."

Jonah frowned, puzzled by his friend's comment. She'd been going to a training session, then meeting via holo-link with the other senators. "I... I don't know, Mike. I mean, it's not like she's telling me everything she does. There was supposed to be a training session."

Michael dragged his fingers through his hair. "I can't make her stay away, Jonah. David isn't here at the moment, and you're about the only one she'll listen to."

Jonah barked a laugh at that. "Listen to me? She's the leader of the Free Republic movement. I'm merely a pen pusher and—"

"Garbage! She's in love with you. Every time you're in the same room, her face kind of lights up. Clarissa reckons she's gone, and so do I."

His stomach contracted, the hard, painful knot in his belly—the one he'd been carrying since the first day on the base—trying to squeeze its way up his esophagus. "I don't have time to talk about this. I've read through the files you prepared on the children. I don't understand some of the things you're talking about but—"

Before he could speak further, a massive boom reverberated. The building shook, glass chinking and tinkling, files sliding to the floor.

Jonah was up, pushing away from the desk as the sound echoed once more, a sonic style boom. Knowledge flared. "They're attempting to break into the base." He wrenched the door open. People moved swiftly, an attitude of banked anxiety wafted on the air.

"We're under attack, sir!" A young, dark-haired aide, probably only nineteen, trotted up to him.

"Find the senator. Get her sequestered and contact the base commander. I want teams on the kids. No one gets near them. No one gets them out." He ground out the words and reached for his sidearm. "Michael, get back to your office. Lock it down, along with Clarissa. You're both targets. I can't afford to lose you as either a medic or anything else."

Spinning on his heel, Jonah headed to the end of the building, where the protective armor was stored. He'd go out there and—

"Sir? We need you here. You're the only one who knows the full extent of the situation." McNally loomed before him, where she'd been handing out the protective suits. "We lose you, and so much knowledge will be gone. All the planning you've done. The contacts you've got. We can't afford to lose you." The words hammered into him like a physical blow.

"I need to—"

"With all due respect, Jonah. You're needed here more. We're going to move you into the building with the senator. This is the first attack they've made on the base. We aren't sure the extent of their force. Right now, we're calling up everyone we can spare."

General DuSaint turned the corner and peered at both of them. "You think you should be out there. Yes?"

Jonah seethed and nodded. "Yes, sir."

The older man shook his head. "You'd be wrong, because right now, we need you where you're safe and able to help with the defensive efforts. Hell, they're sending me back too." The general screwed his face up as if he'd been sucking lemons. "We still need protective suiting."

"I'd agree. McNally?"

She wordlessly handed the general and himself a suit as the aide sped toward him.

"Sir, I have a vehicle waiting for you and the general. We'll take you to a secured location on the base, where the senator awaits you. She's getting ready to do a vid-cast. Says it might help to throw the combatants off."

"If she weren't a senator, I'd probably see if we couldn't train her as a strategist," muttered DuSaint.

Another thud followed a boom. The building rattled as if the foundations were compromised. "I need my backup data unit," Jonah said.

Moving quickly, legs pumping, he ran to his office, then pulled up short at the sight of a gaping hole in the wall. The desk lay in ruins, the data backup missing in the debris.

"We need to get you out of here." McNally grabbed his arm, the general ahead of them disappearing around the corner and out the far door.

A compact utilitarian vehicle revved, and Jonah allowed the woman to push him in, then she clambered in beside the general.

McNally slapped the side of the car. "Go!"

DANIELLA'S STOMACH clenched in knots. Where was Jonah? Michael? She tracked back and forth as the female soldier watched her. The camera sat in position, ready for her to begin the transmission. The door opened with a squeak, and Jonah entered. She didn't look for anyone else, just launched herself into his arms.

"Oh God! Davies here says they're attempting to get into the base? Do we have—"

Someone cleared their throat, and she looked up to see the general. "Ma'am, it seems they are, and they aren't. They got a single rocket off and hit Jonah's office. Interesting that they knew exactly where that was. But they've begun retreating according to our people fortifying the fences. The initial attack didn't work well. They hit the patch we'd already seeded with mines. Their losses are greater than ours. I don't suppose..." He stopped and shook his head.

"What, general?"

"The girl, LV-1? Can she give us any information on how many..."

Horror seeped into her marrow, freezing her. "You want me to use the child to gain—"

"LV might have information that will allow us to make informed choices. Daniella, we really can't afford to ignore that." Jonah laid a gentle hand on her arm, and her vision tunneled. His darker skin stood out against her paler one.

Differences.

Opposites.

"I... How can you ask that? She's a child!" Daniella's voice vibrated with barely suppressed emotion. Anger and revulsion warred inside her, each overlaying the other while the greasiness in her belly roiled.

"Senator, she might be able to give us the information we can't —" He spoke forcefully, face hard and eyes burning with intensity, and Daniella flinched.

"If—that's only an *if* at this stage, gentlemen—I want an assurance that she will not be used again."

Hot tears burned in her eyes as Jonah shook his head. "I can't promise anything, senator. This is a war. We have to do things..."

Shaking her head, Daniella shut him down. "Let me talk to her. Bring her here."

Jonah stared, then shrugged. "McNally? Escort LV up here. Remain on guard, and above all, protect the senator." He marched to the door, wrenched it open, and turned back, burnt her with his searing gaze, then left the room.

Her breath hitched as the general and McNally trotted after him. She'd gone toe-to-toe but hadn't achieved anything positive. Instead, she had the nasty feeling that she'd damaged the tenuous strands of emotion between them.

Her personal communicator blared. She frowned and lifted it, checked the ID, and growled her greeting. "What do you want, Gravely?"

"Sadly, Gravely can no longer use this communicator. Such a shame. He was such a nice man before he made the deal. Know what I mean? Go on. Turn on the news line." The voice dripped with false emotion, and the nausea she'd mostly held at bay struck her as the line disconnected.

She stumbled to the viewer and engaged it, found the newscast, and slumped into her chair, horrified by the vision before her.

"Yes, Gareth, it has been confirmed by sources within the assembly chambers that Senator Gravely was assassinated this morning. The massed army of Senator Daniella Villede are thought to be behind the action that resulted in a total loss of the building. Over forty staffers are presently unaccounted for." Daniella's image filled the screen as the voiceover continued.

When her image disappeared, the camera panned to a man standing beside the pile of rubble who'd assumed a stern facial expression. "Jenna, there is widespread unrest in the capital today. People are worried about their safety. Since the assassination of Yin, and with the death of Gravely, many suggest it's Senator Villede who is pulling strings. That she's hiding out while she masses troops. Privately, others are talking about gangs of children roaming the streets. Sources within the political circles are also stating that…"

The screen turned grainy. Then the test pattern overlaid the viewer. It lasted for around thirty seconds, then the newsroom and reader returned. She looked disheveled as if something had occurred and she'd run her fingers through her hair.

"We apologize for the interruption. We have just received word from Prime Senator Delspar's office." She cleared her throat and shuffled in her chair. "This is an official communique from the office of Prime Senator Delspar. At approximately three o'clock today, Senator Daniella Villede enacted war on the peoples of this planet and the republic. She and her troops refused to lay down arms and to cease their hostilities peacefully. Any man, woman, or child offering assistance will be brought to trial on charges of treason. If found guilty, no clemency will be granted. The new republic will not tolerate any undermining of their laws or decisions. Long live the republic!"

Daniella shut it off and slumped to the chair, hand over her mouth as she dry-heaved.

The door opened wide, and LV stood there. Jonah took one look at her face and crashed in. "What's happened? Daniella?"

"He's... He's declared open war. Delspar has assassinated Gravely. Anyone they think involved in our actions is to be jailed and tried for treason. He means to clear any opposition at all. What do we do, Jonah?"

The sensations and stresses she'd carefully banked over the last week crashed down on her, smothering her. She wanted to cry and scream, but the child stood there, watching with a weird, unblinking gaze.

Jonah moved forward, crouched down beside Daniella, and enfolded her in his strong arms. The feeling of being cared for and home soothed some of the raggedness. She breathed slower, forcing her body to settle while soaking up the calm he emanated.

"They don't want to just clear opposition. They mean to repopulate the world. Make it stronger and defend what they take by force." The words, incongruous on the lips of such a young girl, stilled the grief and anguish.

Daniella pulled away and stared at LV. "What do you mean?"

"We are taught that our generation will be stronger than the last. It's our birthright. We are chosen, enhanced, and trained. Your kind is weak and unsuited to governing, particularly given your outburst. My kind will take and build. Create a whole new world. One suitable for those such as us. Then we'll take to the stars and populate planets."

Daniella tugged away from Jonah and staggered to LV. "Why? I mean, there was no need for this kind of action. Why do you want to do this?"

LV hugged herself, arms wrapped around her slight body, elbows and wrists shining white with pressure and strain. "It's not what I want. None of this is about me. It's what they taught us. But I don't know how..." The child faltered, and Daniella felt her heart crack for a young girl, far more knowledgeable than any child should be in the art of war. "I don't know how to be like you. Like any of you."

Daniella pulled the child into the room and closed the door. "What do you want, LV?"

LV lifted miserable eyes to Daniella. "I want to be normal. I want to make friends. I want to be something different and do something that helps others. I don't just want to grow up and have babies."

Daniella wrapped her arms around the child. LV held herself stiff, clearly unused to this sort of interaction. Daniella persisted. "Help us, LV. Let us help you."

A hiccup, loud and clear, echoed in the room as the child started to shake. "I... I don't know how."

"Let's start with your designation. We can get rid of it. We don't use designations, but names. You need one. Let's get rid of LV, and you can be something else. What about Liv?"

The scalding dampness of tears soaked through Daniella's clothes, and she stepped back, retaining hold of the girl's hand.

"Come on. Let's do something now, Liv. Help me. We'll send a message out. Tell people that—"

"*No!*" the girl shouted and hurled herself out of Daniella's grip.

Confusion washed over her. "What? What's wrong?"

"You want to use me, like everyone else. You want me to go on camera and—"

"No, Liv. She's not aiming to use you. If you don't want to do that, it's fine. You don't have to. The senator wants to help you. Let her find a way." Jonah spoke quietly, and Daniella glanced at him, willing him to see the appreciation in her gaze.

She turned her gaze back to the girl. "I don't want to use you. I tell you what. I'm about to do a broadcast. You sit there, watch me. You don't have to do or say anything, Liv."

The child shot a disbelieving look in her direction as Daniella turned, tugged on her official robe, and stood before the camera, hand extended so the remote would turn on the record function.

"This is Senator Daniella Villede. This evening you were addressed by Senator Delspar. He calls himself Prime Senator, but that's because he knows his position is not truly that of President of the Republic. What he's proposing is merely Government Lite. There is no substance. The children roaming the streets in gangs are his to control. Whether he pulls strings or someone else, my people are investigating and coming closer every day."

She took a long breath her gaze sweeping over the destruction before she turned back and looked into the camera.

"It is true that I'm in a secure location. As the last senior officer of the true republic, I have assumed the mantle of leadership, but though I am in a secure location, I am not so far away that I do not understand and feel the deprivations and fears of the ordinary people. My people are working tirelessly, seeking to overcome the tyranny being forced on you. Every day we grow closer to the point of resolution. Hold fast. Teach your children. Protect yours, because we will not give up until we are once again free."

She clicked the screen off and sucked in a deep breath.

"Well done, senator. As far as gauntlets go, I think that one was a winner!"

"I hope so, Jonah. I hope so."

***

THE NIGHT CLOSED IN, and Jonah stripped his clothes off, then stepped into the shower cubicle. He felt grimy and gritty, as if the explosion in the office, the high tensions, Daniella's fury and subsequent explosion had scoured his skin.

He stepped beneath the stinging spray, letting it hit his body and scalp, washing away his cares. His eyes closed. *What am I going to do with her?*

Michael was sure Daniella loved Jonah, then the outburst made him think that any hope he had there was smashed. His feelings confused him. He felt a deep attraction for the woman. It felt a lot like the word he was avoiding. She made him feel—he hunted for a word that he could stamp on his emotions, something that explained it all and clarified his fascination. He felt more. More than himself, more than fulfillment. Was this love?

He jerked up a container of hair cleanser, squirted it into his hand, and the scent of wildflowers invaded his senses.

"Dammit, wrong one."

"Well, not if you want to wash my hair."

The echo of her voice tantalized his whole being. Pulse rate suddenly spiking to the now- familiar rhythm he associated with physically wanting her. Jonah felt the slide of silken skin against his own as she joined him, wound her arms around his waist and held on.

"Would you wash my hair, please?"

He opened his eyes and glanced down, took up handfuls of golden tresses, the ones he'd slid his fingers into during times of sensual pleasure. The beat of arousal heating him through.

"What do you want from me?" Jonah controlled the growl of self-reproach, wholly unsure where that request had come from.

"I'm not sure what you're asking, exactly, Jonah—but being with you? It makes me feel not just secure and wanted, but it also feeds my soul. I love you."

That rocked the last of his senses, and all that remained was to turn her in his arms. He slammed her body against his and crushed her lips with his own. Feasted on the bounty that was Daniella.

His hands slid down her body, gripped her waist, and lifted her. She wrapped her legs around his waist as the hunger roared, met and found its mate in her eyes.

"Fill me, Jonah. Make me whole. Love me."

He did, shoving himself deep within her, felt the glorious milking of her orgasm while her nipples scraped against his flesh.

He kissed her, deep and starving, as if he'd not seen sustenance in so long. Their tongues danced as his fingers bit into soft flesh, hips flexing until she tore herself away, the cry echoing in his ears. The sensation of rhythmic clenching, fthe glorious milking of her orgasm as he let go, filled her with every drop of hunger inside himself.

They stayed there, suspended as muscles cooled, then he released her so she slid down his body.

"Jonah?" The lack of assurance in her voice tore at him. "We're going to be okay, aren't we?"

Jonah took a moment, turning to cease the flow of water as he muddled through an answer to her question, then he sighed. "I hope so, Daniella. I really do."

Deep in his mind, he wondered if they had met as ordinary people and a relationship formed, how it would have worked out. *Not the time, Jonah.* He dismissed the thought and reached for a towel and folded it around her, then slung another about his hips.

Chapter 19

Daniella tugged at the bulletproof suit that covered her from head to toe. Jonah had refused to allow her to make this appearance without being swathed in the ballistic-stopping outfit.

Heat radiated from the dark material, so she felt as if she were dripping buckets of perspiration. Dark clouds gathered above them as they rode into town in an unmarked vehicle. Her earpiece squawked imperiously.

"Once you're there, follow every instruction given. If they move to pull you out, do as you're told," Jonah growled through the earpiece.

McNally sat beside her, cradling her rifle, a snub-nosed piece of equipment that weighed very little but was highly effective. Or so Jonah had informed her.

Her attention splintered as McNally thrust a similar rifle into her grasp. "Now remember, it has an immediate acquisition mode. Before you engage it, make sure it's not one of us or a civilian. Depress the trigger—"

"Slowly and respectfully. A sharp jerk could cause a misfire, and that leads to an opening for the bad guys. Got it," Daniella finished the phrase McNally had drilled into her.

McNally gave a small nod. "Okay, remember to stick close to me. Jonah is antsy enough that you're going out of the base without him to protect you. Let's make my job easy, yeah?"

Daniella inhaled. "Of course. Me glue, you the thing I'm sticking to."

McNally loosed a tinkling laugh and settled back in her seat. "She'll do fine, Jonah. Daniella reminds me of myself on my first mission. Nerves controlled but not stupid enough to think it's a walk in the park."

Daniella rolled her eyes as she heard Jonah swearing through the headphone. The vehicle jerked to a stop, and her grip tightened on the ML571 weapon.

McNally thrust two more clips into her hand. "If we get separated, make your way to the old factory, and make sure you engage your placer device now."

Daniella tapped the tiny bracelet that wound around her left wrist, activating the locater. If things went really bad, Jonah and a strike team were prepared to follow the tracker to her location. She just hoped that wouldn't be necessary.

The door at the rear of the vehicle opened. Daniella shrugged on the tiny backpack she'd carried with her from the base. The filming should only take a few minutes, then they'd make their getaway.

Jonah had argued hard that it was a foolish risk to go to the site of the ruined Republic Assembly, but Daniella had countered that the people needed to see that she was there, on the ground. That she wasn't dead. They would use this new vision of her as a device to encourage people to fight if hope was exhausted into the future.

Her gaze took in the mounds of rubble. Several older people picked through the remains as she surreptitiously took up position by what remained of the entry to the public gallery. She dropped the bag on the ground, swept up the camera, and engaged the feed so it beamed live. Daniella hadn't explained that part of her plan to Jonah. She was taking a huge risk but felt it was necessary.

"I'm standing outside the remains of the Republic Assembly building. I need to share with you, the people of the republic, my horror and anger at what has passed. Delspar has indicated this was my doing. I'm going to say categorically right now, that's not true." Daniella lifted the visor of her helmet as McNally swore. "I know he's made threats, and those who assist us face the full weight of his troops, but without your help, this form of martial law he's imposing is all there will be. This is not what the republic was meant to be. Join us. Help us."

The roar of incoming vehicles captured her attention, and she quickly turned the camera off and stashed it in the bag as McNally hauled her away from the site of the earlier explosion.

"We gotta get out of here now!"

They hurried, stumbling over smashed masonry, feet pounding as they moved in the opposite direction of their vehicle. Daniella's breath came in jerking pants. "Where... Where are we...going?"

McNally didn't answer, merely towed her into a dark alley. A door opened when McNally pushed on it, and they dashed within. "What the hell were you doing out there? You put us both in extreme danger. Jonah only agreed to this because you were going to tape then air later today."

McNally's words scalded her, every word crashing into her with force. She shrank back. "I didn't think they'd find us so quickly."

She genuinely hadn't. Her calculations had led her to believe she'd have maybe another five minutes before Delspar's people arrived. Her contacts hadn't been aware of combatants hiding nearby.

"I'm sorry. Jonah?" She tapped her finger to her earpiece, frowning as she realized that the connection had disappeared at some point she hadn't noticed. "I can't reach him."

McNally cursed. "They've probably got a blocker on it. We should get rid of these in case they can trace our transmissions."

McNally tugged her earpiece out and threw it to the floor before grabbing Daniella's.

Then she stomped them. Hard.

They crackled as they smashed, and McNally snarled. "We can't stay here. There's a small tunnel in the building next door. It was used when this area was full of hotels and part of the access way for deliveries. If we can get there." She sidled to the window, peeked through the curtain and let it drop back. "We're surrounded. Upstairs now."

They pushed past a startled woman and scurried up the old, wooden staircase. Their feet were clattering as the banging started on the door. At the top, they shoved through a doorway and into a guestroom.

McNally fished about in her pockets and tugged something out. "Okay, this is going to be quick and dirty. And dangerous. If we don't get out of here though, they'll have us." She shoved the window open and fastened the tiny implement to the muzzle of her rifle while disengaging the clip. McNally aimed, and the projectile landed with a twang and a thud. "Swing your rifle over your shoulder. We can't afford to lose it."

Daniella did as instructed. Meanwhile, McNally fumbled with the end of her rifle, lifting the tiny attachment with the long, thin metallic line and started securing it to the window.

"Get your gloves on. This'll cut your hands otherwise. And whatever you do, don't look down. Treat it like one of those training exercises we've been doing."

Daniella slipped on the gloves and watched as McNally swung her feet through the window. They were at least five stories up and dread gathered. "But what if we—"

"We don't have time. Come on."

She followed McNally, arms quivering and her mind filled with terror as they slid over, gripping onto the cord. Hand over hand they moved, dangling in the air. Every movement felt like her arms were being ripped from their sockets. The sway of the line with each action sending another dart of dread through her.

McNally crooned, "Follow me. We're almost there. Eyes up," until they reached the edge of the building. In a single, graceful move McNally grappled her way over the edge to safety.

Daniella gripped the line. "I can't."

McNally sighed, reached down, and hauled on the suit. It moved, and Daniella squeaked.

"Almost there."

The woman tugged, her face scarlet with exertion as Daniella released one hand and gripped the overhang, her foot searching for purchase, and McNally towed Daniella over to safety. The need to flop down was pulled short as McNally grabbed the tiny, metal clamp and released the high tensile metallic cord. "Don't want to make it too easy for them. Now come on!"

Daniella hurried behind McNally, and they'd just rounded the corner of the stairs when they heard shouts behind them.

"Help me!" The sound echoed from inside the building, probably the woman they'd pushed past.

As one, they crashed through the door, the wood rotten with age, and McNally called, "We're going to have to move. Quickly now!"

They ran, pelting down the stairs, one flight followed by another until they reached the basement, and once again, McNally pulled something from her belt. She inserted it into the lock, and it turned.

They slid into the tunnel, and McNally closed the door, locking it with a loud click. "We need to hurry down here. It'll bring us out by the factory."

They clattered down the tunnel, and the further they moved the louder McNally and Daniella became.

The tunnel led off in multiple directions. "Each of the hotels had their own entrance. We need to keep going straight ahead though."

Daniella's heart raced in her chest, thudding as if it were going to jump out when McNally raised a hand and waited for silence. The gloom of the tunnels took on an eeriness now that their wild flight was over, and McNally turned off the tiny torch she wore.

"What are we—" Daniella started to question, but McNally stopped her.

"Shhh."

Daniella waited. Shuffling footsteps echoed, and cold sweat broke out on Daniella's brow.

"McNally? Is that you?" a voice called through a small communicator in McNally's pocket.

McNally pressed the key to answer. "Yeah." She closed her hands around Daniella's. "We're safe. Ready to go?"

"I need a minute," moaned Daniella, and they slumped to the floor. She gratefully accepted the water McNally pressed into her hands as they panted.

McNally grabbed the communication device. "Someone needs to tell Jonah—"

"Already done. He's on the warpath and wants you back on base, ASAP."

Daniella sighed. She'd have to face his anger, given she'd caused the mess that nearly had them both captured.

A soldier appeared out of the gloom, his face in tight lines of fear, motioning to them. "We need to move now. Our location's compromised."

Daniella shoved to her feet seconds behind McNally.

"The trackers. Lose them now."

She complied, shoving the bracelet from her wrist, then following McNally's lead by smashing it under her boot. They followed the soldier out of the tunnel and to a small van and climbed inside.

McNally slid into the front seat. "Turn the lights off and run dark. It's dusk, so we'll be harder to see in a dark truck."

It moved, accelerating as Daniella peered through the back plas-glass panel.

The light that illuminated their path flickered off, and they drove for a good five minutes, silence overlaid by the whine of the engine.

"Why didn't we just get into the car?" Daniella's voice came out panting as she stilled the frantic race of her heart.

"There wasn't time to get to the car, start it, and get out of there before they would have surrounded us. We would have been sitting ducks, senator." McNally spoke absently, and Daniella watched her eyes darting to and fro, as if looking for someone to detect them before they reached safety.

They arrowed toward the base, but once again McNally ordered a change in direction, leading them back around the heart of the city, so their approach was obscured. "Don't want them to find us easily."

Daniella stayed silent during the fraught circuit, and finally, they were opposite the entrance to the base. The gate opened, and they shot within, the egress closing behind them. Tears of fright dribbled down her face as the vehicle slowed then rolled through the streets.

JONAH WAITED, anger boiling as he prowled the office. The children had almost caught her. They'd had to use resources to pull her and McNally out. Did McNally know what Daniella had planned?

Instinctively, he was sure the agent had been duped, just as he had. The knowledge fed the fury surging through his veins.

When the door opened and Daniella stepped within, he stilled, holding the vicious emotion to himself, warring for mastery of himself.

He bared his teeth. "What the fuck did you think you were doing?" He stalked closer, stopped just out of arm's reach, and let the heat of combined terror and rage engulf her. "You took unnecessary chances. You put everything at risk. They almost had you."

She waited, pale yet contained as he flayed her with his words.

"Didn't it occur to you that they'd be monitoring all transmissions? That they'd expect something like this? All our work—the misery and pain and loss—would have been for nothing."

"You're right, Jonah. I thought I knew but—"

He shut her down, waving an arm in a cutting fashion across the air. "No. You didn't know. You promised me you'd follow the rules." He took one step closer, and she paled further, her eyes large in the too-white face, but he had to impress it on her. Needed her to see how much was at stake.

Tears shimmered in her eyes. "I did."

The thickness of her words and the way she wrung her hands as she apologized started to douse the flames licking at his insides. Not entirely, but the conflagration banked, watching and waiting.

"I was wrong. I should have told you, but I didn't. I didn't even tell McNally. I'd calculated I had a good ten minutes to get the broadcast done and on air. I only meant to get in, get done what I needed to do on-site, then get out." She stepped forward, lips quivering. "I was so wrong. We almost died because I was arrogant. I thought I knew better, and I didn't. I know we used valuable resources, and it's pure luck that I'm still here. I'm so sorry, Jonah." Her hands fluttered in the air as if she wanted—needed—to touch him but wasn't yet game.

Jonah opened his arms, and she rushed in, sobbing. She clutched at him, and he slid his arms around her, hauling her close. His eyes closed for a moment before blinking back open. He swallowed a lump in his throat, eyes burning a little as he savored what he'd nearly lost.

Holding her close, the final flame of violence guttered out, like a candle. The quivering started in Jonah's belly, and he tried hard to ignore it. "I nearly lost you. I can't. I won't, Daniella."

Jonah waited, knowing the storm would pass soon, but it took every ounce of willpower not to haul her up, to strip her naked, and settle himself within her body. The thin layer of veneer he wore about him cracked. The fear—no, terror—had gripped him, stripped him down so all that remained was a man in danger of losing the woman he loved.

It was time to acknowledge that.

When Daniella stilled, he sighed. "I was so afraid you wouldn't get back, Daniella. I don't have the words to describe what I felt..." He ran shaking fingers through his hair. "All I could think was you'd be dead, and I would never have told you I love you."

Daniella nudged him, and he released her. "You what?"

He shifted his legs, shoved his hands in his pocket, and gathered his courage. "I love you, Daniella. I can't conceive of a world without you in it. When I lost contact, a bit of me, something I've ignored for a long time, felt like it was trying to tear me apart from the inside. It hit me like a ton of bricks, and to be honest, I could have done without it." He inhaled deeply. "But it's there, and I can't change it. Don't want to, because you make me whole when I didn't realize I wasn't."

Daniella swiped at her eyes, and he found the handkerchief in his pocket and handed it over. "So, I look like a wreck and—"

His laugh echoed. "You could never look like a wreck."

She snorted. "Let's go back to our quarters. I need a shower and to think some things over."

Jonah reached up and scratched the top of his head. "I can't. I need to work out who tipped them off. Someone from my office or this building has access to our tactical advice and is sharing it with the other side."

"What do you mean?"

"During the attack, only one building was shelled. Only my office. They knew where I worked and where I was keeping my files."

She blanched. "You lost all the files?"

His smile bloomed, but he guessed it wasn't a happy expression when her mouth dropped open with shock. "No. I keep a third backup, they're just the paper copies, but only I, and now you, know that."

"Oh!"

"Yeah."

"You're going to lay a trap?"

Jonah nodded. "I sure am. But we also need to talk about who you saw and what you heard in town today as well. But go take a shower, change, and come back for coffee and debriefing."

"Don't you usually do it straight away?"

"Normally. But I've noticed that you work better after you consider things, so take that break, but be quick."

She kissed him gently on the lips. "I'll be back as soon as I can." Then she was gone.

THE HARD CHAIR and bare room reminded Daniella of a cell. "So, after you spoke with Liv, you knew that the only option was to go to the assembly site and broadcast direct?" The general hunched over his notepad, rubbing his brow.

Jonah remained quiet in the corner of the room, observing the interaction but not actively participating in the debriefing session.

"General, Liv has given us an insight, the details of her training and the eventual plan they have for her."

The general peered at Jonah, and Daniella observed the general. Something in his manner felt disconnected, and it increased her disquiet. "General, we've been over this all before. It's simply a case of she's given us everything she can, and I felt it was better to get the footage so people would know I'm still here. They've been sending messages through the media to destabilize people's belief in me."

"Hmm." He made another notation.

Jonah rose. "I'm going to grab a coffee. Senator? General?"

The man glanced at Jonah and nodded. "Yes. Go get coffee."

As soon as the door closed behind Jonah, the general rose. He walked to the far wall and returned, as if laboring under some significant weight.

"General, is everything okay?"

When he turned, she spied an emotion on his face she'd never seen before. Fear.

What the... "General? What's wrong?" She stood and advanced while he backed away.

"Uh, nothing, senator. Nothing of any consequence." He lied; the way his eyes darted back and forth told her. She'd seen staffers and senators with that same look on their faces when trying to prevaricate in the assembly rooms over the years.

"There is." A seed of doubt rose and refused to be squashed down. "You didn't..."

He turned away, and she knew. Or at least thought she knew. "You sold us out."

His shoulders slumped. "No."

The door re-opened, and two guards and McNally followed Jonah.

"You knew?" The squeaky words erupted as she stared at her lover and friend.

"We guessed. He's been oddly quiet since the planning meeting.

They knew which building. The exact window. They only attempted entry at one point—the only completed minefield—to distract us from the placement of their guns. Three missiles only. All hitting the one building. It was too careful. Too well planned."

Daniella began shaking, biting her lip to stop herself from crying out as she turned back to the general who'd aged nearly ten years in the two to three minutes since she'd worked it out.

"He betrayed us because they have his family. But who was it, general? Who was it that ordered their arrest? Who brought you into the fold?" Jonah stepped forward, his eyes shining bright with condemnation.

The older man shook his head. "They'll kill my family."

"We've already got them in custody, general. Our people were already planning on bringing them to the base when we worked out what happened. Jonah ordered a team to snatch them and take them to a remote location under full guard." McNally laid a soft hand on the general's arm. "They're safe now. Tell us what you know. We can't bring the bad guys in until you do. The longer they have to plan and undermine, the harder it will be in the end to undo what they've achieved."

The general stared at Daniella. "You'll arrest me, won't you?"

Daniella nodded. "We'll have to investigate. Even if everything you tell us is true, that they held your family hostage, there have to be repercussions. You gave them information about us, the base, and who knows what else. We'll need to convene a court, and we don't have time right now. Tell us who you gave the information to, general. Start to undo the wrongs you've personally done."

He staggered to the chair, slumped with head in his hands. "Major Olante. He's one of their top-level military advisors. He didn't return to the base when the call came out, said his family needed him or something like that. That's when he asked about you, Daniella. Your office. Who was here and about your routines. He inferred he knew about my family. Where they were and their safety. I took what he said at face value because I know war finds its mark, sometimes among the innocent. In the past I didn't take any notice of his comment about being an orphan and raised in one of the institutions near Eastcliffe."

Now she started. "The orphanage in Eastcliffe? Jonah? Wasn't the director—what was his name?" She cast around in her mind.

"Corwin? Cording?" McNally was on the same track.

"Corvino. Ellis Corvino," Jonah interrupted.

"I wonder if there's some—kind of connection? Jonah, it needs to be—"

"Followed up. McNally, get hold of David and put him on that immediately."

"On it." The little woman raced from the room, the door slamming behind her.

"What else can you tell us?"

The general shook his head. "Not much. Olante doesn't have a partner, and he lives in a small house in Ironswood."

"That's a bit above his paygrade, isn't it?" Daniella couldn't help the words, and Jonah smiled at her as she turned to look at him.

"I'd say. We need to send a team down there." Jonah advanced on the general. "I need a list of known associates, places he visited, and dates. We need to build a profile and quickly." Now Jonah's eyes softened. "These guards are as much for your protection as to arrest you. You'll be confined to quarters until I'm satisfied with our findings."

Jonah reached out to Daniella, and she gripped his hand tight. Together, they turned and headed for the door.

"For the record, in every other way, I'm loyal to the government. It's not an excuse, just an explanation."

Daniella nodded without looking back at the general, and they left the room.

Chapter 20

Jonah watched Daniella push the food around on her plate. "You're not hungry?"

"It's not that so much as I'm thinking. If the major is a traitor and feeding information, then he knows about our firepower, capabilities, and weaknesses. Could he possibly work out our strategy though?"

Jonah covered her hand, letting his fingers rub in tiny circles as he considered her words, evaluating her unspoken fears. "He could, but I called up his records after we'd finished with the general. He's been in the army for over twenty years yet not progressed past major. There are bumps on file. Misdemeanors. Nothing enough to get him discharged but..."

"Oh. So, he's not totally unknown in these kinds of circumstances. Connections?"

"Not much. The only thing of interest is his nominated NOK."

She squinted. "NOK?"

"Next of kin."

"Oh. And who would that be?"

He couldn't contain his grin. "The director of the Eastcliffe orphanage. Corvino."

"The connection." Daniella nodded as Senna trotted up to the table and slumped down in the empty seat. Jonah sighed.

"So, I didn't think you'd mind me popping by to say hi. Good work on the general. It's the talk of the base."

Daniella pulled back, sitting straight in her chair. "He was under duress."

"Oh, yeah. Coercion is something I know a little about. See, there's some chatter about Major Olante. Is it straight?" Senna had always been a straight shooter and only appreciated reciprocity.

"Yeah," muttered Jonah.

Senna nodded. "Okay then. I have something you might want to know. At the station, before I got kicked, there was a visitor—a stranger with sandy hair and thick glasses. I kind of recognized him but the name didn't twig until after I heard about the major. See, he had this 'friend.'" Senna made quotation marks with her fingers, and Jonah frowned.

"He was gay?"

"What? Oh, I think he dabbled in a bit of everything, to be honest. Liked wild parties and other stuff far too much to allow anyone to label him. But no, while I'm sure the guy was significant to him, there was something odd. He had scars, some deep though he tried to disguise them. Walked oddly, like he was stiff, and kept his gloves on even in summer. It was about the time when Colvert was prevented from practicing. It was in the news night after night there. Anyway, he and the major closeted themselves in the office with the chief. When the men came out, they were talking about the kids. At the time, I honestly didn't think anything of it. I'd known the major only briefly, so it took ages for it to twig."

Jonah opened his mouth, but Senna shook her head before he could speak.

"No, he didn't see me. I was cleaning the truck at the time."

"Oh, what a tangled web we weave," Daniella murmured.

"Huh?" He glanced at Daniella as she stared into the distance, a tiny smile on her lips.

Daniella laughed. "It's an old line. From a poem, I think. I don't remember who wrote it, but it talks about deceit."

"We've got that in buckets," Senna said wryly then rose. "Well, I should leave you two lovebirds to it. Glad you're in one piece, senator." Senna sashayed off, leaving him watching her retreating back.

"She's nice. I like her. It's a good thing she doesn't have designs on you."

"What?" He swooped back, taking in her smile.

"Nothing more than a jest." She speared a bean with her fork. "We should eat before the food gets cold."

***

THIS TIME it was Daniella watching Jonah suiting up, her stomach knotted with worry. "You're sure it will be an easy mission?"

"Find one bad guy. Bring him back here. Sure." He grinned, but even with his light tone she wasn't so sure it would be all that easy.

"Take care then. Don't do anything heroic and get killed. We have things to talk about and decisions to make, okay?"

He grinned at her, then kissed her softly. "I know. When we get back, we need to sort out where we'll live, who takes whose name, stuff like that."

His comment blindsided her. "What do you mean?"

The grin melted away, replaced with intensity and heat. "This isn't a short-term thing. We love each other, and I intend to marry you. Have kids and a house with a white wrought iron gate and look after your security while you take up the position of president."

"I... Uh... You've surprised me." He had indeed, the thud of her heart speeding up. She reached up to her chest, as if to calm the thunder within. "I didn't have any expectations about anything except being together."

Jonah cupped her cheek, his thumb brushing over her lips. "We'll talk when I get back. When we've both got time and privacy." He kissed her again, soft and light, brushing her lips. "I love you." The whisper of his breath slid over her skin, making her shiver as the sensual hunger bloomed.

In a whirl, he turned on the ball of his foot and left her. The room around her stilled. She ignored the sets of eyes and settled into the seat before the screen where they'd watch the feed direct from the action.

Jonah had climbed into the truck, the camera on his helmet now settled into place, and Daniella watched as they rattled back and forth. He hadn't yet engaged his earpiece, so the silence felt eerie.

It seemed to take forever. Then the sound crackled to life. "Can you hear us, base?"

"McNally here. Reading you clear, McDowell. Evidence suggests that the building to the right is his house. Be careful. I see some red on the scanner."

"Red?" Daniella turned to McNally as she fiddled on the tablet on her knee.

"Devices. Likely tripwires, scanners, and the like."

She rested her hand on her stomach and turned back to the viewing screen. Men and women streamed around Jonah on the screen, silent except for urgent hand movements. She knew Jonah was waiting by the vehicle, exactly as they planned.

She caught sight of something from the corner of her eyes. "Jonah?"

"What?" He spoke with a terse voice, but she plowed on, undeterred.

"There's someone there. Window to the right. It..." She swallowed hard, taking in the small face and angry eyes. "It's a child!"

"Shit! Fall back!" he called, voice muffled, and the view bobbed up and down as he moved.

Gunfire rippled.

Terror swamped Daniella as she watched the men and women of their strike team back up. Tiny figures dressed in combat fatigues rappelled from the top of the building.

"It's a fucking trap. Get back!" called Jonah.

One of the soldiers to his right went down, scarlet droplets landing on his camera, and Daniella wanted to retch. She dug her fingernails into the chair instead, refusing to leave, needing to see it all.

Jonah's helmet bobbed as they ran, scurrying up an alley.

"McDowell, go down the next arcade on the left. The antique store. Enter there."

He didn't answer, instead relaying the instructions to his people.

At one point, he turned, and she could see the rage on the children's faces. Deep and intense hatred. She gulped.

He turned back, and they dove into the passage, found the store, and she watched him gesture his people in, tug down the blinds, and bob out of sight.

Daniella bit her hand, holding back the cry. Helpless. The sense of being unable to aid him raged deep inside her. She sweated, and her head felt like it might explode while the burning itch of her eyeballs told her she was holding back an intense urge to cry.

"He's fine, senator. He knows what he's doing."

I don't want him to know I'm falling apart.

As if she'd heard Daniella's thoughts, McNally reached over and patted her knew. "I muted the headset so he wouldn't hear."

"Oh, thank God!" she muttered as the woman smiled.

"Are we clear?" Jonah's voice was tight as McNally returned to her task, fingers flying.

"Not quite. I read two combatants outside. Let me check the nearby scanners. See what..." McNally breathed out, eyes growing wide. "You gotta get out of there *now!*"

"What?"

"Incoming armament. Also, likely up to thirty children. I'm checking building specs now. Seeing if it's connected to a main tunnel system."

Daniella couldn't control the tiny sound of terror that erupted, and McNally glanced up. "Bear up, senator. This is going to get messy." She swiped and tapped. "Go down. Basement entry to the minor tunnel system brings you out at the small store behind. It's a convenience store so open at the moment. You're going to have to move quickly. Head north to the mass transit system on Mallington."

"Got it. Moving now." He did, the sound of feet muffled echoed through the headset.

She saw them head down and move through the reinforced tunnel just in time to hear a boom.

"Can they patch into our headsets?" Jonah asked.

"Negative. Maylin tweaked them."

"Good."

Daniella popped the name Maylin away for asking about later. Right now, she needed to focus on Jonah and the action being played out before her gaze. The tunnel was dark, so she only caught snatches of vision. They reached another door and wrenched it open. His hands moved, navigating them left and right.

The door to the operations room clanged open, and she turned. Senna stood there, dripping blood and shuffling her way forward. "There's a traitor in his team. I just..." She collapsed on Daniella even as McNally yelled into the receiver.

Two people followed her in. "Senator, we apologize, but she was insistent. Said you'd need to know..."

"Get my brother here now!" Daniella barked, and they scurried away as she levered the unconscious woman to the floor. Checking, Daniella found a lump on the side of Senna's head, her skin torn.

Michael dashed into the room. "What the hell is going on?"

"She just turned up like this. Knock to the head, some swelling, and a wound. She said there's a traitor in Jonah's team." Now her lip trembled as her brother cared for the injured woman.

In the background, Jonah roared into his headset as he pushed his people toward the transit station. Her eyes widened as she took in the team. With rifles slung over shoulders, Daniella guessed more than one captured vision with portable devices.

The sign for the station came into view as they clattered on. "Where... Where to now? McNally?" Jonah sounded winded, and Daniella's stomach churned.

"We've got a train coming in two minutes. Platform three. Get on it. It takes you to Ravenscroft. Get off there, and I'll have a team meet you."

She spoke tersely into a communicator as Jonah pelted on, down the stairs, people parting like a sea. "This one! Get on!" His team jumped over the railing as the train stilled before them, doors shushing open. "Is it...automated?"

"Yeah! I've got Maylin on the system now."

A small, Asian woman in the corner nodded, hunched over a keyboard and tapping furiously. "All mine!"

McNally cracked a smile, the first of the day. "It's ours. Doors closing..."

The woman nodded. "Now."

"Move to the front carriage. The eyes and ears are better there."

They did. Daniella could hear the tromp of boots through the sound system married with the vision Jonah supplied as he brought up the rear.

Jonah settled by the door, his face harsh as it mirrored from the train door. "Who is it?"

"I'm looking into that now, Jonah. I need another minute to break individual encryption sequences." Maylin brushed a stray strand of hair from her face and bared her teeth. "Dammit! Nope, we're going to have to get them back here and..."

"Serum?" He spoke wearily.

"Yeah. Jonah, I'm sorry, but we're going to have to find it out asap. We've got more leaks than a sieve and haven't had time to check out who's passing intel since arriving at the base beside the general."

Daniella watched Michael sliding a needle into his patient's arm, McNally furiously working at her tablet, and the other people bent over systems, radars, and security feed. She was untrained for this. What was there for her to achieve?

A thought flashed in her head. "McNally, can you get me a line to Senators Parmenter and Fields? I need to arrange for them to be escorted here."

McNally lifted her head and squinted. "Why?"

"They were judges before their senatorial careers, and I trust them. We need to deal with the traitors. We need to try them then enact their punishment, and do it publicly, so people have trust that we're still open and accountable. And our troops need to know that we won't turn a blind eye to infractions. We're all in this together."

McNally grinned. "As soon as we get the team back here, I'll get it arranged."

"Good." Daniella resumed her seat, confident that she'd made the right decision.

Chapter 21

Jonah's team trudged into the grounds of the base and collapsed on the green grass, tugging helmets off and laying rifles down beside them. They gasped for breath, the wild flight across town to their pickup pushing them all to their limits.

His eyes scanned the group before him.

They were going to be injected with the Serum J—a neuro-exciting chemical. Previously for military use only, it lowered the resistance of those injected, ensuring they answered truthfully and fully during questioning. He'd seen it in action. And the after-effects.

Grim determination filled him. He'd save them all if he could.

"Someone here is a traitor." He spoke carefully, eyeing the team, looking for a hint. Someone who paled, sweated, or couldn't hide the truth from him.

They stared back at him. "What do you mean, sir? We're all loyal," a young woman near him called out, and he turned.

Click.

He knew that sound—a small, hand-held revolver.

Jonah turned slowly around.

The oldest of his crew, one he'd worked with previously, shook his head. "Well, I doubt I'll survive, but taking you out will damage them even further than blowing up your office. The funny thing is, I wanted to kill you then, but they said no. We needed to know just how good you are. We needed to know what LV-1 said. We needed to keep tabs on the others. She's the only one who broke, wasn't she?" He gloated. "Your people will kill me once I drill you. I'll be a martyr, but you'll still be dead."

The crack of a gunshot echoed. The man's eyes opened wide. "What did you do?" He crumpled, landing on his knees, gaze still on Jonah, who watched mesmerized. It hadn't been him.

Glancing up, his gaze rested on a woman, blonde hair hanging down, the perfect foil for her black, fitted pants and shirt. *Daniella.*

"You killed me." The man pitched forward, landing in a heap.

Jonah bent down and rolled him over. The man's eyes stared sightlessly ahead. Dead. Daniella ran over and flung herself into Jonah's arms, the hot metal bouncing over her shoulder. "He didn't shoot you, did he?" She patted and rubbed furiously while he pushed her back.

"No. But he had information."

"McNally and Maylin will find it." She kissed him furiously as his people dropped back down to the ground, chuckling.

"You're going to have to marry me now." He cleared his throat as she tugged back and grinned. "Can't do something like this without ruining a soldier's reputation."

Daniella cocked her head like she was trying to read him. Then her smile turned sly, eyes narrowing, and he wondered what she was up to. "Then maybe you should ask me, soldier. After all, a girl needs a little romance, even in the middle of a war."

The woman who'd spoken up chuckled. "You tell him, sister. I mean, senator."

Jonah turned, eyed the young female soldier before him, and she returned his stare with a thumbs-up gesture. He took a second to compose himself, inhaling deeply and seeking the inner calmness. The level he usually embraced.

It wasn't the way he'd planned to propose. She deserved flowers and dancing—an excellent meal with good music. She should have a night to remember.

Instead, he could give her this—a moment of green in a dark and chaotic world.

Jonah turned and dropped to one knee. Her eyes widened as he reached for her hand. "I'd do anything you wanted and more. Daniella, senator and the woman I adore. Marry me. Live with me forever. Please?"

She stared at him.

Sweat poured down his back.

She waited, the corner of her mouth rising.

She's going to say no.

With a shake of her head—his brain nearly exploded—Daniella dropped to her knees, took both cheeks in her warm hands, and leaned close enough that her lips brushed against his. "Yes, Jonah. I will marry you."

The kiss blew all the fears that had built up within him away. Warmth flushed through, and he slammed his arms around her, only realizing at her *oomph* that maybe it was a bit hard. "Sorry," he muttered.

"Kiss me, soldier."

He did. Thoroughly.

Chapter 22

The door behind Jonah's back banged open.

"McDowell, sir? We have a lead."

Daniella straightened up in her chair on the other side of the desk and stared at the young, eager soldier who nearly quivered with excitement.

Jonah turned his chair around to face the young soldier.

"From?"

"Captain Senna Reed. She was able to use some of her civvie contacts and worked out where the major is. She says we have to move swiftly and your team is best. She's suiting up now at the armory."

The lump that had barely melted after the last abortive mission lodged itself back in Daniella's throat. When Jonah looked at her, she was aware that he knew she too struggled with the knowledge.

"Daniella, I..."

"I know. But I'd like to come with you. I promise I won't be a liability. I'll remain in the vehicle, but..."

"No. You're safer here. If anything happened to you—"

"Same back at you. This is a war, and we're all fighting. I think vision shot of the arrests and subsequent trials will help our cause. People need to see."

Jonah's face scrunched up as he considered her words. "I don't like it."

"I'll wear any protective gear you tell me to. I'll stay quiet and hidden. It's important. I want the people to know I'm not just hiding. Jonah, it's not just about strategy and strength. It's about faith." Daniella rounded the desk to stand in front of him. "I don't like that you're going to put yourself on the line any more than you're going to like it once this is over and the reality of governing sets in. But it's who we are. Two sides of the same coin."

"All right, but you stay with McNally the whole time. In a shielded vehicle. If I tell you to go, you do."

Reaching up, Daniella cupped his head and kissed him. "Thank you."

"We need to move. Contact McNally, and we'll crack this nest."

They moved together, both of their communicators open and murmuring. McNally was eager initially until she realized she'd be stationed with Daniella. "At least it gives you a little more time to recover from our last little skirmish. Besides, you've barely had time to heal from the last injury."

McNally only scowled at him in response.

Arriving at the armory, they trudged inside, the tall Senna forcefully ordering team members into the heavy gear Daniella remembered from last time.

Senna looked at Daniella, blinked, then turned to Jonah. "What's going on?"

"She's coming with us."

"Like hell, J! Have you lost your mind? Taking a non-combatant into—"

Daniella drew herself up, face tight as she responded. "Captain Reed, you may be the one who found the contact and set this up, but I am the head of the government. I am attending as an observer and in recording capacity. Furthermore, Jonah is the senior officer."

Jonah started, and Senna grinned at his stunned reaction. "I'm a lowly captain."

"Not anymore. With the general being stood down, some decisions needed to be taken on rank. I wanted to tell you, but we didn't quite get to that part. It's a field promotion of sorts."

There was a rumble of congratulations, brief and ended effectively by Jonah. "Right, we need to move. McNally will remain with the senator at all times. She will take on the role of her personal guard until we return to base. We've got five vehicles to transport. Maylin has arranged intel on the building. The eyes surrounding it…"

Daniella watched as he laid out the plan. Every step methodical, and each question considered and answered as they donned the tactical suits, inserted earpieces, and jammed on helmets.

Within ten minutes, they were moving out to the waiting trucks. Jonah grabbed her hand and pulled her to the central people mover. "You'll be in this one. I'll travel with you, but we'll plant you a little further away. It's fitted with armor plating, and your driver, Santos, is an expert at defensive driving. He's the best."

They climbed into the center of the vehicle, and Jonah took her hand in his.

"This vehicle also has an inbuilt recording device within the interior and four exterior vision." Jonah indicated to a tiny console hidden within the seat ahead. "You can record, but I had Maylin disengage the broadcast facility." He spoke drily, and she couldn't help the tiny laugh that escaped.

"I've already learned that lesson, Jonah."

The drive turned silent, and she let him settle his mind to the task ahead. Moving into Eastcliffe, she noted the loitering children with dull eyes, sitting as if they had no idea what to do with themselves.

"Do they think we won't enter their area?"

Jonah shrugged. "While they're taught some strategy, and there's a single point of command, I'm not sure they're ready for what's happening. These kids look to be about ten or eleven. Michael's research leads me to believe Liv is at least twelve, even though her maturational age is likely younger. I'd say they haven't …"

"Been trained yet? So, they're sending their better and more seasoned warriors out to attack our base and..."

"They can only have so many."

Jonah tugged out his communicator and contacted Michael while Daniella watched the play on his features, the dawning realization of something, she guessed.

"Michael? How big was the initial implantation group?"

"What? Umm, I need to check."

"Be quick." Jonah's fingers drummed on his lap as he waited impatiently.

"Uh, the records show the original group, where the subjects would be aged around twelve, is thirty-nine. Subsequent groups are—"

"Michael, follow the numbers. Get me an indication of how many surrogates and if any carried more than one child. Factor in the possibility of..." Sucking in a breath, it took a moment to clear away the fury. "Dammit, how long should they wait between pregnancies and how many could a woman have in her lifetime. You know that stuff better than me. Get me figures. Find out from Liv whether the ones with the same designation were implanted in the same surrogate. I've got an idea."

He clicked off the communicator but the suggestions he'd made turned Daniella's stomach. "You think they're breeding again and again from the same women, but increasing the numbers of surrogates each year?"

"It makes sense. He'd take those who'd sworn loyalty and implant the women. Have the men given a role, likely as a trainer for the children."

"That's just...sick!"

"But it's been well thought out. I mean, look at it this way, you grow your army. The women feel they've achieved something because they're bearing the next generation of warriors. The men, who may or may not be the biological father, are also rewarded with positions in the new order. They probably think they'll be promoted when the time comes to positions of power. They don't realize just how expendable they'll be once this lot is fully matured. Michael said he thinks the maturational advancement speeds up with the new iteration."

Jonah looked out the window, like he was considering what might be next.

"If possible, I'd like to get my hands on one or two of the younger group. We need to know more." His voice dripped with frustration. "Michael and Professor Venos would be best for that. Clarissa and the psyche guy—what's his name—will be able to give us a view of their emotional maturity. I don't get how they do the scientific stuff, but it all makes sense to them, and they can explain it to us later."

The convoy pulled up outside a warehouse, and Jonah slid on his helmet. "Stay here and be safe." He didn't kiss her now, fully immersed in the mission, and she understood even if her chest ached a little.

Sitting in the vehicle as the door slid open and he jumped out was the hardest thing she'd done yet. This operation was dangerous. They could be ambushed, the feeds from the headsets compromised. He climbed into another vehicle, and she watched as it slowly drew off, heading to the rear of the building.

McNally slid forward and filled Jonah's seat. "We can take the feed on these screens, see what Maylin does."

McNally touched a button, and the screens rose on hydraulic arms, lifting out of the armrests.

Daniella settled back, her screen showing five different views. One from each of the building security cameras and the front of the vehicle.

The vehicles slid into position, waited.

"Vehicle one in position."

"Vehicle two in position."

One by one, four of the five reported in.

Her driver tapped a button. "Vehicle five. Acknowledged."

The doors slid open, and carefully, sliding into view, came the operatives, black-suited and weapons held upright as they scanned. This time one of the other men carried the camera. It made Jonah less of a target, Daniella surmised.

A hand signal at the rear—Jonah, she guessed—and they moved forward. "Engage on all fronts."

They swarmed, and Daniella held her breath.

Doors slid open, the people rushed inside, camera feeds from the helmets filling her screens. Each room, sparsely furnished, led to a long hallway.

⸻

JONAH SWEPT THE ROOM, his rifle moving left and right while he gestured to his people to fan out.

"Sir, we located the steps and are moving now." The leader of his eastern force would secure the first floor while he and Senna's team would take on the main tactical room, which he'd been led to believe was on the ground floor.

"Excellent. Western force? Check the basement. Be alert," he murmured, but Maylin had tweaked the specs of the audio.

A long corridor waited, and he crept along with it, adrenalin pumping in his chest. If they could take the major, they'd have a hope of picking off whoever was the highest-ranking officer. He hoped like hell it was one he didn't know. If they could close down the military arm and chief strategists, they could go after the king-pin. He couldn't see the military heads going into this blindly, without an awareness of who put together the masterplan.

They reached a doorway, and he snatched up the small, hand-held scanner on his belt. The last thing they needed was to find it was wired to some security device.

The light glowed a determined green, and he exhaled. "Entry this side clear."

Senna repeated his words, and he gave a tiny nod. "Green for go."

He turned the knob, and the door opened. For just a second he stopped. The room before him resembled a bunker, with maps scattered, personnel pinning notes to boards, and electronic operators seated before communications devices.

"Maylin, block signals now!" His bark had people scattering, but his team was better prepared. They lunged and rushed, grappled and snatched.

Jonah spied the major and headed in his direction. The man was chalky white, panic clear in the way his mouth hung open.

Major Olante reached down for his sidearm, and Jonah flung himself across the chasm between them. He reached him as the man tugged the small snub-nosed item from his holster.

Time slowed; his hand clamped on the major's arm.

"Get off me!" the major screamed with horror.

Jonah hung on, using his body to ram the man from his seat and into the wall.

Olante oomphed and reached up with the other arm, telegraphing the punch he aimed at Jonah's unarmored neck, at the point where the helmet didn't meet the top of the suit.

Jonah dodged, breath coming in pants.

"Get him down!" Senna screamed into his earpiece, but the grapple continued as Olante swept out with his foot and unbalanced Jonah.

They fell, bodies crashing together and landing heavily. "Fuck!" The epithet joined with the rocketing pain, but Jonah jerked at a hand, smashing left and right against the floor while rolling on top of the squirming man. "Give it up, Olante!"

"I won't!"

Jonah balled his free hand and thrust it into the man's face. A crunch echoed, and a spurt of blood landed on his visor. He didn't have time to clear it as Olante bucked. With a savage move, Jonah grabbed the man's hair and whacked his head against the floor. Wheezing, the man went down.

Jonah waited, his breath squeezing from his overtaxed lungs, and checked the man. "Still breathing."

He glanced around to see his people had subdued the others. "Eastern team? Western?"

"Sir, you really need to come up to the first floor."

With a grunt and more than a twinge of pain, he rose slowly, spied one of this team.

"Secure Olante and get them loaded into the van. I'm heading up. Senna?"

A form separated from the others slid up her visor, and the grinning woman spoke. "I forgot how much fun this was. Maybe I was getting a little stale in the arson investigation unit. Once the war is over, I'm not sure I'll return."

He merely grunted and headed to the back of the building, and for the stairs he'd spied earlier.

One of the team waited and lifted a visor. "Sir? We found a whole bloody maternity ward...or something like that."

They made their way down a corridor of white walls and frosted glass, and panic congealed in his belly. A maternity ward? They'd had no idea about... His thought stopped as he stepped into the room.

Cradles lay in rows, tiny babies slept one to each cot. He did a quick tally. Twenty-four. "Holy shit!" The fact that unnerved him was that each child lay supine, a tiny cord running from ceiling to the mask laid over each child's face.

"That's not all, sir. I think they've been attempting an artificial womb. In the next room, there's like maturational chambers—that's the only term I can think of."

He followed the soldier, feeling somehow old and infirm in the face of such a sight.

Five tanks met his gaze, each with a viewing screen. He walked up to one and peered within then reared back in horror. "What is that?"

"It's a fetus. Early in pregnancy."

He started at Senna's voice. "How the hell did you know that?"

She pointed to the screen attached to the unit. "Says here 'eighteen weeks' on the chart. And even I know it won't survive if we try to move it. It'll require whatever is in the liquid being fed down through that tube up there, and who knows what else?"

Above them, a transparent tube carried a gray-green liquid. "Shit! You're probably right. But we can't leave them here, can we? I mean they'll just reinforce this and continue making them. We have to..." The thought curdled in his belly.

"Yeah. We will, Jonah."

He shook his head. "What about the infants?"

"How the hell would I know?"

He grunted and slid down his visor. "Michael, are you seeing this?"

"Yeah." The answer was infused with rage and loathing.

"They won't survive, according to Senna. Your take?"

"No. If you can grab a mask off one of the infants, we should be able to run an initial test through your scanner. But I'd say they should be okay to transport. Maylin says you're going to have to hurry. There's a force headed your way."

Jonah grunted and hurried back to the room. He whipped off the mask on the infant nearest and held the scanner to it. "Michael?"

"It's nutrients. Load them up, Jonah. You've only got minutes."

"Are the prisoners from the ground floor secured?"

"Yes, Jonah. Do you require—"

"I need about ten men. We have to get these babies transferred to the vehicle and get out of here. Senna? I need to blow the building. Can you—"

"On it now, J."

The people in the room began transferring the sleeping infants, snatching the tags and sliding them under the nappies, placing them three to a crib. They carefully lifted them. With the assistance of members of his team, each crib was carried from the building. With care, they were raised into the vehicles waiting to transport them to the base.

"Everyone accounted for?" Jonah squeezed up close to Daniela who gawked at the basket containing three infants thrust into the floor space.

"Everyone is loaded up," Senna answered.

"Good. Light it up and let's get out of here."

The vehicles started sliding forward, as a light followed by a boom shook the ground. They sped up and into the night.

DANIELLA WAITED as they came to a stop by the health center on the base. "What are you going to do?"

"First, we're going to drop these babies off to Michael and Clarissa, then we'll need to visit the armory and divest ourselves. And I need a shower. And a stiff drink."

He looked as ragged as she felt. Watching him in the maternity wing had both educated and sickened. "We couldn't have saved them?"

Jonah shook his head. "You got it all on the vid?"

"Yeah. But to be honest, I'm not sure we should play all of it. Maybe show the maturational chambers, the children we've..." No words seemed appropriate to describe how they'd liberated these children and given them hope for the future. Or what had become of those they'd left behind.

"We can't think like that. Now come on. The others should have arrived at the base now, and we'll need to interrogate Olante when he comes to."

By the time they'd showered and settled into the small office Daniella had claimed as her own, Michael and Clarissa had arrived.

"Their status?" She leaned forward in her seat.

"They're all in prime condition, well-fed and matured," Michael replied. "They only have minimal tech in them, the vision you got briefly. Maylin was able to break into their system, which according to her is substandard and without high-level encryption, and shows that they planned to insert more once they'd achieved maturity. The infants were all awaiting implantation. There is still only a twenty-five percent success rate. The others are..."

"What?"

"Don't ask."

Now Daniella's stomach roiled. "They treat those infants as disposable."

Jonah crouched before her. "Look, I can't say that any of this is palatable, but we got some useful medical data. We know now, how they increase the maturity of the children, force the evolutionary push. We also have hard data on the testing regime, and so on. We still don't know how many there are or where they're scattered. But this mission was a success. Together with the footage, the intelligence we've received, and what we'd gleaned previously, we can release bits to the public. Hopefully enough to educate them. We need more assistance than we currently have, Daniella. We're fighting an urban war, and there's going to be casualties. People will blame us. Some will understand the reason we fight is for their freedom and others won't. We can't let our emotional hang-ups strangle what we're doing. We're the good guys, and they need to know that."

Daniella bit her lip. "What will happen to the infants?"

"I've spoken with Doctor Aros, and we think they need families. He suggests a form of adoption. Only, they're going to be more like special needs babies. We can't let them off the base in case they end up in the wrong hands. He's suggested the married and committed relationship couples should be asked if they'd be willing to take them on." Michael rubbed his brow, as if it ached viciously.

Daniella glanced at Jonah, and he smiled, gave a tiny nod.

"Michael and I are going to seek one. We're probably in the best position to understand their needs." Clarissa settled herself on the seat opposite Daniella.

"How soon do you think they'll be ready for families?" Jonah lowered himself to the corner of the desk.

"I'd like to keep them under observation for the next few days. We'll need to stabilize a nutritional supplement and schedule. Plus, we're going to need to find a way to get our hands on the stuff they need."

"Makes sense. On another note, I guess we'd better organize ourselves, Jonah." She grinned and fluttered her ring hand until Clarissa's eyes lit up.

"A wedding? How exciting."

The conversation turned personal, and when Clarissa and Michael left the room, they remained still, basking in the happiness until Daniella cleared her throat. "It's a shame my parents can't be here. I guess when David and McNally sort their complicated relationship out, maybe things will be settled."

"As much as I'd like for your parents to be here, they're safer where they are. But I'm sure if we asked Maylin..."

"I like the way you think, Jonah."

She slid out of her seat and stepped in front of him. He opened his arms, and she leaned in. "We should probably call it a night."

The rumble of his chest and the poking of an inevitable part of his anatomy told her why.

"I'm sure that can be arranged, soldier."

Chapter 23

The room was sparse—a table, several chairs, and the recording equipment—and Jonah rested back in his seat, the battered major opposite. The cuffs likely chafed and the seat had no padding.

"So, we have recovered the rest of the team on the premises. Several are already singing, major. We also found the maturational chambers and infants. My people were able to hack the systems, so we have invaluable information. But you're not clever enough to organize and run such a plan."

The major blanched but remained silent as he had since being fastened to the heavy metal table.

Daniella, the admiral, and even the subdued and chastened ex-general shifted in their chairs, but Jonah remained calm and quiet.

"We also managed to hack into the system you were using. It seems Operation Break Point was not as successful as you hoped. Why did you continue when your attack on the base brought forward no rewards? Your attempt to capture the senator was also a failure. Your booby- trapped residence also yielded no results. I can't see any superior officer settling for that, can you?"

"We didn't need to." The major spat his answer at them, and

Jonah restrained the smile. Needling the man clearly would yield more results than an intelligence line of questioning.

"You're career army. An officer but languishing at the rank of major. How many years?"

"I didn't sleep with a senator to achieve promotion."

A bubble of anger rose, but he buried it. *Keep your cool. He's getting frustrated—the red tide on his neck the most useful indicator.*

"No. You didn't stand out. You've got bumps and numerous instances of being disciplined."

Before the major could do more than open his mouth to remonstrate, Jonah raised his hand to stop him.

"Come on, major. Do you think we wouldn't realize that you, with your skills and contacts, wouldn't find a way to get even? To be more than some low-level, desk-based jockey? You were born for greater things. To do and be more than these has-beens would allow you to be. Weren't you?"

"I'm going to be a senior officer in the forces once you and your puny resources are crushed. Once Cassington realizes that I..."

"Cassington, Lieutenant General?"

Olante stopped, opened his mouth like a floundering fish, then seemed to shrink in his seat.

"You've got no spine, Olante! I worked out pretty quickly that the best way to get you to spill what I needed to know was to needle you. That's why you've been passed over. You've got a big mouth and bigger ego." Jonah hunched over the desk, face tight. The man quivered before his fury. "Now you're going to tell me who else."

The man turned purple and shook his head, and Jonah laughed.

"We'll find them all, clear out the nest. This is your only chance. Give us the names or face the full force of the court-martial process."

Olante's eyes widened further, wheeling with terror.

"Do you know what happens to traitors of the republic? There is only one sentence, Olante. Death. It's pretty damned final, and you don't strike me as someone who'd handle a firing squad well. They chain them and—"

"Ah, McDowell, do we need to..." Daniella intercepted just as he'd requested.

"He could turn informer. Give us the rest of the names. Might get hard labor, but at least..."

Olante shuddered in his chair. "Okay, fine! I have names, but I want to be sure—" "Names first, then we can agree."

"But they'll kill me! If they get hold of me, I'm dead. Come on, McDowell, you know how it works."

The unpleasant whine and the ripeness of fear made Jonah want to edge away from the man. He had to finish the job because they had to cut the head off this hydra before it could rise again.

"Names first. If the ones you give us ring true, I am authorized to offer you a deal." He shrugged and settled back.

"Get me paper and a pen. I'll give you everything I have."

THE DAY dawned bright and fine. Clarissa hovered at Daniella's shoulder, fluffing her hair one more time.

"The last time we did this, you and Michael had a big celebrity wedding. Now Jonah and I. It was only weeks ago, but feels like a lifetime."

Clarissa stared over Daniella's shoulder, capturing her gaze in the mirror. "You wanted all the pomp and circumstance?"

Daniella considered her words. "Maybe twenty years ago, but now I know the important thing is Jonah and I will be married. You and Michael, even David and McNally, will be there. My parents will attend via vid link."

The door crashed open, and Kallee hurried in, stopping dead. "Oh damn, did I interrupt?"

"No, Kallee. You're just in time. Now we need to do your hair too."

"Mine?" The voice squeaked.

"Yes. And you need to get into the dress."

Kallee let a shriek loose. "I'm going to be in the wedding?"

"Yeah. Now, we don't have a huge amount of time, so get into the dress. Clarissa will do your hair. We've only got about thirty minutes. Hand me the box you've got."

Daniella knew that the box contained flowers. Her mother had arranged for them to be shipped over. She privately thought it a waste of resources, but the admiral, Jonah, and even Senna had encouraged her to see the PR value in the wedding.

Once Kallee scrambled into the seafoam green gown and stood beside Clarissa, Daniella rose from her seat, smoothing down the cream pantsuit. They hadn't had time to find a wedding gown, but she didn't care. The suit was one she hadn't worn before. Besides which, it fit her perfectly. Her only adornment was a small silver and enamel hair clip in her hair.

Daniella opened the box, handed each of her bridesmaids a posy of tea roses, and took up the tea rose and chrysanthemum bouquet. The scent filled her senses.

A knock at the door told her it was time.

"Nervous?" Clarissa asked.

"No. Excited more. Let's get out of here."

The three women hurried from the room, followed the young aide to the idling vehicle festooned with white crepe, and climbed inside. "Drive slowly! You don't want to ruin the bride's hair!" demanded Kallee.

The journey was swift, bringing them to a small chapel near the center of the base. They alighted and formed up.

"You've got no one to walk with," mentioned Kallee.

Daniella laughed. "No, but he's waiting for me in there. I'm all good with that." Then she hugged her friends.

The music swelled, doors opened, and they moved forward with Daniella entering last. She didn't look left or right. Her future waited at the altar.

She took the first step to a life she never would have thought would be hers.

The End

Did you enjoy ***Children of a Greater Evil***? Read on for some excerpts of Imogene's titles!

BioCybe by Imogene Nix

Levia scanned the long line of other hopefuls entering the testing chamber. The large building in the center of town was cold, and she dragged her wrap around her body, even as she craned her head, looking to the high ceiling. She'd never before had an occasion to enter the testing complex, yet she'd seen the lines of teenagers every time they passed the building.

Once she'd asked her parents why the teens were lined up and her mother's face had shuttered. Her stepfather had just shaken his head and growled. They'd stopped her questions with a carefully uttered, "You'll know soon enough, Levia." The pain in her mother's eyes had been enough to shush her questions. For endless months afterward, her parents had traveled different routes to the educational facility she attended and Levia lost interest in the puzzle of that building.

Now, as she looked around, remembering that long ago spring day, it was her opportunity to find out. But she felt a surge of concern at what lay ahead. She likely wasn't the only one, given that there were probably two to three hundred seventeen-year-olds gathered in the one place. Ahead of her, she caught sight of a couple of girls, their arms linked together and wide smiles on their faces. Scanning the crowd, she became aware that, by far, a majority of those gathered displayed both fear and trepidation.

"All female subjects will enter through doors three, six, and seven. All male subjects will enter through gates four, eight, and ten." The speaker above her was loud, and she jumped before checking the numbers etched on the black metal sign over her head.

The massive doors beside her swung open, and now an uncertain silence reigned. Many of the youngsters hung back, clearly discomforted by whatever testing regime lay ahead. This was where they'd been told their futures would be determined.

"Oh gosh, I hope they only have an aptitude and psych eval. I don't think..." Levia turned to see the white face of the girl behind her. The girl had uttered what many must silently be thinking.

Levia dragged an unsteady breath in, her hand resting flat against the plane of her belly as she looked around. No one had entered yet. It was clear many were on the verge of taking the step, but still they hung back.

She straightened her shoulders. "I'm not afraid." It was always wiser to approach things head-on, she believed. When her biological father had died, she'd been one of the few to view his capsule before it was sent into the massive gray structure built to accommodate those who'd moved onto the next life realm.

Her legs shook as she wobbled toward the entrance. Beyond the doorway, she spied sealed cubicles and her heart stuttered. Why cubicles? Usually testing—med and psych—were in eval-units, hidden only by billowing white curtains. She glanced back, noting that others had taken the first step.

"Move along, subjects." Once again, the androgynous voice of the address system blared.

Of course, given it was her seventeenth anniversary of birth, she was technically considered an adult now.

She thought longingly of baby Rald and her half-sister, Elda, waiting at home for her to return, and the celebrations to be held that night. That made her smile. She would need to make them proud of her.

She entered a row and the tall Educational Specialist, the edu-specs as her peers laughingly called them, stopped her. "Present your credentials to the scanner."

She'd done this many times since the tiny implant had been slipped below the dermal layer of her skin at birth. The small unit in her wrist heated as her details were checked.

"Enter the first cubicle, Levia Endrado, and follow the instructions to complete your assessment."

Thus dismissed, Levia moved to the first unit, laid her palm against the scanner, and the door slid open soundlessly.

"Welcome, Levia Endrado. Take your place in the eval-unit." The soft contralto of the voice echoed after the door closed silently behind her.

"What are you evaluating?" Her voice was breathy, and she peered around.

"Your skills—physical and psychological. Your emotional and medical status. Your educational attainment levels."

It was an answer that shed little insight into the many things she was hungry to know. "Why do all seventeen year olds—"

"Take a seat, Levia. Then we may begin your testing."

If she'd expected an answer, she was sadly mistaken, she considered sourly. She dropped into the seat, the soft leather-like surface molding to her body.

"Levia Endrado, you are required to remove all non-specified apparel."

She jolted in the chair. "It's cold."

"The temperature will be amended. Remove the non-specified apparel."

Her misgivings grew as she dragged off the light wrap she'd brought with her, and then threw it to the floor at the side of the unit.

"We will begin, Levia Endrado. At any time, should you experience any malfunctions of the unit, simply depress the red button." It glowed and she grimaced.

Levia reclined against the chair and waited for the testing to begin.

The first examination was based on her understanding of the political system, where she saw herself, and her knowledge of the rights and responsibilities accorded through citizenship of both her planet and the commonwealth.

The second test was mathematical and scientific proficiency. It felt like hours had passed by the time she'd finished, and she lay limp on the seat, exhausted.

"Levia Endrado, you may rise. The sanitary unit will emerge once you trigger the yellow button at the door. Should you require refreshment, press the blue button and a restorative will be made available."

"Can I leave?"

"Negative, Levia Endrado. Your needs will be catered for in this capsule."

"Why?" Her voice hitched and true fear rose for the first time. Why did they keep her in the alcove?

"All will be revealed at the end of the testing cycle."

Levia looked at the now empty screen before hurling a curse word. It was met with silence.

The urgent throb of her bladder reminded her that she needed to use the facilities, so, with

a sigh, she rose and clambered from the seat. After attending to the needs of her body, she walked around the unit, peering at the door, but it was obviously programmed remotely. She poked and prodded, but it made no difference. With a huff, she headed back to the chair.

The moment she'd settled in, the viewing screen shone bright. "Welcome back, Levia. The next sequence will evaluate your psychological reflexes, then that will be followed up with the general knowledge portion of the evaluation."

"When can I leave?" It seemed better to ask bluntly, she told herself.

"Once the examination is completed. After the next set of evaluations, you will be subjected to the physical aspect."

"Then I can go home?"

"Levia Endrado, you will now complete the psychological test. This will be undertaken by one of the center's personal evaluators."

She frowned. Personal evaluators? She bit her lip, and the sting reminded her that this wasn't something to joke about. In her seventeen years, she'd only heard of personal evaluators being brought in once before, and that was when one of the girls at her academy had been in a serious accident. Both legs were amputated and her body's ability to keep her alive had been gravely compromised. Her peers had been informed that the girl had requested the assessment before she could request her support systems be disconnected.

"Levia Endrado, are you ready to recommence processing?" The emotionless voice echoed once more and she gulped.

"Yes."

Available from Beachwalk Press
   www.beachwalkpress.com
   http://bit.ly/BioCybe

Starline by Imogene Nix

Duvall McCord stepped out of line as the parade was dis- missed, inwardly wincing as his new boots rubbed his feet and his new uniform scratched his neck. He looked at his

family, considering and measuring. He'd worked hard to attain the grades needed to be able to enter the academy, but it was all he'd ever wanted and dreamed of. To travel the stars and eventually captain his own ship. Now there he was on the cusp. Even as a fosterling, his room had been decorated with the ships he one day wanted to command, and at the age of twenty-three he was finally on the way.

His father, Captain Gentry, who had given up the chance of a plum command to keep his family happy, was always in the back of his mind. He now captained inter-galaxy runs for the Admiralty. He'd even given up his Star Destroyer for his wife's peace of mind. Duvall promised himself he'd never do that.

He belonged somewhere out there, among the biggest, the boldest, and the best.

His little sister, Meredith, bounced up and down, squeaking excitedly, and his parents smiled. He felt their genuine fondness for him, their foster son. They were proud of his many achievements, and if there were doubts in their minds, they were never spoken of.

Duvall was driven, almost obsessive in his desire to become the best of the best. That was why, now at the end of his time in the academy, he had been nominated as Best of his Class. The Top Graduate. The one his peers looked up to. The question had been asked and answered: was he good enough? His answer was always an unequivocal "yes." His family, peers, and instructors saw the drive and accepted it for what it was—an integral part of who he was.

His mentor, Captain Gustav Elphin, had requested that he serve aboard the Star of Ishtar, and had taken a great personal interest in this cadet.

It was acknowledged he would be on the fast-track to the stars. And, as Elphin told him again and again, emotional entanglements grounded a man; a piece of advice Duvall took seriously, so he had been careful in his social encounters. Always keeping a light touch with his lovers. Love 'em and leave 'em was his motto. He refused to let anything get in the way of his achievements and the desire to captain his own ship.

If privately his parents had any doubts about his lack of emotional ties to the women he was seen with, they kept them to themselves. No doubt they believed that one day a woman would change his mind and the attitude he had worked so hard to foster.

For now, he accepted their belief that he knew what he wanted and had the drive to achieve it.

War was finally over and there was time to settle down. Long days of peace stretched out before them. The uneasy truce between the Earth Empire and the Ru'Edan, while new and tenuous, meant that there were opportunities diplomatically for the right kind of man and woman.

The rogue Admiral of the Ru'Edan Empire, Crick Sur Banden, might still be on the loose, but there was a belief that soon he would be brought to ground and that a true peace might be the outcome. Well, that was the opinion of the hopeful in the Empire anyway. The Empire held its collective breath as the newest graduates of the Earth Empire Academy marched out. They hoped to reap the benefits of those who came before.

Available from Beachwalk Press
   www.beachwalkpress.com
   http://bit.ly/StarlineNix

Cyborg: Redux by Imogene Nix

At the monotonous whine techs rushed the room.

They didn't come to save her, but to harvest the body and organs while her body would be utilised for cybe-organic treatment.

Beyond the room, in a viewing platform over top, Jeremy watched, satisfied with what he saw as the medical technicians began the process. The slicing of the flesh, exposing what to him were unnecessary organs. They hurried, hands flying, blood spurting while inserting chips and wiring.

He watched his assistants replace her liver, damaged in the accident that had stolen her life. Instead, they mounted smooth replacements, carefully built just for her.

Each move was carefully orchestrated and he braced himself against the glass. "This one should be successful."

The surgical intern beside him —his Personal Assistant— glanced at him and shrugged. "Who knows. So far, we've had only limited success."

Ah yes, limited success. He clenched his fist, aware of the curling with a level of interest that only lightly impinged on his senses. Everything else, every fiber of his being remained focused on the surgical procedure taking place in the room beyond.

Three had died, one had resurrected but the brain deficiencies were extreme, resulting in the need for termination of the specimen. A shame really, he'd been strong in his body, but the mind had utterly failed. Things would be better this time, he was sure.

The surgeons below, the best and brightest of those committed to his cause continued their work, disposing of the organs they replaced. Those that were recyclable were stashed in white cooler boxes, filled with cold sterile ice and packed protectively. Even as he watched, they were whisked away.

He grunted looked back to the operating table, considered the only one other had survived. She would too.

"Make it work." Jeremy turned and glanced at his hand, silver glinting under the dim lights of the viewing platform. The whir clank of his personal hydraulics system filling the air.

If only I'd been a candidate. Sadly, his injuries had left him with two cybernetic legs, a cyber-enhanced hand and a hunger to build bigger and better. It had ended his official surgical career, but not his brain. Instead, he'd gone underground. Working only with the most damaged, the ones society and the medical community deemed to be beyond assistance. It allowed him a new level of freedom. The medical community at large turned a blind eye to his experimentation, though few realised the extreme limits of it.

Their imaginations were so limited, he thought and chortled, then left the room, heading for his office where he'd work on his latest batch of refinements.

She blinked, eyes opening and closing in quick succession while her vision flashed blue and white. *I died. Why am I here?*

Her body felt heavy and alien, yet stronger. *Strange.*

The small thought exhausted her and she slipped away to rise again some time later. "Where... Where am I?" She licked her dry lips, felt the cracked sting as they moistened the parched flesh.

The beeps echoed and she glanced up, the ceiling above her bright white and dotted with harsh lighting.

Clarissa stretched, aching down to her bones at the unfamiliar sensations that flashed through her. "What..." Her throat closed and it took a moment to force the moisture from her mouth down her throat. "What happened to me?"

A voice echoed in her mind. "Clarissa, you're awake. Wonderful. I'll send a technician in to check your fittings."

Confusion filled her. Fittings? Technician?

She waited, body not quite vibrating but with the overwhelming sensation of renewing strength.

A door opened, but she couldn't move her head, it remained in some contraption that held her still. Clarissa struggled for a word to describe the feeling. *Vice.* It felt like the vice her father kept in his small workshop at the back of the house. "Where am I?"

A white smocked and capped tech popped into her vision. "You're in the Colvert Clinic. Remember?" The smile seemed odd, as if they were watching for some kind of negative response and reaction. She sensed a tension about them, as if they were suffering from an adrenalin surge.

"What happened to me?"

"Oh, I'm not able to discuss that with you. You'll need to meet with Doctor Colvert at a later time. He'll explain everything."

Now the technician scurried around, tapping details into a hand held computer, tugging on cords but not releasing her. Clarissa struggled, fear ballooning in her chest, pushing against her lungs and she heaved, trying to suck in oxygen.

"Breathe slowly. It'll help." That voice in her brain again, stern and strong.

Stars exploded in her vision and she struggled, fingers curving but not grasping anything. "I can't..."

Confusion warred, her heart sped up, bellowing fit to burst in her chest. Perspiration dotted on her upper lip. "Breathe, damn it! Control your oxygen intake or you'll sleep again." His voice echoed and she fought against the sensation that Jeremy was somehow there, inhabiting her brain. The wild thought scattered to the four winds as Clarissa tried to regain control of her body and mind.

"I want out of here!" Her weak cry was married with a burst of terrifying emotions. Tears dribbled down her face as she heard the man cursing.

A sensation of cold trickled through her and the grey loomed. "No! I don't want to sleeeee..."

Available from Beachwalk Press & Imogene Nix
   www.beachwalkpress.com
   https://books2read.com/cyborg-redux
   http://bit.ly/cyborgredux

Also by Imogene Nix

<u>Warriors of the Elector</u>

- Star of Ishtar
- Starline
- Starfire
- Star of the Fleet
- Starburst
- The Star of Eternity

The Star of Ishtar & Starline - Print

Starfire & Star of the Fleet - Print

Starburst & The Star of Eternity - Print

<u>Blood Secrets (Re-releasing 2020)</u>

- The Blood Bride
- The Illuminated Witch
- The Sorcerer's Touch

<u>The Search Duology</u>

- Miss Elspeth's Desire
- Miss Isabelle's Craving (Not Yet Released)

<u>Reunion Trilogy</u>

- War's End
- The Assassin
- Executing Justice

The Reunion Trilogy in Paperback

<u>Sex Love & Aliens</u>

- Tangled Webs
- False Webs
- Covert Webs

21st Testing Protocol

- Cyborg: Redux
- Children Of A Greater Evil
- When Evil Came To Stay (Not Yet Released)
- Finis: The War To End All Wars (Not Yet Released)

Celtic Cupid Trilogy

- Blame The Wine
- A Stranger's Embrace
- Revenge On Cupid

The Celtic Cupid Trilogy in Paperback

Zombieology

- The Reset (2018)
- I Dream of Zombies (2019)
- The Six Million Dollar Zombie (Not Yet Released)

Knights of Pleasure

- Silken Knights (Not Yet Released)

Single Titles

The Chocolate Affair (also in Print)

Falling In Love Again (Previously A Sapphire For Karina)

BioCybe (also in Print)

Hesparia's Tears (also in Print)

Tomorrow's Promise

A Bar In Paris (also in Print)

Inheritance Of The Blood (also in Print)

The Plan

Loving Memories (also in Print)

Hero of Heartbreak Hill (also in Print)

Raspberry Dreams (Not Yet Released)

Non Fiction

Self Publishing: Absolute Beginners Guide (With Suzi Love)

Written as Ciara Cave

25 Curated Ways To Get Rid Of Telemarketers

Book Signings for Absolute Beginners

About the Author

 Imogene is published in a range of romance genres including Paranormal, Science Fiction and Contemporary. She is mainly published in the UK and USA and says her readers "Rock Big Time."

She adores meeting her readers at signings and has a page on her website where you can find out where she'll be attending next!

In 2011, Imogene Nix (the author not the person) was born in Bondi and since then, there's been no stopping her! Imogene sat down and worked tirelessly for 3 months culminating in the books Starline. This book became the first in a trilogy titled, "Warriors of the Elector." Since then, she's dabbled in just about every romance genre, written lots more words and had a ball as she's continued on the publishing path.

Imogene has successfully been contracted for well over 30 titles and has even self published others, under this pseudonym. She's also working on other books with differing pen names.

Imogene is a member of a range of professional organisations, including the Science Fiction Romance Brigade (SFRB), Dark Siders Down Under (the Australian Paranormal, Erotic Writers of Australia, (ALLi) Alliance of Independent Authors and Romance Writers of New Zealand.

She mentors new writers, participates in NanoWriMo (and is a Municipal Liaison) and love to drink coffee, wine & eat chocolate. When she's not working she's probably in the kitchen or the vegetable garden and is parenting a spoiled dog and a ferocious cat, a flock of chickens and recently added a clat of worms!

To keep up to date, why not subscribe to her newsletter? You will find the sign up on her website.

To contact Imogene:
www.imogenenix.net
imogene@imogenenix.net